Praise for Maya Banks's *Into the Lair*

Rating: 5 Angels and a Recommended Read *"Into the Lair* is a fast paced, action and sex packed book that left me trembling and breathless. ...I highly recommend this book to anyone who loves erotic paranormal romance!"

~ *Melissa C., Fallen Angel Reviews*

Rating: 87 *"Into The Lair* is a naughty romp with a plot that complements the sensual aspects of the story well enough to make it a most entertaining read. ...When it comes to fun and entertaining stories that make me want to fan myself, I can be a pushover and Ms Banks always seems to know how to exploit that weakness of mine."

~ *Mrs. Giggles*

Blue Ribbon Rating: 5 "I've been anxiously awaiting the next book in the FALCON MERCENARY GROUP ever since I read INTO THE MIST. INTO THE LAIR is a thrillingly intense story full of all the passion, wonder, and paranormal elements that I've come to love about this series. Maya Banks pulls out all the stops with this book..."

~ *Chrissy Dionne, Romance Junkies*

Rating: 4 cups "Ms. Banks takes you on a wild ride of love, lust, and erotic description that will make your fingers tingle. ...From cold St. Louis, Missouri to the wilds of Austria, to the South American jungle, Into the Lair will bring the reader's beast to the forefront with this pulse pounding action tale. Filled with ménage a trois, light bondage, and some one-on-one sex scenes, this erotic tale is perfect for any red hot romance reader."

~ *Danielle, Coffee Time Romance*

"This book had me from page one and kept my attention right to the end. ...This series has it all, action, hot sex, incredible alpha men, a strong heroine and wonderful paranormal elements that promise you a read you will not be able to put down. If you adore shape shifters as much as I do, you have to read this series. Ms. Banks just can't write a bad book. Some books are better than others, as with any author, but this book, and this series, is by far one of her best."

~ *Stephanie Q. McGrath, ParaNormalRomance*

Rating: 4 Hearts "The always exhilarating Maya Banks has once again created a compelling, edgy, and dangerous plotline filled with the right level of danger and erotically sizzling action to keep the reader hooked from the first chapter to the last. ...The sparks fly with the delightful battle of the sexes! The ménage element of the relationship seems like a natural thing. Warning, the sex is volatile, rough, edgy, and erotically shocking, pushing the boundaries to heights of delightful pleasure. ...It is nice to re-visit characters from Into the Mist, book one of this stunning series! Do not miss this delightful tale!"

~ *Shannon, The Romance Studio*

"*Into the Lair* is a thrilling ride and although the second in a series – it stands alone and will give reader a fantastic feel of what a brilliant author Ms. Banks is. If however you are looking for a bit more depth and knowledge about the situation that the men have found themselves in, it's highly recommended to start with the first in the series."

~ *Sandra, Ck2s Kwips and Kritics*

Look for these titles by *Maya Banks*

Now Available:

Seducing Simon
Colters' Woman
Understood
Overheard
Love Me, Still
Undenied
Love Me Still
Stay With Me
Amber Eyes
Songbird

Brazen
Reckless *(stand-alone sequel to Brazen)*

Falcon Mercenary Group Series
Into the Mist (Book 1)
Into the Lair (Book 2)

Print Anthologies
The Perfect Gift
Caught by Cupid
Unbroken

Into the Lair

Maya Banks

A SAmhAIN PUBLIShING, LTD. publication.

Samhain Publishing, Ltd.
577 Mulberry Street, Suite 1520
Macon, GA 31201
www.samhainpublishing.com

Into the Lair
Copyright © 2009 by Maya Banks
Print ISBN: 978-1-60504-321-0
Digital ISBN: 978-1-60504-210-7

Editing by Jennifer Miller
Cover by Anne Cain

First Samhain Publishing, Ltd. electronic publication: October 2008
First Samhain Publishing, Ltd. print publication: July 2009

Dedication

To Valerie, who I finally got to meet in person.

Chapter One

Katie Buchanan stared at the clock with growing dread. A knot of panic—and grief—swelled in her stomach until she feared vomiting.

He wasn't going to call.

Despair rolled over her shoulders, and she slumped forward, dropping her head into her arms. *Don't cry. You can't cry. You can't lose it now.*

Her teeth sank into her bottom lip. Gabe was all she had left. Her only family. And now he was gone.

You don't know that. Maybe something went wrong on a mission.

But no, he'd missed both call times, and he'd never missed the second. He once told her that the only reason he would miss his check-in was death. His. And in her heart she knew that. He'd never let her down.

The cell phone that was clutched tightly in her hand rang, and she lunged upward, grabbing at it to flip it open.

"Gabe, thank God!" she babbled into the phone as a rush of relief so strong it made her weak stormed through her veins. "I thought you were dead."

Heavy silence settled over the line. Her brow furrowed as dread took hold once more. "Gabe?"

"Katie, this is Ian Thomas."

She slammed the phone shut, fear-induced adrenaline sparking and flowing fast through her veins. She scrambled out of her chair and looked wildly around the tiny apartment.

"Okay, calm down," she said as she tried to steady her

breathing. No one had that number. Gabe had arranged for the high-tech phone, and it had an international number from a remote country at the ends of the earth.

It started ringing again, and she nearly hyperventilated. And then as quickly as panic had gripped her, an eerie calm descended.

Gabe was gone. He couldn't help her now. He hadn't spent the last several years teaching her independence for her to crumble when he was no longer around to help her pick up the pieces.

First she had to get the hell out of here.

She went through the room, throwing her clothes into a backpack. She only packed the necessities. Everything else would have to stay. The phone began ringing again, and she ignored it.

She pocketed the ATM card for the account Gabe had opened for her. Her first stop would be to drain what cash she could, and then she'd be out of town in less than an hour.

West. She'd go west. Maybe some isolated mountain town. Montana. Or Colorado. There had to be some place she would be safe.

She zipped up her backpack, her heart heavy. Gabe had been working on getting her out of the country. A year ago, he'd been prepared to take her to Argentina, but then things had gotten weird. He'd become distant. Worried and anxious.

Her departure was delayed, and Gabe became more paranoid, more cautious. She moved constantly, once every couple of months, and he'd enacted their call system.

He drilled into her over and over what to do if he failed to make his monthly call. Oh God. Maybe that was it! Was he testing her? Making sure she followed through with their escape plan?

A flutter of hope swelled in her throat. It would be just like Gabe to force her through the steps of a plan they'd gone over until it was branded into her mind.

She snagged the now-silent phone, hauled her backpack over her shoulder, and then, taking one last look at the apartment that had been home for the last two months, she took a deep breath and started for the door.

Early morning sunlight shone bright, causing her to squint as she hustled down the rickety steps toward the street. As she turned onto the cracked sidewalk, a black SUV pulled to a stop alongside her.

The passenger door opened, and a large man stepped out. She froze as they stared at each other. Slowly, he removed dark sunglasses, giving her a glimpse of deep green eyes. His expression was indecipherable.

Power radiated from those broad shoulders. Tall, muscular and intimidating as hell.

"Katie," he said in a low voice.

Anger, fear, panic. They all swamped her, and she didn't wait around to figure out which would prevail.

Dropping her backpack, she turned and ran.

Curses rang out behind her, and then he called out to her. "Katie! Katie, wait!"

God, they knew who she was. Bile rose in her throat. Gabe wasn't testing her, and he hadn't warned her. Which meant he hadn't been able to.

She could hear her pursuer behind her, and he was gaining ground. She threw a look over her shoulder and wished she hadn't. Two men were closing in on her.

Her chest on fire, she pushed herself harder, faster. Her tennis shoes pounded the pavement. The park loomed ahead of her, a study in lush green grass and playground equipment. The men chasing her wouldn't want to take her down with a dozen children and their mothers looking on.

She turned onto the jogging trail and poured on the speed. To anyone else, she'd look like she was out for a run. She was dressed the part in athletic shorts, T-shirt and tennis shoes.

Her phone and ATM card, all she needed, were in her pocket, and she reached down to make sure the phone didn't fall out. When she got to the other side of the park, she chanced another glimpse behind her and nearly fainted with relief. They weren't there.

Not that she could count on them to be gone for long. They'd find her again. She'd been a fool to ever think Ricardo would forgive the fact that she'd killed his brother.

Chapter Two

"Piece of cake, huh?" Braden Thomas snorted derisively as he and his brother Ian drove down yet another street paralleling the park. "This was supposed to be a simple extraction. We show up, she falls gratefully into our arms and we haul ass out of the country."

Ian ground his teeth as he contemplated the pleasure he'd take in shoving Braden out of the moving vehicle.

"It's your damn fault," Ian growled. "You had to barrel out of the truck and scare her shitless. What the hell was she supposed to think?"

Braden snorted. "Yeah, like you did any better on the phone? She hung up before you finished telling her your name."

"Spooky flake," Ian muttered. "I'm not convinced she's worth all this trouble. We're risking a lot to fulfill a promise to a guy who betrayed us."

Even as the thought crossed his mind, a wave of grief consumed him. Gabe was gone. Yeah, he'd betrayed his team, and that was hard to swallow. They'd been through a lot together. But until he knew the full truth behind Gabe's defection, he couldn't bring himself to condemn a man he'd called friend for so many years.

"Yeah, but if we have her, sooner or later, Esteban will come calling. We'll kill two birds with one stone."

Ian nodded. Braden had a point. They'd talked it over with Eli and with Falcon, and it was decided that Katie was too good an angle not to exploit. Worst case scenario, they were stuck babysitting for a few weeks. Best case scenario, they nailed Esteban and could then send Katie Buchanan on her way.

Where the hell was she? She'd taken off like a scalded cat, and she was damn fast. He had to give her that. He would have caught her, but in the midst of the chase, he'd felt the prickle up his spine, a sign he was fast associating with the need to shift.

His heart had damn near pounded out of his chest, and vivid images of a cat stalking its prey had come to mind. He'd been just a few seconds from transforming to jaguar. He would have hunted her and probably killed her.

A resigned sigh escaped him, and Braden cast a sidelong glance at him.

"You okay, man?"

Ian grunted in return. He didn't want to admit to Braden how close he'd come to losing control. They both battled the beast on a daily basis.

"Something happened back there, Ian."

Ian raised an eyebrow and stared over at his brother in question.

Braden's face twisted into a scowl. "When I was running after her...it was as if I was the cat and she was the prey, only I didn't have an urge to hurt her. Just the opposite. I can't explain it," he finished lamely.

Ian frowned. It was similar to the way he'd felt, not that he was about to admit that to Braden. But he wasn't so sure that he wouldn't have hurt her. "Maybe you need another injection. We should go back to her apartment and see if she shows."

He glanced down at the bag Katie had dropped. They'd go back to her apartment and wait inside. He could give Braden an injection and hope to hell he held out until he could take one himself later. While they waited, he'd poke around and see what he could discover about Gabe's little sister. And figure out her next move.

Katie stood at the ATM and jammed the cash into her pocket. Stupid daily limits pissed her off. She'd need to make several more withdrawals before she'd have enough money to fund her getaway. In the meantime, she had no choice but to get the hell out of town, no matter how dire her finances.

The evening air chilled her sweat-dampened skin, and she shivered. She'd been stupid to drop her pack, but then escaping the two men would have been more difficult carrying it. Warmer clothes would have to wait until she'd cleared town.

She took off down the street, weighing her options. The bus station was too obvious. Airport even more so. Hitchhiking, though something she'd done in the past, gave her too much exposure, not to mention it was dangerous as hell.

A resigned sigh escaped her. Walking it was. She was in shape, thanks to rigorous workouts and training sessions. But fitness didn't help with the cold. And it wasn't like she hadn't walked all damn day already.

Though heading west held certain appeal, she'd be better off going east, to some large city she could disappear in. Small towns made her too noticeable.

Some place warm. Florida sounded heavenly. But it left her too boxed in. Not enough escape options. Atlanta maybe? Anything beat the cold of Missouri.

St. Louis had seemed like a good idea when she'd arrived. How had they found her? She'd been so careful. Or so she'd thought.

She picked up her pace. A cab could take her out of the city. It would cripple her monetarily, but it would be worth it. She could pick up some light camping equipment and parallel the interstate south to Cape Girardeau. It would take her several days, but it would give her time to hit ATMs and build her cash flow. From Cape, she could buy a cheap vehicle and drive wherever she wanted to go.

Bolstered by her plan, she crossed a busy intersection and started looking for an available cab. Clutching her arms with her hands, she rubbed up and down to infuse much-needed warmth.

Note to self: Don't relax your guard. Ever.

It was appropriate that at the moment she administered the reprimand, a man stepped in front of her, his hands flying out to grip her shoulders.

She lashed out with her foot and kicked him squarely in

the balls. A harsh curse split her ears as he doubled over. She didn't waste any time. Turning around, she launched into a full run.

Only to collide with a heavily muscled wall of male flesh. Steel bands wrapped around her none too gently. She reacted violently, kicking and flailing, but he didn't loosen his hold.

Her eyes met his and she found fire. Angry determination glittered in his green eyes. Bracing herself, she reared back and rammed her head into his nose. Pain exploded through her skull, and her vision blurred.

To her dismay, he didn't budge. If anything he crushed her tighter against him, and she whimpered in pain.

"I've had about all I can take from you," he bit out.

She struggled harder as she fought the dizzying effects of her head-butt. She managed to wiggle enough to bring her knee up between his legs.

Fingers dug into her knee, squeezing until she yelped.

"You give me no choice, sweetheart," he said grimly.

Before she had time to try and figure out that cryptic remark, she felt a prick against her shoulder. She went rigid in his arms, and fear hissed through her veins. Oh God, no. He'd drugged her.

His face swam in her vision, and she went slack against him. And then she heard another voice, close to her ear.

"We won't hurt you, Katie. We're here to help you."

Her eyelids fluttered, and no matter how she fought the drug, it was too much. Everything went dark.

Chapter Three

Ian frowned as he stared down at Katie Buchanan. She lay on the seat, her body curled into a defensive posture even in sleep. Strain lined her forehead, and a frown tugged her lips downward. He reached down to touch the short blonde wisps that lay raggedly on her neck. Then before giving it any thought, his finger traveled over her jaw to her lips where he smoothed the downward curve.

Her hair was an interesting assortment of lengths, like she cut it herself with no regard for appearance. The strands stuck out, each going a different direction, but on her it fit. She didn't strike him as the sleek, always-styled type at all.

Hearing Braden behind him, he yanked his hand away and frowned in annoyance. His head ached like a mother, his eyes were crossing with fatigue, and yet he was standing here like a nimrod entertaining himself with her hairdo.

Grumbling to himself about psycho females, he gathered her limp body in his arms and hauled her out of the SUV. Braden walked ahead and opened the door to her apartment. They hadn't wanted to risk getting a hotel room, and her apartment was unassuming.

Katie was an enigma. Cautious. Extremely so. Spooky as a bat, and she kept a very low profile. Looking around her apartment earlier, he'd discovered that she lived a very barebones existence. Odd for a woman. Did she know she was a target? Had Gabe warned her?

He shouldered his way into her small living room and gently laid her on the couch. Then he stepped away as Braden leaned in to check her pulse and peel back her eyelids.

16

"She's going to have one hell of a bruise on her forehead," Braden said as he straightened.

"She damn near broke my nose. You'll forgive me if I'm not terribly sympathetic," Ian said darkly.

"At least you aren't walking funny and singing soprano," Braden grumbled.

Ian grimaced and felt a sympathy twinge in the region of his groin. He'd seen how hard she'd kicked Braden in the balls. He'd be lucky if he ever fathered children after that.

"So what now?" Braden asked as he slumped down in one of the armchairs.

Ian lowered himself into a chair as well and eyed his brother. "We get some damn sleep, and tomorrow we get the hell out of the country."

"You call Eli yet?"

Ian frowned. "And when would I have had time to do that when we've been chasing the hellcat down all day?"

"And where are we taking her exactly?"

"You're full of questions today, little brother."

Braden grinned. "Am I annoying you?"

Ian scowled.

"Then my duty is done."

"For someone who just got their balls relocated you sure are a cheerful son of a bitch."

Braden shrugged. "Maybe I'm looking forward to being done with this. Makes me edgy being back in the good ole U.S. of A. I somehow doubt Uncle Sam will roll out the welcome mat, you know?"

Ian's lips tightened. "Yeah, well fuck 'em. We'll be out of here tomorrow."

"Going where?" Braden asked again.

Ian sighed. "Eli's supposed to be working on it. Evidently Falcon has a few safe houses across Europe. I liked Argentina, but that's fucked now that Esteban knows where it is."

"Isn't the point of this exercise to lure Esteban?" Braden asked.

Ian nodded. "Yeah, but he's not supposed to know he's

being lured. Going to Argentina would be tipping our hand, not to mention making us look like complete nimrods."

Braden grew quiet for a moment. "Tell me something, Ian. Do you think this whole merger with Falcon is a good idea? I mean I know why Eli is there. Tyana's fingers are wrapped tight around his nuts, and he's content to be led around like a lapdog."

Ian's gaze narrowed. This was the first time he'd heard Braden express doubts about joining ranks with Falcon Mercenary Group. Their former team leader, Eli Chance, had fallen head over ass for Tyana Berezovsky, a member of Falcon, and with the way their hostage recovery team had gone to shit when they all turned into a bunch of unstable shifters, it made sense to team up with the merc group.

Eli wasn't unstable, though. Resentment bubbled up before Ian could control it. He and Braden hadn't been as lucky as Eli and Gabe. While the two other men had full control over their newfound abilities, Ian and Braden struggled with their instability on a daily basis.

Braden was watching him closely, and Ian tried to school his features. "Are you having doubts?" he asked Braden.

Braden looked thoughtful for a long moment. "Honestly? I don't know. Too much has changed in too short a time. I don't think Falcon will fuck us, if that's what you're asking. I just wonder how we fit into the picture. I don't like the idea of being some fucking charity case and having their doctor shoved at us at regular intervals."

"Yeah, I hear you," Ian muttered.

"Are we going to end up like Damiano?" Braden asked softly.

Ian swore under his breath. Damiano was a member of Falcon, and like Ian and Braden, a victim of the chemical agent that had changed them all into shifters. He was even more unstable than Ian and Braden, and if D's future was their own, it wasn't pretty.

Damn Esteban Morales. Damn him to hell. Ian glanced over at Katie again, and his resolve hardened. If she was their key to nailing Esteban's ass, then he'd have no compunction about using her in any way necessary to achieve their means.

"Let's get some sleep," Ian said, ignoring Braden's question. "You can take the couch. I'll take Miss Psycho into the bedroom and make sure she isn't going anywhere for the night."

Katie came awake with a start. Her eyes flew open, and despite the fogginess surrounding her mind, she felt alert. Fear could do that to you. Adrenaline coursed through her veins as she took stock of her situation.

She tried to move and then froze, feeling rope around one wrist. The next thing she registered was the large body of a man next to her. The third thing she realized was that she was in her own bed in her apartment.

As far as *what-the-fuck* moments went, this was a big one.

Her eyes rapidly adjusted to the darkness, and she looked down again to see that she was tied to the man's wrist. He was sound asleep, his soft, even breathing filling the room.

Then she frowned. There had been two of them. She remembered that much. Which meant that somewhere close, there was another one. As if one wasn't enough to deal with.

She gritted her teeth then turned her attention to the rope binding her to the mountain of muscle lying next to her. With her free hand, she carefully slid her fingers under the neckline of her T-shirt and into the sports bra to find the tiny pocketknife underneath the curve of her right breast.

Dumb bastards hadn't patted her down, but then why would they feel the need to search the poor defenseless little woman?

She pulled the razor-sharp blade free of the clasp with her teeth then ever so carefully, she lowered it to the length of rope between their wrists.

As it passed through the twines like butter, she gave herself a mental pat on the back for being prepared and making sure she kept the blade sharp. Gabe would be proud.

Deep sadness clogged her chest, pulling painfully at her heart. No, she wouldn't think about him now. Later. When she was safe, she'd mourn. For now she had to make sure they didn't both end up dead.

If it weren't for the fact that she had no idea where the other guy was, she'd bolt out of bed and run. She'd have the element of surprise, and by the time sleeping dude figured out she was free, she'd be two blocks away.

Instead she inched her way off the bed. Slowly, carefully, moving the tiniest bit with each breath. Every time he stirred she froze. When he flinched, she held her breath. Until finally, she slid the remaining way.

Not wasting a moment, she hurried across the floor, damning the fact that the bastard had removed her shoes. She didn't have time to find them.

She halted in the doorway to the living room when she saw the second man's too-large body sprawled on her too-small couch. He didn't appear to be sleeping as deeply as the man in her bed. Getting by him and out the door could be a problem.

She felt in her pockets and nearly cursed aloud. All her cash was gone. She trembled with rage and curled her fingers into tight fists at her sides. Her bankcard was gone along with her cash.

Tears of frustration burned her eyes, pissing her off even more as she made her way quietly across the living room floor.

Her hand was on the knob, and she held her breath as she made her bid for freedom.

"Tell me you aren't going to make me chase your ass across town again."

She yanked her head toward the couch to see the man leaning up on one elbow, staring balefully at her. Foregoing any attempt at stealth, she threw open the door and bolted into the night.

The pounding of footsteps behind her told her that she was being pursued. She put her head down and turned on the speed. At the end of the block, she darted across the deserted street and veered away from the direction of the park. They'd expect her to go the familiar route.

She'd only gone another block when she heard the groan of an engine. As she went to cross another street, the squeal of tires sounded deafeningly close, and she pulled up short just in time for a silver Mercedes to careen in front of her.

A man jumped from the driver's seat, and even in the dark, his identity was unmistakable.

Fear, vicious and stark, pooled in her stomach and swelled outward until nausea overwhelmed her.

"Katie, my love. Out for a late-night jog? I've always thought you were in impeccable shape, but one would think you were running from someone. Surely not me? We have a lot to clear up, you and me."

She stared dully at Ricardo de la Cruz. It was only a matter of time before he showed up. His henchmen had sat on her long enough for him to arrive.

Cocky and arrogant as ever. His perfect white teeth flashed in the glare of the streetlights. His smile was sinister, with the promise of retribution. If only she'd killed him instead of Paulo.

Bitterness welled in her mouth, hard to swallow.

She turned to run when a strange sound shattered the night. Her entire body jerked and went stiff as agony fired through every one of her nerves. She couldn't move, couldn't speak, couldn't think. So much pain. She was on fire.

For a moment, she stood locked in the grip of hell, her body refusing to respond to her commands. As she stared into the darkness, she saw the man who'd chased her from her apartment standing in the shadows a distance away.

His expression wasn't one of triumph, however. Concern creased his brow, and he looked angry.

Then she sagged to the ground, gasps of pain spilling from her mouth. Desperately, she sucked in air, trying to drag more into her lungs. Lungs that felt as though they'd been torched.

Rough hands hauled her up. Fingers twisted in her hair, yanking her head back. She found herself staring into Ricardo's handsome face right before his spit hit her on the cheek.

"You will pay for killing my brother, whore."

Chapter Four

Tyana Berezovsky awkwardly made her way down the hallway to Jonah Pearson's office. The going was slow, thanks to the crutches and heavy cast encasing her right leg.

She faltered for a moment when she got to the door but regained her footing and shoved the door open with one crutch.

Jonah looked up as she entered. "Should you be up and around?"

She glared and hobbled forward. When she got to his desk, she leaned on one crutch and brought the other one up until she prodded his chest with the rubber tip. Jonah glanced down at the crutch then back up at her with a raised eyebrow.

"You've got to do something about Eli. He's driving me insane."

Jonah shoved the crutch away and smirked at her. "Eli is your problem. Not mine."

Tyana sagged into a chair and dropped the crutches with a clatter. "Surely you can find something for him to do?" She frowned at the pleading note in her voice. She sounded desperate.

Hell, who was she kidding? She *was* desperate.

Jonah chuckled. "It was your idea to fall in love with the guy."

She closed her eyes. No, it wasn't her idea. If she'd had a choice, she wouldn't have waded into all those messy emotions.

It was one thing to be accountable to herself and to her team. She could deal with that just fine. But now she was accountable to someone else. Someone she was emotionally involved with. In short, it sucked.

"He's smothering me," she grumbled. "I can't take a piss without him hovering."

Jonah put his fingers together at his chin and stared hard at her. "As much as you know I don't love to play armchair psychologist, may I point out that A. the guy loves you, and B. he damn near lost you. He's entitled to hover a bit."

She closed her eyes and groaned. "Jonah, please. There has to be something you can give him to do just for a couple of days. You're supposed to be bringing him into Falcon. Isn't there some bullshit assignment you can throw at him? Have him go make the arrangements for the safe house for Ian and Braden. Something, anything. I just need him out of my hair for a little while or I'm going to pull it all out."

He studied her for a long moment. She was begging, and she knew it wasn't a pretty sight. She never begged for anything. Maybe he sensed her desperation, not that it would take much brilliance to figure out she was at the end of her rope, because he sighed and leveled a resigned eye roll in her direction.

"I'll see what I can do, Ty. But damn it, Eli isn't my problem. He's yours. I'd thank you to remember that in the future."

She grinned. "If I could get up, I'd hug you."

He managed a look of horror. "You've gotten soft on me. You fell in love, and it turned your brain to mush."

"Could we stop going on and on about the L-word?"

Jonah shrugged. "You're going to owe me one for this, and don't think I won't collect from your invalid ass."

She nodded and made a grab for her crutches only to realize she couldn't reach to the floor from her chair. She shifted and reached again only to come up short.

"Damn it," she muttered.

"Problem?" Jonah asked with ill-suppressed humor.

She flipped her middle finger at him as she strained with her other hand to snag her crutch.

"And you wonder why Eli is hovering," Jonah said dryly as he walked around the desk. He bent and picked up her crutches and then handed them to her.

"Thanks," she mumbled.

She heaved herself upward, sweat breaking out on her forehead as she bobbled. Her continued weakness bugged the hell out of her. She was ready to be a hundred percent again.

Jonah caught her arm to steady her and frowned. "Might I suggest you stay off your feet for a while longer? You're clearly not ready to be up and around so damn much."

Tyana sighed. "Now you sound like Eli."

"Heaven forbid."

She hobbled toward the door, ignoring his sarcasm. Up to now he hadn't fussed over her much, and he hadn't cut her any slack. Just the way she liked it.

"Don't you get soft on me, Jonah," she said when she got to the door. She turned to look at him. "I much prefer you being the big asshole."

He lifted one brow. "And you expect me to do you a favor?"

She winced. "Yeah well, forget the asshole part."

He smiled again. "Don't let the door hit you on the ass on the way out."

Chapter Five

A sharp slap to her face brought Katie awake. She tried to raise a palm to her stinging cheek, but rough hands gripped her wrists, holding her immobile.

Ricardo stood in front of her as two men hauled her to her feet. Annoyance ticked his cheek even as satisfaction carved a smile on his sensual lips.

He was an extraordinarily handsome man, as Paulo had been. Olive, sun-kissed skin, raven hair and startling blue eyes, crystal clear, like a Caribbean sea.

She wanted to laugh at the idea that she was standing here, waiting to die and remarking on the beauty of the man holding her life in his hands.

Instead of striking her again, he cupped her cheek in his palm and lightly caressed her skin.

"Paulo was a fool to think he could ever tame you," Ricardo murmured. "He was too weak, too trusting. You unmanned him in every way."

She had to bite her tongue to keep from retorting. Let him bait her. She wasn't going to give him a reason to hit her again.

His fingers trailed down her skin and hooked into the neckline of her tank top. He slid his palm inside, cupping her breast. Every muscle in her body tensed. She couldn't control the shudder of revulsion, and it angered him.

"I, on the other hand, am more than capable of bringing you to heel," he said silkily.

Bile rose in her throat. He didn't mean to kill her at all. Merely make her wish for death.

"Take her upstairs and make her bathe." He withdrew his hand and stepped back. Then to her he said, "I've taken the liberty of laying out some clothes for you. I expect you to clean yourself up and change. You look a mess."

She pressed her lips together and looked away. It was a mistake.

His palm cracked against her exposed cheek, knocking her back into the men who held her arms.

"Don't you ever look away from me, whore."

Slowly, she turned to stare him in the eye, doing nothing to disguise her hatred.

"Yes, you'd like to kill me wouldn't you?" he said in a deceptively soft tone. "Just like you killed Paulo. I will make you beg, Katie. You will beg me to kill you before I'm finished."

He waved his hand. "Take her away."

The two men dragged Katie toward the stairs. She scrambled to get her feet under her, but they walked too fast. They hauled her up to the bathroom and shoved her inside.

"Do as the boss says," one of them ordered. "Your clothes are on the counter."

They retreated, closing the door behind them.

Katie took quick stock of the bathroom. There wasn't a single window. Most of the rooms in the house didn't have any. The first time she'd seen Ricardo's compound, she'd remarked to Paulo how it reminded her of some clichéd drug dealer's fortress. Paulo hadn't been amused, but then she hadn't realized until later how on-target her assessment had been.

Her hopes plummeted at the thought of how difficult escape would be. Even if she did manage to gain freedom from the house, she would have to deal with the surrounding terrain. Ricardo would have no compunction about ordering his men to bathe her if she refused to do it herself. With that in mind, she turned on the shower and stripped out of her shorts and shirt.

Her body ached from the Taser Ricardo had used to prevent her from fleeing. She checked her appearance in the mirror and winced at the bruises on her face, neck and arms.

She turned away and climbed into the shower.

What the hell was she going to do? She washed rapidly,

knowing Ricardo could very well show up in the bathroom. He thrived on being unpredictable, on keeping people off balance.

The little weasel had wanted her from the moment Paulo had brought her home and introduced her as his girlfriend. He'd played into Paulo's insecurities and convinced his younger brother that Katie was having an affair with him.

If only she could have killed Ricardo instead. If only. It was a regret she'd carry to her grave. And if she ever got the chance to rectify her mistake, she'd take it without a moment's hesitation.

As she rinsed the last of the soap from her hair, she ran her hand over the back of her neck, sliding the wet strands away from her skin. Her fingers glanced over something at her nape, and she frowned.

She backtracked and ran her finger over the slight protrusion again. It felt like a splinter. Gripping it with her fingernails, she tugged, and after a slight twinge, it came free.

She pulled her hand around so she could look at the tiny object. What the hell was it? It was metal, needlelike but not very long.

Opening the door to the shower, she stepped out, the sliver still in her palm. She laid it on the counter then reached for a towel to dry off.

After she hastily pulled on the jeans and shirt—the bastard hadn't included any underwear, his way of humiliating her, no doubt—she turned her attention back to the thing she'd taken out of her neck.

There was no way she'd gotten it by accident, which meant someone had inserted it on purpose. Was it a tracking device? And why put one in now, after she'd been captured? Unless Ricardo was afraid she'd escape again...

Carefully, she inserted the device back into the hollow of her neck. She didn't want Ricardo to know she'd found it. If she did manage to escape—and she had every intention of doing so—the tracking device could buy her valuable time if she sent him looking in the wrong direction.

First she had to regain her strength then she'd bide her time until she found a way to escape. Whatever she had to endure from Ricardo was a price she'd have to pay.

"I knew this was a bad idea," Braden grumbled. "This has been one pain in the ass after another." He glanced up at Ian who wore a similar look of irritation. "Is Tits sure Esteban hasn't made a move on Katie yet?"

Ian shrugged. "Word is Esteban offered a reward for her—alive—yesterday. These assholes nabbed Katie two days ago. You do the math."

"Fuck."

"He's reportedly no longer interested in Eli—alive, anyway. I'm guessing that us teaming up with Falcon has deterred Esteban. After the last ass-kicking he received at our hands, I doubt he wants to pick any more fights. He's focusing all his resources on finding Katie, which has to make us the biggest dumbasses alive for sticking our necks into this one. It'll make us targets all over again."

Braden shook his head and put the binoculars back to his eyes. He focused on the sprawling mansion nestled in the small valley below. He and Ian were stationed in the densely wooded area just above the house, keeping close watch on the goings-on. They were still getting a signal from the tracking device Ian had planted on Katie, but there had been little to no movement in the last twenty-four hours.

Ian wanted to wait, watch, learn the lay of the land. Braden? He just wanted to get it the fuck over with, go in, put down some serious lead, hogtie Katie before she could cause any more trouble and then get the hell out of the country.

He lowered the binoculars and looked up again at Ian. "Are we going to stare at the damn house for another day or are we going to get our heads out of our asses and make a move?"

Ian's lips tightened. "I'm not getting my ass shot over her. It's bad enough we've had to chase her across the damn country after spending weeks looking for her, but now apparently she's pissed off some jacked-up coke dealer with an ego the size of Canada." He shook his head in disgust.

"Yeah, it would seem Esteban is the *least* of her worries,"

Braden muttered.

He put down the binoculars and rose from his knee. As he stretched and worked the kinks out, he glanced back at the house.

"So what's the plan, big brother? We going in or not?"

Ian heaved a disgruntled sigh. "Yeah. We've fucked off enough time already. We'll move in just before dusk. We're going to have to be quick and not too picky about piling up the bodies. We grab Katie and get the hell out then book it to the Delta. Our pilot is on standby there."

Braden shrugged. The bodies didn't bother him. Scum-sucking drug dealers did, however. What he really wanted to know was what connection Gabe's little sister had to Ricardo de la Cruz. She was still alive which told Braden that de la Cruz wanted her that way.

She was pretty enough in a psycho, hellcat sort of way, that is if you liked your women with claws. He preferred them slightly more biddable.

"Let's do a weapons check and then..." Ian stared at Braden as his voice trailed off.

"Then?" Braden prompted.

"We should probably take a low dose of the sedative," Ian said quietly. "We can't afford a shift."

How ridiculous that Braden hadn't even considered it. No matter how long he dealt with the limitations of living his life as half man and half panther, it still managed to creep up on him. Stupid.

"Where are we flying to?" Braden asked as he watched Ian take out the syringes and the small vial of medication.

"Paris," Ian said in a tight voice. "Falcon has a safe house there."

Braden nodded. He knew Ian was uncomfortable relying on Falcon. Braden wasn't entirely down with it himself. They'd spent too many years as their own team, Covert Hostage Recovery. Eli had led the team, no doubt there, but everyone knew their job and they did it, no babysitting required.

Now, suddenly they were faced with new people, new personalities to learn and a new leadership. Jonah had

Braden's respect, but he didn't have Braden's complete trust. Yet.

Ian checked his watch. "We'll wait two more hours then take the sedative. The doses are light enough not to impair our judgment, so we should be fine."

Still, Braden would feel more comfortable if they had back-up. Even Falcon. Against ordinary civilians, he and Ian were more than capable of taking down the entire house, but these weren't ordinary people. They were drug dealers. Armed to the teeth and not bashful about shooting first and asking questions later.

"So I guess falling asleep just before go time probably wouldn't be a good idea," Braden joked, knowing it would annoy Ian.

Ian scowled. "Very funny." Then his scowl deepened. "I sure hope to hell she's worth all this aggravation. She better damn well serve Esteban up on a platter or I'm going to be pissed."

Braden shrugged. "We owe it to Gabe to make sure she's safe."

Ian's eyes hardened. "We owe him nothing."

"You wouldn't have betrayed the team for me?" Braden asked. "Because I would have for you. No question."

Ian looked surprised, and then he grew pensive. Instead of responding, he glanced away, busying himself with the two syringes. He packed them into one of the bags and then started a weapons check.

Subject closed. Typical Ian. If he didn't want to talk about it, he just ignored it until it went away. Braden sighed and walked to the back of the SUV to run down his own weapons.

They needed to view Katie as a key to a cure, to figuring out how to rid themselves of the beasts lurking inside, waiting to be released at any moment. If they did that, they could put up with any amount of inconvenience.

And really, if they couldn't handle one slip of a woman, they needed to fucking quit anyway.

Chapter Six

Katie lay on Ricardo's big bed with a sense of purpose. Even as pain whipped and coiled through her body, her mind focused on what had to be done.

She shifted and sucked in a painful breath as the movement jarred her abdomen. Ricardo had enjoyed watching as his men hit her. But that wasn't as bad as what he planned next.

He wanted her helpless and hurting, completely at his whim and mercy. His men had carried her to Ricardo's bed and left her. He was going to rape her. There was no pretense, no false arrogance that told him she really wanted him and would welcome his advances. He didn't want that. He enjoyed inflicting pain and humiliation. Her enjoyment would ruin the experience for him.

Her gaze fastened on the one window. Her escape route. Few of the other rooms had windows, but here in Ricardo's domain, there was a large picture window overlooking the rugged terrain of the Uncompahgre Plateau.

She heard his footsteps, and she tensed in anticipation. She would escape or force him to kill her, but either way, he wouldn't have her, would not take from her by force what she wasn't willing to give.

She'd spent the last two years running, constantly looking over her shoulder, and for what? So she could end up Ricardo's whore until he tired of torturing her?

Fuck him and fuck that.

He appeared at the foot of the bed in a silk robe. How cliché was that? Clearly the man had watched too many mafia movies.

There was nothing put-on about the look of lust that crowded his eyes or the way he stared at her. The lapels of his robe parted as he pulled at the silk and let it fall to the floor.

He was aroused, but violence had always been a huge turn-on for him. Katie was convinced that he couldn't get it up unless he inflicted pain.

She shrank into the bed, careful to affect the pitiful, injured look she was trying to maintain. Let him see her fear. It would only make him more confident of his power. He underestimated her. He always had.

The bed dipped under his weight as he climbed onto the mattress. She didn't move. She waited.

She adopted an appropriate look of meekness and fear. When he reached out to touch her, she held back the flinch.

"I told you to undress," he said in a menacing whisper.

Yeah, he had, but she couldn't very well escape naked.

"But I'm glad you didn't," he continued on as his fingers trailed up her arm. "I rather like the idea of tearing your clothes off myself."

Just a little further, asshole. Just a little further.

She held her breath as he leaned forward. His engorged cock brushed against her hip, and she bolted into action.

She grabbed his erect penis in one hand and twisted violently. She smashed her other hand into his nose.

His howl of pain was immediate. She rolled until they both fell onto the floor, her on top of him, her hand still wrapped tight around his dick and balls.

Not giving him any time to recover, she leaped up, grabbed the lamp off the bedside table and smashed it over his head as hard as she could.

He went limp.

She didn't take even a second to savor her victory. She lunged for the bedroom door, flipping the bolt to lock it. His men would have heard him bellow and would be beating down his door in a matter of seconds. She needed those precious seconds.

After securing the door, she went back to the bed and yanked the comforter off. She moved toward the window, wrapping the blanket around her body as she went.

The window didn't open. She'd already tried it. So the only way out was through it. She just hoped she didn't break anything in the fall from the second story.

Desperate times and desperate measures and all that jazz. *Yeah, stop thinking about it. Just go.*

She backed from the window, clenched the blanket tighter around her and took off running. When she got to the window, she jumped, ramming her body as hard against the glass as she could.

It shattered on impact. For a moment, it felt as though she was suspended, but the air rushed over her face and a second later, she hit the ground with a resounding thump.

Pain speared through her body. Her arm. God, the one she landed on. It hurt like a mother. She hoped to hell she hadn't broken it.

There was no time to take stock of her injuries or lack thereof. She scrambled to her feet, wincing when she cut her hand on one of the many shards of glass surrounding her.

She discarded the blanket and took off through the courtyard toward the stone barrier surrounding Ricardo's estate. She held her bleeding hand against her shirt so she wouldn't drip on the ground.

It wasn't going to be easy to get over that wall but then what the hell had been easy for her so far?

She lowered her arm and took a running start. When she got to the wall, she leaped, doing a quick run up the stones. Her momentum carried her up, and she grasped the ledge with her fingers. Barely.

She hung there for several long seconds, catching her breath and praying she didn't fall. Her hands ached, and she couldn't even feel her fingers as she clawed for better leverage.

Her feet swinging, she boosted her body until she managed to scrape her elbows over the top, and then she used her arms to haul herself the rest of the way up.

As she rolled over the side, part of the stone by her head exploded, sending sharp pieces of rock into her face and neck. It took her a second to realize she was being shot at.

She dropped over the other side and took off running. She ignored the pain, her injuries, the fact that she had no shoes and that her clothing offered little protection from the bushes and shrubbery she flung herself through.

Only one thing mattered. Escape.

Sucking in mouthfuls of air, she ran, dodging tree branches and jumping over rocks. She didn't know where she was running. That didn't matter. As long as she was away from Ricardo, she could figure out the rest later.

She topped a slight rise and paused only to work the stitch out of her side before she started down again. She skidded to a halt when a large man stepped directly into her path.

A frightened moan escaped her lips. God, not him again. She glanced frantically around for the other one and sure enough, he was circling behind her.

Against Ricardo she had a fighting chance. Though bigger than her, he had a slim build. These two? Hulking masses of muscle-bound humanity. She'd bounce off them like a quarter.

She tightened her shoulders. No matter what, they weren't taking her down without a fight, and she damn sure wouldn't let them get close enough to drug her again.

Ian's gaze traveled over Katie's tense body as Braden circled behind her. He didn't miss anything. Not the bruise on her cheek, the bruises around her neck and the fingerprint-shaped bruises marring her upper arms.

Her blue eyes were wild with fear—and determination.

He put a placating hand out. "Now, Katie—"

He couldn't even get the words past his lips before she was off like a shot. Braden cursed as he gave chase. Ian took off after her as well. The last thing they needed was a damn long pursuit when de la Cruz's men were going to be after them.

This was not how this was supposed to go down. They were supposed to go in, shooting anything that moved, and haul her out on the route they'd planned. She wasn't supposed to have already escaped with Ricardo's men all still accounted for. Difficult wench.

Braden managed to bolt ahead of her, effectively cutting her off. The moment she paused to change direction gave Ian the chance he needed.

He took her down with a tackle. Her cry of pain hit him right in the chest. Damn it, he hadn't wanted to hurt her.

She struggled beneath him as he tried to pry most of his weight off her.

"Get off me!" she cried.

He grabbed her wrists, careful not to squeeze too tightly as he tucked both hands into one of his and held them over her head.

"Stop fighting me," he said through gritted teeth. "I'm trying not to hurt you here."

"I won't go back to that bastard," she hissed. "You'll have to kill me."

Braden made a noise that sounded like a snarl. Ian yanked his head up to see Braden scowling beside him. Ian glanced back down at Katie in surprise. She thought they worked for de la Cruz. And why wouldn't she? They both showed up at the same time and both had made a grab for her.

He eased his hold on her and backed away, determined not to terrify her any more than he already had.

"Katie, listen to me. Gabe sent us."

Her eyes widened in shock, and all the fight went out of her in one big whoosh. She stared dumbly at him for a long second as he rose to his feet. She scooted along the ground on her behind then picked herself up as if she was prepared to flee again.

Braden stepped forward, but Ian held out a hand to stop him.

"Is he alive?" she demanded.

There was so much fear in her gaze that he couldn't stand the thought of telling her Gabe was dead. Right now his priority had to be keeping *her* alive.

Braden glanced over his shoulder as the staccato of machine gun fire sounded in the distance. Then to Ian's surprise, he strode over to Katie, hoisted her over his shoulder and took off into the brush.

Ian jogged after them just about the time Katie started to fight. But it was her pained grunt when Braden hopped over a fallen log that made him pause.

"Braden, wait, you're hurting her," Ian called out.

Braden stopped and swung around to stare at his brother in surprise. Ian grimaced. Whether she was hurt or not wasn't the issue. If Braden wasn't killing her then Ian should have just let him go. The sooner they got the hell out of here the better.

But Braden eased her off his shoulder and set her on her feet, though he gripped her arm so she couldn't take off. Her pale, shaken face and her short gasps of breath made it obvious that she was indeed in a lot of pain.

Braden cursed and touched her cheek with one hand. "I'm sorry, Katie. But we've got to get the hell out of here. *Now*. We can't fuck around waiting for you to decide if you can trust us. It's either your buddy de la Cruz or us. I need you to decide so we can escape without an ass full of lead."

There was a brief flash of uncertainty in her wide eyes as she studied Braden first and then Ian. She glanced back toward the house, and her expression hardened.

"If you betray me, I'll kill you," she said in a voice that sent chills down Ian's spine.

Funny thing was, he absolutely believed her.

"You can certainly try," Ian said as he moved toward her again.

He took her arm and turned her in the direction of the SUV. Braden took her other arm and they hustled her up the incline. By the time they reached the SUV, Katie was stumbling to keep up. As he glanced down at her bare feet, he cursed to see one was bleeding. He hadn't even considered her feet. He'd told Braden to put her down because she was in pain, and he had no idea the extent of her injuries, but in his boneheadedness he hadn't considered the fact she'd been running through the woods with no shoes.

He reached for her, sweeping her into his arms as he walked the remaining distance to the truck. Her face went pale, and sweat beaded her forehead.

He stalked over to the SUV and sat her on top of the hood. Before she could utter a sound, he yanked at her T-shirt, baring her ribcage and breasts to his view.

"Hey!" she shouted as she took a swing at him. She shoved furiously at the shirt, but he held tight.

"What the hell did he do to you?" Ian growled.

Her full, pink-tipped breasts bounced slightly as she struggled to cover herself, but Ian's gaze was drawn to the dark bruises that marred her belly. He put his hands over her ribs, checking for breakage.

Beside him, Braden muttered a dark obscenity as he stared at her chest.

Her hands trembled as she gripped the T-shirt, trying to pull it away from Ian.

"Can we just get out of here?" she asked in a shaky voice.

Ian gently arranged her T-shirt back over her stomach then plucked her off the hood of the truck. He carried her around to the passenger side and deposited her into the backseat.

"Stay down," he ordered.

To his surprise, she complied, lying on the seat as Braden slid into the front seat.

Ian hurried around to the driver's side and got in. He shoved his gun at Braden. Seconds later, he peeled out down the rugged path they'd taken to the ridge overlooking de la Cruz's house.

As soon as he pulled onto the divide road, they were nearly run over by two black SUVs. He careened sharply to the left to avoid being hit and then stomped on the accelerator, fishtailing in the loose dirt.

"Holy fuck," Braden spit out as he almost landed in Ian's lap. Then he hit the deck when a barrage of bullets pelted the passenger door.

"What the hell did you do to piss him off so bad, sweetheart?" Braden called back to Katie.

"I'm breathing," she muttered.

"Not for long if I can't shake these assholes," Ian said grimly. "Anytime you want to take some heat off us would be nice, little brother."

Braden cracked a grin. "Well, you do always say I'm too quick to start shooting shit. Figured I'd show some restraint."

"Restraint, my ass. Now ain't the time for it. Shoot the fuckers."

Braden laughed, and Ian shook his head. How on earth he

37

could always crack jokes in high-pressure situations was beyond Ian, but he was used to it by now. It used to drive Gabe up the wall, while Eli just chuckled and went on.

Braden cracked the window, angled his rifle and squeezed off several rounds. Ian checked his rearview mirror to see one of the SUVs hit the ditch. The bad news, however, was that two more had joined the chase.

"Son of a bitch," Ian swore.

"I'd say the airport is out," Braden said as he steadied himself for another shot. "We're going away from Delta, and it's not like they're going to let us on a plane to calmly fly out of there."

"Aren't you the observant one," Ian said snidely.

"Can we dispense with the adolescent bickering and get the fuck down the road?" Katie bit out.

"Aah, I'd almost forgotten about her," Braden said cheerfully as he took out another SUV.

"We're saving your sweet ass, so I don't want to hear any bitching," Ian said in a tight voice.

She snorted. Actually snorted.

"Would you like me to let you out so you can hitch a ride with your buddies back there?" Ian asked.

Braden arched an eyebrow as he glanced sideways at Ian. Ian ignored him.

"Don't expect me on my knees with gratitude. I don't know who the hell you are, only that you've chased me all over St. Louis, you drugged me, tied me to you in my bed and stole my cash. Now you show up here in Colorado and tell me Gabe sent you. That's the only reason why I didn't take your goddamn heads off back there."

Ian laughed. He couldn't help himself. "You talk big for such a little woman."

He heard her hiss of anger and smiled even bigger, and all the while, Braden was looking at him like he'd lost his mind.

"Need I remind you that there are people behind us that would love to reshape our bodies with assault rifles?" Braden pointed out.

Ian grunted and focused his attention on the road. He

needed to lose these assholes and fast. Preferably before they picked up a police tail. And then there was the problem of their pilot waiting at the airport. They couldn't very well lead de la Cruz's men to the airstrip and expect them to let the airplane take off. Which meant that their departure from U.S. soil was going to be delayed.

This was turning into one long-ass mission. Goddamn Gabe. Why the hell had he kept Katie a secret, and what the hell kind of mess had he dumped Ian and Braden into by asking them to protect her?

This was supposed to be easy. He'd thought it no less than a dozen times since this shitstorm had started.

"They're slowing down, Ian," Braden said.

Ian checked his rearview mirror to see that, sure enough, they were putting more distance between them and their pursuers. He frowned. Why were they giving up?

Katie cautiously rose and glanced back at the fading vehicles. Evidently satisfied that it was safe to sit up, she reclined rigidly against the seat. Ian watched her in the rearview mirror out of the corner of his eye as she gave a weary sigh and closed her eyes.

She looked exhausted. It was obvious she was in a great deal of pain. Unexpectedly, his gut clenched. What had the little bastard done to her?

If he'd expected her to be an easy acquisition—and he had—he'd never been more wrong in his life. She wasn't a shrinking violet. She had courage—and a spine made of steel. Some of his earlier annoyance faded. He admired guts, especially in a woman who looked way too small to ever fend for herself.

"Are you okay?" he asked softly.

She opened one eye and stared back at him. "Honestly?"

"Yeah."

"No. But I'll get there."

His lips quirked upward in a smile.

Braden turned in his seat to stare at Katie. "What the hell did you do to Ricardo de la Cruz, lady?"

"The name is Katie. Use it."

He gave her a lazy grin. "Sure thing, sweetheart."

"Asshole," she muttered.

Ian chuckled under his breath. Braden the babe magnet was failing in the charm department.

"Look, can you just pull over and let me out?" she asked. "It's obvious neither of you understand the seriousness of the situation. Maybe you have time to sit around and make stupid remarks and laugh at your own lame-ass humor, but I really need to put as much distance between me and Ricardo de la Cruz as possible."

Ian's eyes narrowed. "Keep your panties on. Braden's way of dealing with any tense situation is with lameness. What can I say? He's a lame guy."

"Hey, fuck you," Braden said. "And good God, don't tell me you're getting a sense of humor in the middle of a mission gone to shit."

Ian ignored his brother. "We hauled your pretty ass out of Ricardo's grasp, so the least you can do is show a little gratitude."

Her mouth gaped open. It was a pretty mouth too. One he could easily fantasize about. He blinked as the absurdity of his thoughts hit him.

"You pompous, dumb-as-shit moron. If it weren't for you, Ricardo would have never caught me. I wouldn't be in this situation. I'd be halfway across the country with money and means of transportation."

She heaved a breath, and he saw her wince, but her face was mottled with anger, and her eyes glittered.

"And as for hauling my ass anywhere, I had already taken Ricardo down and escaped through a window, thank you very much. I'd gotten over the wall and would have escaped the grounds on my own. Where the hell do you get off thinking you're some kind of goddamn hero when all you've done is cause me endless pain and grief at that asshole's hands?"

"This would probably be a good time for you to shut up, dude," Braden said out of the corner of his mouth as he surveyed Katie with an amused expression.

Suddenly Braden's head snapped back as Katie decked him. All amusement vanished, replaced by astonishment.

"She hit me!"

"Let. Me. Out. Now." Fury glinted in her eyes as she gave her dictate through gritted teeth.

Ian didn't know whether to throw back his head and laugh his ass off—and he probably would if he wasn't sure she'd deck him next—or gag her. He was seriously leaning toward the latter.

"I hate to break it to you, but you're stuck with us." He stared at her in the rearview mirror. "Gabe asked us to come," he said quietly.

Raw grief swamped her eyes. "Is he alive?"

Ian hesitated a moment too long. He watched her fold inward, hunching her body into a ball. She turned her face away, pressed her cheek into the seat and closed her eyes.

"I'm sorry," he said, though he doubted she heard him.

He exchanged uneasy glances with Braden then returned his attention to the road. He listened for the sounds of her weeping, but she didn't make a single peep.

Every once in a while he glanced back at her, but she remained huddled against the seat, her expression one of deep pain.

Something in his chest softened. She was prickly as hell, but then who could blame her? She was right. He and Braden had likely been the cause of her falling into de la Cruz's hands, and she'd suffered a lot at those hands.

His jaw tightened as his gaze flickered over the bruises on her face and neck. He'd like to meet up with Ricardo. Severing the asshole's dick with a rusty knife held a certain appeal.

At some point she drifted off to sleep. Her body language changed from the tense, defensive *don't fucking touch me* stance to a more relaxed posture. Her eyelashes rested on her cheeks, but even in sleep, there was such an expression of sorrow that it formed a knot in his throat.

"What the hell are we going to do with her?" Braden murmured.

Ian looked at his brother in surprise. "Nothing's changed. Esteban is still our priority. We get her the hell out of the country then wait for him to make his move."

Braden nodded, but something in his expression bothered Ian. Neither of them could afford to grow soft. Not when so much was riding on them finding a cure.

Remembering their pilot, he yanked up his cell phone and put in a quick call. Ian didn't want to be exposed for a prolonged period of time. The more time they spent on the ground, the more likely they were to have run-ins like they had with de la Cruz and company. But at the same time, he didn't want to risk their pilot landing in an area where they would have to risk their asses to fly out of.

After he explained the problem, the pilot suggested a rendezvous at a small airstrip outside Chama, New Mexico.

It was a long-ass drive, and he and Braden were both fighting the effects of the sedative, but they couldn't afford to stop.

He glanced one more time back at Katie. Hopefully she'd sleep for a good long while. The sooner they got her on the plane—preferably without any more drama—the better.

Chapter Seven

Katie stared dully out the window as the scenery passed in a blur. Dead. Gabe was *dead*. She'd known it when he hadn't called, but hearing it confirmed sent a fresh wave of grief splintering through her system.

Dusk had fallen, and the stars were gradually popping in the sky. She'd listened as the two men murmured between them, but they hadn't said anything that told her who they were, why Gabe had sent them to her nor had they given her any indication she could trust them. She knew their names only from listening to their conversation, but nothing else. Gabe had never talked about his teammates. Once he'd mentioned someone named Eli, but that was it.

She assumed they were brothers because of the strong resemblance. Both had black hair and green eyes, though Braden's were a lighter shade than the deep emerald of Ian's. They obviously took their military training to heart because they were built like brick houses. Ian was taller than Braden, but Braden was the stockier, more muscular of the two.

Clearly they were the lesser of two evils. No, she wasn't entirely sure of their motives or intentions, but she *knew* what her fate was with Ricardo. That in itself was good enough reason to go along for the ride. Ian had seemed appalled by her bruises, so maybe he wasn't a complete dickhead.

She dragged a tired hand through her matted hair. Dried blood was smeared on her fingers, and her arm screamed as she tried to figure out how injured it was. It didn't feel broken, but it was swollen. Just great.

Her ribs protested as she gently probed. Breathing was

painful but not hindered. All in all, she was damn lucky to escape with only bruises.

She closed her eyes briefly and sucked in her breath. When she opened them again, Braden was staring back at her.

"You okay?" he asked in a tone that suggested he actually gave a damn.

"I'm fine," she mumbled.

He turned to Ian as though she hadn't spoken. "We need to stop. She's a mess, and we need to make sure her injuries aren't severe."

She aimed a glare at the back of his head. Funny how he hadn't appeared very concerned with the severity of her injuries when he'd tossed her over his shoulder and bounced her to hell and back.

On the other hand, if they didn't stop, she couldn't very well escape. Granted she'd like to be a little further away from Ricardo and company before she bolted, but she'd take whatever opportunity was presented.

Gabe sent us.

Why?

Did she want to know? And did it matter now that he was dead? She was on her own. Not that she hadn't been for the last few years, but there had been comfort in knowing that Gabe was a phone call away, that if she really needed him, he would come.

Trust no one. Ever.

Gabe's words came back to her. Words to live by.

She glanced toward Ian and Braden again as they went back and forth as to whether they were going to stop. She wasn't a gut person when it came to forming opinions. Obviously she had the sense of a moron when it came to men. No, there wasn't some nifty little feeling steering her emotions. She dealt in concrete evidence, and nothing had shown her that these men were anything but dangerous.

A pitiful little moan worked its way past her lips. She was careful to make sure her gaze was focused out the window, so they wouldn't suspect she was paying them any attention. She even managed an appropriate wince as she moved her arm, not that she had to work too hard, because damn, it really did hurt.

She heard Ian sigh, and a few seconds later, he turned off the road. The headlights bounced over the wooded area as they came to a stop on the makeshift path.

"I don't want to stop anywhere close to a town," Ian said gruffly. "We're only a couple hours from de la Cruz's place, and I'll feel better when we're a lot further. We'll get you cleaned up and checked out, and we'll worry about finding better accommodations later."

Said like she was a child in need of coddling after a bad fall. She blew out an exasperated breath and plotted her move. She studied the area. Lots of trees and brush. As best as she could tell, they'd already bypassed Nucla and Naturita and were probably approaching Norwood.

Their size was to their advantage, though she'd already proven she was faster when she had a good lead. But they weren't injured, and she was.

Gabe sent us.

She closed her eyes. Yes, she wanted to know why, but at the same time, she couldn't discount what Gabe had drilled into her head. Trust no one.

It had been proven to her over and over that trust was not something to be given lightly, if at all. She couldn't even trust herself or her judgment, so how the hell was she supposed to hand her wellbeing over to complete strangers? Strangers who had drugged her, tied her and tackled her.

No thanks.

The SUV ground to an abrupt halt, jarring her uncomfortably. Before she could react, Ian got out and yanked open her door. As soon as he touched her, she shrank away.

His stare grew menacing, but it was clear he wasn't angry at her. No, he was focused on her battered appearance with a frown that would scare the hell out of the boogeyman.

His touch grew gentle as he slid his hand up her arm. Then he simply reached in and picked her up off the seat. He carried her around back where Braden had popped the door.

"I'm afraid this will have to do," Ian said as he lowered her to sit just above the bumper.

Her legs dangled over the edge of the truck, and he urged her to lie back. Panic set in as she processed the vulnerability of her position. Her hands flailed, but she found them restrained by his firm grip.

"Look at me, Katie," Ian said in a quiet, firm tone.

She stopped for a moment, unwittingly lured by the strength in his voice. For just a moment, she felt *safe*. It had been so long since she'd gotten even a fleeting taste of what it felt like to live without fear that she grabbed on to the feeling and absorbed it hungrily.

His eyes bore into hers. "I won't hurt you, at least not intentionally. We haven't gotten off to the best of starts, but I'm not a bastard who beats up women."

Her mouth went dry as his fingers slowly pulled at her shirt.

"Shine the flashlight over here, Braden," he said.

Ian scowled when the beam of light hit the splotches of discolored flesh on her abdomen. In an effort not to make her uncomfortable, he tried to keep as much of her breasts covered as he could.

It amazed him that such a slender, slight woman would have so much in the boob department, and he couldn't help that his gaze kept returning to the lush mounds. If he moved his finger at all, it would brush the soft underswell.

With gentle hands, he probed her ribs. She winced in a few spots, but it didn't feel like she had broken anything. Satisfied that at worst she'd suffered painful bruising, he tugged down her shirt then turned his attention to her arm.

The area above her elbow and the elbow itself was swollen. He could tell it hurt when he moved it, but she remained motionless and stoic.

"This could use some ice," he said as he carefully lowered her arm back to her side.

She averted her gaze. "I'll be fine. It's not broken."

Braden reached out and ran his fingers lightly over her bruised cheek. His expression was bland, but Ian could see how tightly his jaw was drawn.

"What does Ricardo de la Cruz want with you, Katie?"

Braden asked.

Her blue eyes became ice crystals. She visibly retreated behind a mask of indifference. It was a lot like watching a brick wall go up.

Ian pulled a T-shirt from one of the bags then opened a bottle of water. He poured it over one corner of the shirt and set to work wiping the dried blood from the cut on her hand.

She had small hands, dainty almost, and as soon as he made that observation he wanted to laugh. She was about as far from dainty as a woman could get.

When he was through cleaning the wound, he let his hands trail down her leg until he got to her foot. It was dirty, and there was a large cut on the bottom. It had to hurt like hell.

He felt her tremble when he began wiping at it, and he glanced back up at her to see that she'd relaxed her guard somewhat. Pain glittered in her eyes, and he was gripped by an odd, fierce rage for what she'd endured.

How the hell did he know she wasn't some drug-running floozie in league with de la Cruz? For all he knew, he and Braden had walked into the middle of a lover's quarrel. Still, no matter what her sins were, no woman deserved to be a man's punching bag.

He swabbed the T-shirt over her small feet, and he was fascinated by the incongruity of her pink toenails. They looked decidedly feminine on a woman who was as prickly as a hedgehog.

"Get me something to bandage her hand and foot with," he said to Braden.

Braden dug around in a first-aid kit, pulled out a roll of gauze and thrust it at Ian. Ian eyed Braden's hand resting on Katie's other knee. It was a possessive grip, and he moved his thumb in a soothing up-and-down motion over her skin.

Ian rolled his shoulder then began winding the gauze around the instep of her foot. When he was satisfied with the result, he taped it and cut the end.

He reached again for her hand that was now resting on her taut abdomen. For a brief moment, her fingers curled trustingly around his, but then she flexed them, the tips flying off the back of his hand as if she'd realized what she was doing.

A few seconds later, he had her hand wrapped, and he tossed the gauze into the truck.

Braden slid an arm underneath her and eased her forward. She regarded him with wary eyes as she gingerly sat up. Her gaze flickered to Ian, and for a moment he saw fear—of him—shadowed in her face. Before he could offer any reassurance, the vulnerability was gone, replaced by a look of annoyance.

It was fascinating to watch her, because she was like an open book. Every thought, every emotion played out in her eyes. You only had to watch closely enough to see the changes.

Somehow he didn't think she'd appreciate his analysis, or that she was so easily read.

"We should get on the road," Ian said.

He started to help her up, but she shrugged off his hand.

"I can make it," she said as she slid from the back of the SUV.

She hung back as he and Braden started for their seats. He saw her hesitate as she rounded the corner of the truck, and before he could blink, she bolted.

"Well goddamn," Braden swore. "Not again."

Ian let out a frustrated growl as he and Braden both ran after her. His nostrils flared, and her scent carried to him on the wind. Lightning-fast images cascaded through his mind.

Predator and prey.

God.

His breaths came faster as he closed the gap between him and the fleeing woman.

He wanted her.

She was his.

A low snarl tore from his mouth.

And suddenly Braden slammed into him, knocking him to the ground.

"Hold it back, Ian." Braden's voice came hoarse and urgent close to his ear.

"Go after her," Ian managed to say. "Don't let me hurt her, Braden. Swear it."

"Forget her. She still has the tracking device. Come back to the truck with me so I can give you an injection."

"Too...late," he rasped. "Get away from me. *Now.*"

Braden's face contorted and rippled in Ian's vision. The change began to ricochet over his body. Painful.

Bones popped, muscles spasmed and reshaped. He closed his eyes and panted as he fought the shift with everything he had. It was a battle he knew he wouldn't win.

Braden sped after Katie's retreating figure. Stupid twit had no idea what she'd started. He'd be lucky if Ian didn't eat them both for dinner.

Adrenaline-laced fury rocketed through his veins as he focused on the chase.

Don't shift. Don't shift. Don't shift.

The chant swam fluidly through his brain as if by saying it, willing it, he could escape his brother's fate.

He was gaining on her. He sucked in air through flared nostrils as her scent grew stronger.

Mine. Mine. Mine.

He shook off the hum of arousal as it surged, hot and steady through his groin.

This had to end now.

As he topped the next rise, he dove for her. He slammed into her back, knocking her to the ground. Her body absorbed the shock of both their landings, and her cry of pain echoed in his ears.

He rolled, wrapping his arms protectively around her even while he wanted nothing more than to shake some sense into her. She rammed her knee in the direction of his balls, and his hand shot downward, halting her inches from his groin.

He squeezed her knee until her leg went limp. She sagged against him, but he wasn't in the least bit fooled by her sudden capitulation. He locked his other arm around her body and held her flush against him, so that absolutely no space existed between them.

"I can't breathe," she gasped.

"And right now I don't give a damn," he snarled. "I've about had it with you, lady."

She squirmed against him, and he tightened his grip until she could no longer move.

In one quick movement, he flipped her over, threw one leg over hers and wrapped both his arms around her, trapping her arms against her sides. Her ass was pressing hard into his groin, and that wasn't the only thing hard. Goddamn it. What a time for a freaking erection.

She felt it too, and for a moment she went completely still. He felt her quick intake of air and then she exploded into action, kicking and writhing.

"For the love of God, chill the fuck out," he barked. "I'm not going to hurt you."

"Let. Me. Go."

"Not on your life."

She went limp against him.

"Now we can do this one of two ways," he said through gritted teeth. "You can give in and walk back with me to the truck, or I can hogtie your ass, carry you back and stuff you into the cargo space."

She stiffened again. "Fuck you."

"No, fuck *you*, sister. I'm usually a good-natured guy, but I swear you're doing your best to piss me off. Now what's it going to be? If I don't get an answer in three seconds, I'm choosing option B. God knows it'll be a lot easier on me if you're trussed up like a turkey."

"Fine," she muttered.

"What's that? I didn't hear you."

"I'll go back with you," she spit.

He almost grinned. Sounded like a pissed-off kitten. Then he frowned. He had no idea where Ian was which meant the trip back to the truck was going to be interesting. The sooner he could get her locked in, though, the safer she'd be. For that matter, he wasn't crazy about skulking around in the dark with a jaguar on the loose.

He loosened his grip and cautiously got to his feet. She lay there in the darkness, her breaths shallow and pained. He refused to feel any guilt over it.

Pale moonlight streamed through the treetops, softly

illuminating her skin. The forest was quiet except for the short gasps of her breath as her shoulders heaved up and down.

She rolled to her back, and a shadow fell over her face. He moved so he could see her and then extended his hand down to help her up. For a long moment, she stared at him as if not believing he was acting so civilized. Hell, he wasn't an ax murderer.

When he shrugged his shoulders and started to lean down to pick her up, she quickly thrust her hand toward his. He curled his fingers around her wrist and pulled so she stood in front of him.

He cupped her chin and tilted it upward until the moonlight better illuminated her face. "You're a mess."

Her lips thinned, and she jerked away from his grip. "You're not looking so hot yourself. And you smell like a goat."

A light chuckle escaped him, and it seemed to irritate her even more. He cupped her uninjured elbow and herded her back toward the truck.

Though he made an effort to relax and not give away his concern over where Ian was, his gaze shot left to right as they walked back. Halfway there, he heard a low growl emanate from about thirty yards to his right.

Fuck.

"Listen up, sister. When I tell you to run, you haul your pretty ass back to the truck. I'll be right behind you. Don't pull any stupid tricks or I swear to God I'll leave you for the critters to eat."

She tensed beside him but didn't argue, thank God.

A hiss shot through the night.

"Run!"

Thankfully, she didn't hesitate. She took off like a jackrabbit, and Braden pounded the ground after her, his hand at her back urging her faster.

Metal glinted in the moonlight ahead. The SUV came into view, and he grasped her arm and dragged her the remaining way.

He yanked open the door and tossed her inside. She landed with a thump then rapidly turned over to glare at him.

"Don't get out of this truck," he said. "I don't care what you hear or see. You don't leave. You got me?"

"Yeah, I got it," she returned softly.

For a moment, fear lurked in her eyes.

"What's out there?" she asked.

He grimaced. "I'm not entirely sure."

He glanced once over his shoulder to make sure Ian hadn't stalked them back to the truck, and then he turned back to Katie.

"I'll be back in a few minutes."

Without giving her a chance to respond, he shut the door, bathing the interior in darkness once more. The night air blew down his spine, eliciting a shiver.

He listened closely, tuning in to the sounds around him. There in the distance—the slow, methodical sound of a predator creeping through the underbrush.

Braden turned and ran in the direction of the noise. He shoved aside branches and bushes then leaped over a fallen log. It was stupid to confront the jaguar, but he wouldn't leave Ian out here alone.

He burst into a clearing and came to an abrupt halt when the luminescent eyes of the cat stared back at him.

Shit.

They stared at one another, both so still. Then the jaguar raised its head and sniffed in his direction. The ears that had lain flat against his head slowly rose.

The cat stepped forward, and he hastily backed up. He reached for a gun that wasn't there, not that he'd use it. Then he nearly laughed. What was he going to do, threaten the cat with it?

The jaguar stopped, his nostrils flaring. His head bobbed up and down as he inhaled Braden's scent. Then he started pacing from side to side, his eyes never leaving Braden.

"Ian, man this sucks. Come on. Shift back. Katie's probably setting the truck on fire as we speak."

At the sound of his voice, the cat hunched down and let out a growl.

"Shutting up now," Braden murmured.

He remained stock-still, not wanting to alarm the jaguar any more than he already had. He couldn't bring himself to think of the cat as Ian. That wasn't Ian.

The jaguar padded forward again, his steps cautious and slow. His ears flicked and twitched, and occasionally he tossed his head in the direction of a distant noise.

Braden held his breath and hoped he wasn't about to kiss his ass goodbye.

When the cat was just a few yards away, he stopped again and settled on his haunches. He simply stared at Braden, his tail lazily flopping around his paws.

Afraid to say anything that might set him off, Braden just stood there, waiting.

His chest grew tight. Sorrow squeezed his throat even as anger lit fire to his veins. This was bullshit. It was no way for him and Ian to live—worried that at any given moment they could shift to beast and kill the other, or someone else.

"Come back, Ian," Braden whispered. "Goddamn it, shift back."

To Braden's surprise, the cat eased down and gingerly rested his head on his front paws as he stretched out his lithe body. In the next moment, his body gave a shudder, and a garbled sound of pain—half human, half animal—shattered the stillness.

Braden raced forward, dropping to his knees as Ian's body contorted and stretched. Fur melted away, replaced by pinkened skin. Sweat popped and beaded on his flesh as the muscles contracted, seized and finally went limp.

Ian's mouth stretched into a ghastly grimace, and a more human-sounding cry of pain escaped, carried away on the breeze.

Ian's head fell to the ground. Harsh breaths danced in rapid staccato, escaping in a thin puff of smoke against the increasing coldness in the air.

Braden leaned over his brother, fear like a vise gripping his chest. "Ian. Ian, talk to me, man."

"It hurts," Ian said with a tortured groan. "Goddamn, it

hurts."

"Come on, let me help you up before you freeze," Braden muttered.

With Braden's help, Ian staggered to his feet, his naked skin illuminated by the full moon. A hunting moon. Did it call to the predator inside them both? Was it the reason, along with Katie's flight, that they battled the beasts so fiercely?

"Katie," Ian gasped out. "Did I hurt her?"

Braden snorted. "My money might be on her in a showdown between her and the jag."

"Not funny."

A half smile quirked Braden's lips. "You never think I'm funny."

"Clothes. I need clothes."

Braden sighed. "Yeah well, between chasing after Katie, running from you and stuffing her into the truck, I didn't exactly stop and get you an extra pair of underwear, you know?"

"Go," Ian bit out.

Braden shook his head. "I'm not leaving you, so deal with it. It's dark. Your maidenly modesty will survive intact. You can get into your clothes at the truck."

"I'm not too wiped out to kick your ass, little brother," Ian growled.

Braden smirked. "You couldn't fight your way out of a paper bag right now."

He promptly doubled over when Ian planted a fist in his gut.

"Damn but you're a cranky son of a bitch."

"I could have killed you, Braden. Think about that the next time you decide to play babysitter. I told you to get the hell away from me."

Braden wrapped an arm around Ian's shoulders and ignored Ian's attempt to shake him off. He shoved his brother forward.

"Yeah, you told me, but when have I ever listened to you?"

Ian shook his head, but he stumbled and leaned wearily

against Braden. They walked back in silence. When the SUV came into view, Braden halted and leaned Ian against a tree.

"Wait here. I'll get you some clothes."

Chapter Eight

Eli Chance let himself into the bedroom he shared with Tyana and glanced over to see her propped on the bed, her casted leg elevated on a pillow.

She looked up, her eyes flickering with both welcome and wariness she still hadn't shed when it came to him.

She kept it interesting which was one of the things he liked most about her. He damn sure never had to worry about being bored.

"Glad to see you found your way back to bed, sugar."

She rolled her eyes, but he could see the pain and fatigue etched in her brow.

Not waiting for an invitation, he stretched out beside her, careful not to bump her cast. Her body settled comfortably into his, and he felt her go soft around him.

Enjoying the quiet and stillness, he brushed his lips across hers, tasting her mouth with his tongue.

"Jonah tells me you're getting tired of me already," he murmured.

Her eyes widened and she stared at him in horror. "He said what?"

He chuckled. "You're way too easy, sugar."

She frowned, but he saw a glimmer of guilt before she looked away.

"Ah, so you did put him up to getting rid of me."

"Hell," she muttered. "It wasn't quite like that."

He lifted one brow as he trailed a finger down the softness

of her cheek. "So how is it? Come on, Tyana. We've always been honest with each other. Don't start holding out on me now."

She sighed and slumped back into her pillows in defeat. "I'm just not used to all the hovering, Eli. Don't take it personally. This whole relationship thing is new to me. I don't handle convalescence very well."

He laughed. "That's an understatement if I ever heard one. Okay, so I'm getting on your nerves."

She gazed curiously at him. "You don't seem offended."

"Should I be? I'm assuming you don't want to get rid of me on a permanent basis."

"Don't be stupid," she growled.

He grinned. "I love it when you get cranky."

He propped his head in his palm and let his other hand wander down her midriff, enjoying the way she tightened beneath his fingers.

"So what's up, Tyana?" he asked softly. "What's really going on here?"

There was a flash of vulnerability followed by a quick masking of her features. The tough exterior he was so used to pushed itself outward until not a trace of uncertainty remained.

And then just as quickly, as though she made the conscious decision to let him see inside, she crumbled, and she closed her eyes.

"I hate this," she said honestly. "I hate not being able to face you as an equal. I hate being out of action. I hate not being able to help D. I want to go after Esteban so damn bad, and instead I'm stuck here with you babysitting me while Mad Dog and Jonah play the indulgent older brothers. It sucks!"

Eli knew better than to tease her at this point. He touched her chin with one fingertip to gain her attention. Her green eyes locked with his. He could read the conflict loud and clear. He understood it because he'd feel the same damn way in her position.

"So Jonah wants me to hook up with Tits and meet Ian and Braden in Austria instead of Paris, at the safe house he's arranged. As soon as Ian checks in again, I'll head out."

Instead of looking relieved, Tyana grimaced. "You know he

did it for me," she muttered.

"Sending me on a pussy errand? Yeah, I know he did. He wasn't any happier about it than I was. But we both love you, so I guess we can both suck it up."

She visibly winced. "Christ. Now I feel about an inch tall."

Eli took pity on her and leaned in to kiss her. "Quit being so hard on yourself, sugar. I knew when we started that things wouldn't be easy, and our issues wouldn't be resolved overnight. We're both too used to doing things our own way."

Tyana kissed him back. Not gently because that just wouldn't be her. She took possession of his mouth like she owned it. Hell, he loved that. And he did belong to her.

When she pulled away, her eyes were glazed with passion, kind of foggy. "I'm not being fair. This has been so much more difficult for you, Eli. Having to cede control to Jonah, to someone you don't fully trust yet. Having to rely on Falcon for the safety and wellbeing of your men. In your position, I know I couldn't do it. Neither could Jonah. He's too much of a control freak. And yet we all expect you to make sacrifices because you were dumb enough to fall...to get involved with me," she finished uncomfortably.

He bit the inside of his cheek to keep from smiling at her slip. She'd never said she loved him. Nor had she really acknowledged that he loved her. Hell, he couldn't remember if he'd ever said the words either, mainly because he knew how uncomfortable they'd make her.

It was enough that she was here with him. They were together. She was having a difficult time adjusting, but never once had she hinted that she didn't want to make it work.

He could be a patient man when the end result was worth it. Tyana was.

"I'll be gone for a while," he said casually, ignoring the awkwardness of her rambling. "Why don't you hang out with D and recover so we can go kick some Esteban ass together?"

Her eyes flashed and brightened and a broad smile lit her face. Trust her to get all excited over the prospect of a good fight.

And then she sobered and touched his cheek with her slender fingers. "I want you to come back, Eli. I hope you know that. It's not that I don't want you here. It's just that I hate for you to see me this way. So helpless. I hate seeing me this way."

He captured her hand and kissed the tips of her fingers. "I won't be going immediately, and don't worry. You're going to have to do more than whine to Jonah to get rid of me."

She growled under her breath. "I didn't whine to Jonah."

He raised his eyebrows and quirked his lip at her. "Oh? That's not the way he tells it."

"Rat bastard," she muttered.

"Oh, and Tyana? I assure you, Mad Dog and Jonah will be every bit as watchful as I am. So don't get any crazy ideas."

She actually looked disappointed.

"Now, you want me to carry you downstairs so you can drink and smoke weed with the other fools?"

"Carry?" she sputtered. "I'm down but not dead, Chance."

Chapter Nine

Katie shoved her hair out of her eyes as she stared out the window into the darkness. Where the hell had Braden gone, and for that matter where had Ian disappeared to? Was he out looking for her?

Honest to God, she'd never met two more bizarre men in her life, and lord knew she'd met some doozies.

She pressed her palms to the glass, but Braden had disappeared. She frowned as she realized she was worried. What should it matter to her if he got his ass killed?

Then it dawned on her that she was in the truck alone. And she was sitting here harboring ridiculous concerns for a complete stranger when she should be driving as fast and as far away as possible.

She clambered over the seat, settling behind the wheel. To her dismay, the keys weren't in the ignition. Of course. Because God forbid anything be easy.

A snarl of frustration ripped past her lips. She placed her hands on the wheel and rested her forehead against the horn.

She was starving, she hurt like hell, and she'd give her eyeteeth for a bed and a good night's sleep.

Whiney ass. Just be glad you're alive and not in bed with Ricardo right now.

That sobered her quickly.

The door swung open, startling her. She let out a yelp and threw up her arms in defense. Braden stood outside, a smirk on his face.

"You don't think I was stupid enough to leave the keys, now

do you?"

She scowled even as relief hit her so hard she went weak. She wasn't glad to see him. Not at all. And she wasn't worried about where Ian was or that he'd been eaten by whatever the hell was out there.

"You don't look happy to see me," he said dryly. "Is that the thanks I get for saving your pretty ass again?"

She started to hit him until she figured out he was yanking her chain. Royally. She took a deep breath and smiled sweetly at him.

"I'll be happy to take this pretty ass elsewhere. Just get the hell out of my way."

He leaned in, his body pressing hard to hers. She shoved at him, but he was intent on reaching beyond her to the other seat.

"Get off, damn it," she gasped out as he squeezed the air from her lungs. "Big oaf."

He snatched a duffel bag then slowly eased away from her, a cocky grin on his face.

"I wouldn't get out if I were you. Your delicate sensibilities might be offended."

Then he was gone, shutting the door behind him. What the hell? What sensibilities? Then she glanced in the rearview mirror to see a naked Ian thrusting a leg into a pair of jeans.

Naked? What the ever-loving fuck is he doing naked?

She continued to stare until she realized she was still staring, and then she jerked her gaze away, looking at the windshield, the seat, her hands...anything but back at the naked man.

What is he doing naked?

And why was she sitting here like a docile moron?

She peeked up at the mirror and to her relief saw that Ian was dressed and talking to Braden. Braden gestured toward the truck and her and then both men started toward the front.

Shit.

Ian reached her door first and yanked it open. He took one look at her and a feral light entered his eyes. A shiver skated down her spine and sent an odd tingling into her womb. She honestly didn't know whether to be terrified or intrigued by the dangerous fire in his gaze.

He sucked in air through his nose, his nostrils flaring and quivering. His fists curled and clenched and then he rubbed his open palms up and down his pants legs.

Braden jerked him backward, and the truck shook as Braden thrust Ian against the hood.

"Goddamn it, Ian, what the hell is wrong with you?" Braden demanded.

"It's *her*," Ian said hoarsely.

Braden snapped his gaze to her and scowled. Then he quickly turned his attention back to his brother. "You're getting an injection and then you're going night-night. Are we clear?"

Katie watched in open-mouthed fascination as Braden strode to the back of the truck and then returned a moment later with a syringe. She winced when, without preamble, he stuck the needle in Ian's arm. There was so much wrong with this scene she didn't even know where to start. And she'd thought things were weird with Ricardo.

Braden left Ian leaning against the truck as he headed to the backseat to open the door. Katie's gaze was drawn to Ian as he stared up at the sky, his face a brooding mold.

"Slide over," Braden ordered.

She blinked and yanked her concentration from Ian to stare at Braden.

"Ian's going in back. You get over in the passenger seat. No arguments."

She immediately bristled but forced air through her nose and stifled the protest dancing on her lips. Part of survival was knowing when the hell to keep your mouth shut. This was one of those times.

She moved into the passenger seat as Braden went back to Ian. A few seconds later, Braden herded him into the backseat and shoved him into a lying position.

As she glanced casually over her shoulder, she saw Ian staring at her, those eyes flashing despite the lethargy from whatever Braden had injected him with.

Determined not to back down, she boldly met his gaze. For

a long moment, they just stared at one another until discomfort skittered over her skin. When Braden opened the driver's door, it gave her an excuse to look away.

He slid in beside her and started the engine. His hands curled around the steering wheel, but he made no move to put the truck into drive.

She shifted uncomfortably and forced her gaze away.

"This shit has to stop, Katie," he said in a firm voice.

That pissed her off. She whirled around to glare at him. "Where the hell do you get off giving me orders? I don't even know who you are or why you've taken it upon yourself to irritate the living shit out of me. Don't you think you've caused me enough grief?"

He rammed the gearshift down and took off, the SUV rocking over the bumpy terrain.

"You're a piece of work, you know that?"

She gaped at him, speechless.

"You haven't even asked about Gabe."

Rage and grief grabbed hold of her throat and squeezed. Hard.

"You said he was dead," she said through gritted teeth. "What else is there to know?"

He glanced sideways at her. "You're a cold bitch. He was your brother."

She shook her head and turned away. "What do you want me to do, cry? Would it make you feel better for me to fall at your feet in a weeping, wailing mass of femininity? Would that appeal to your manly ego?"

Her fingers curled into tight fists in her lap. "Well, let me tell you, none of that is going to keep me alive, and if Gabe taught me nothing else, he taught me to survive. The last thing he'd want is for me to rely on a complete stranger. Trust no one."

"Christ, you even sound like him," Braden muttered. "The most suspicious bastard I ever knew."

For a moment she wanted to do just what she scorned and ask Braden about Gabe. Details. Information she was hungry for. Yes, Gabe was her brother, and he'd saved her, but she hadn't seen him in two years. Their phone calls were always brief and to the point.

"Gabe sent us to find you," Braden said. "Now, you can believe that or not, but I'll be damned if I'm going to risk my ass or my brother's just because you can't decide whether you'd rather hang out with us or your buddy Ricardo." He snorted and shook his head. "Yeah, that's a hard choice."

"You don't get it, do you?" she said softly. "I don't want to hang out with either of you. Do I think you're a better choice than Ricardo? I don't know."

She stopped when he sucked in an angry breath.

"I don't deal in instincts, Braden. I look at irrefutable evidence, and I'm sorry, but so far, I'm not seeing anything that screams to me I can trust you. I've been burned and burned bad. If you think I'm going to put my life in your hands because you say Gabe sent you then you're out of luck."

Much like the Taser Ricardo had used on her, sudden remembrance hit her with enough force to knock the breath from her. Her hands flew to the back of her neck, frantically feeling for the protrusion.

"Oh fuck. Fuck, fuck, fuck," she breathed.

"What the hell is wrong with you?" Braden demanded.

All the blood squeezed itself from her cheeks until they grew tight. She was an idiot, and she deserved to die for such stupidity.

Her fingertips fumbled over her nape until finally she found the thin piece of metal.

Braden's hand circled her wrist, and he yanked downward. "What are you doing?"

"Tracking device," she croaked. "I fucked up. I found it but left it in because I intended to use it to throw them off my trail. That's why they backed off, I'm sure. Because they know how to find us."

Braden chuckled.

"What the hell is so funny?" she demanded.

"Ian and I planted the tracking device. I'm surprised you found it."

"You *what?*"

She jerked her hand out of his grasp and reached for the device again.

"Leave it," he ordered.

She stared at him in astonishment. "You're out of your mind. Like I want you knowing my every movement? Don't you get the whole point of escape?"

He laughed again, much to her irritation.

"You're not escaping, Katie. But that tracking device has already saved your damn life once. How do you think we knew where to find you when Ricardo swooped in and carried you off to his love nest?"

She threw up her hands in exasperation. "You didn't save shit!"

"Ricardo is not your only concern," Braden said quietly. "In fact, I'd go so far as to say he's a little fish compared to what else you're up against."

She made a rude noise. "If this is some sort of bullshit attempt to scare me into sticking around, save it."

"You don't have a choice," Braden said in a clipped tone.

A dart of fear scurried from her belly into her throat.

Braden's hands tightened around the steering wheel as he navigated back onto the highway. She waited in silence for him to explain, to give her something other than a tersely worded dictate.

It pissed her off that he had the power to frighten her, but she'd long given up trying to deny her fears. Being helpless and powerless *did* scare the hell out of her.

When it was clear he wasn't going to offer anything further, she reached over to touch his arm. He flinched and quickly glanced over at her. She retracted her hand in silent apology.

"What were you talking about, Braden? Why did Gabe send you when he's told me under no circumstances was I to ever trust anyone? No exceptions."

"And why is that, Katie? What the hell is going on between you and Ricardo?"

She pressed her lips together and shook her head. "I don't want to talk about Ricardo. You wanted to talk about Gabe earlier, so talk. Why did he send you after me, and what else am I up against?"

His eyes narrowed in the dim glow of the headlights. "Seems to me we both have information the other wants. You up for a trade?"

A trade. He had to be joking. Like this was some game. Her life was on the line, damn it, and that wasn't something she took lightly.

But still, uncertainty warred with her determination not to offer him anything at all. What if Gabe really had sent them? What could possibly be worse than being pursued by Ricardo and company?

She wasn't sure she wanted to know.

"Look, Katie, I get that you don't trust me and Ian. I don't expect you to. But believe it or not, we're trying to help you. Now, you can accept that, and we can work together, or you can keep fighting, which only puts you in more danger. We can't protect you if we're constantly having to chase you down."

She sighed and looked away to stare out her window at the passing scenery. He was asking her to trust him even while saying he understood her *not* trusting him.

If only Gabe hadn't died.

That was a stupid thing to say. His being alive wouldn't change her present circumstances. He'd taught her a lot, but she'd been on her own for years. Dead or alive, Gabe wouldn't save her. It was up to her to save herself.

"We're not adversaries, Katie, despite what you might believe. You don't have to trust us, but it would be stupid not to take the help we're offering."

And that was it in a nutshell. Stupid. She had a lot of experience in being stupid. She made such a big deal over not trusting her instincts. Well, her instincts screamed for her not to have anything to do with Ian or Braden.

God, what a mess.

She looked at what was concrete, what was tangible. Ian and Braden hadn't tried to hurt her, and they had done their best to keep her away from Ricardo, despite her early confusion that they worked together.

She couldn't believe she was even contemplating going

along with this.

She glanced over her shoulder at Ian, who was unconscious, and then back to Braden.

"I'll tell you what you want to know if you answer all my questions. *All*. But I won't do it until he's awake," she said, jerking her thumb in Ian's direction. "I want to hear what both of you have to say, and I want to look you in the eye while you're talking."

"Fair enough," Braden said with a shrug. "Why don't you get some rest. I promise not to try and kill you while you sleep."

She slouched down in her seat, weariness seeping into her bones. She wanted rest, needed it. If she didn't refuel, she was going to crash and burn.

"Will you be okay to drive?" she asked and immediately cursed the fact that she sounded concerned.

He cracked a half smile. "Go to sleep, Katie. I'll be fine."

Chapter Ten

Ian dragged himself from the remnants of a drugged sleep. Dark images assaulted him, pulling at him. Memories of the hunt. The overwhelming urge to claim what was his.

Katie.

He put a hand to his throbbing head and shook the cobwebs free. He was losing his grip on sanity. Katie wasn't his, and moreover he didn't *want* her to be.

Slowly he sat up and blinked to bring his surroundings into focus.

"You feeling any better?" Braden asked from the driver's seat.

Ian leaned forward to stare out the windshield. The eastern sky was lightening as the first rays of sunlight eased over the horizon.

Then he looked over to see Katie scooted over as far against the door as she could go. She was curled into a tiny ball, her hands in a defensive position, and her eyes were tightly closed.

She slept, but even in sleep she was tense and rigid.

"Ian?"

He turned to his brother. "I'm good. I think."

Braden's troubled gaze found Ian in the rearview mirror. "That was a bad one, Ian. What the fuck happened?"

Ian rubbed the back of his neck and closed his eyes for a moment. "It's her. I can't explain it. There's something about her that sets me off. Been that way since the beginning."

Braden sighed. "Yeah, I know. Me too."

"Where are we?" Ian asked as he studied the roadway.

"Almost to Durango."

"Pull over. I'll drive. You need to get some sleep."

Braden rolled one shoulder and worked his head from side to side. "I thought we'd snag a room just long enough to grab showers and touch base with Eli."

Braden glanced over at Katie and said in a quieter voice, "She's wiped, and she needs to eat. The bandages came off when she ran, and she needs tending to."

Despite his irritation with her, Ian softened a little when his gaze swept over Katie's huddled form.

"Okay, but we need to make it quick."

Braden nodded.

Thirty minutes later, they pulled into a roadside hotel. Braden hopped out and looked back at Ian. "Will you be okay with her?"

Ian swallowed the retort and motioned for Braden to go. As his brother walked away, Ian stared down at Katie who hadn't stirred.

What was it about her that got him so fired up? He wasn't unused to the instability or the sudden urge to shift, but this was different. Something dark and feral came over him. A drive inside him that had nothing to do with danger or risk.

He wanted her. Badly. It pissed him off to no end. How could his body, his beast, want something so badly when his mind was screaming hell no? And why was Braden similarly affected?

Unable to stand the confines of the truck, he eased the door open, careful not to make too much noise. He stepped into the early morning coolness and breathed deep of the cleansing air. He took several gulps before he gently shut the door and walked a few steps toward the front of the truck where he could still see Katie through the windshield.

Would he have hurt her? It was hard to say. He couldn't trust the jaguar because he retained no memories of being the beast. He only knew the overwhelming desire to possess her, to mark her, to make her his, that swamped him just prior to his shift.

The best thing would be to stay as far away from her as he could, but that wasn't exactly a possibility when he and Braden would be spending every waking minute with her until Esteban made his move.

As he watched, she came awake. There was no slow build to awareness. No sleepy stretch or lazy yawn. She bolted forward, her eyes wide, and he could see the tension billowing off her in waves.

Her gaze connected with his, and for a moment, he saw relief. That surprised him because she'd made no bones about the fact she didn't trust him or Braden one iota. No sooner had he reflected on the apparent relief in her expression, her eyes hardened as she stared back at him through the glass.

With a sigh, he sauntered around to her door.

"Why are we stopped?" she asked as soon as he swung it open.

"Braden is getting us a room so we can shower, and then we've got phone calls to make and we—you—need to eat."

She wiped a hand over her face, drawing his attention to the still-vivid bruising on her cheek and on her slender neck.

"What's wrong?" she asked.

It took him a minute to realize he was scowling.

"Nothing," he muttered. But anger he couldn't quite control quivered and snaked through his veins, whispering to him and calling to the predator.

They both looked up as Braden strode out to the truck.

"Let's go," he said as he walked to the back to pop the trunk.

He tossed a set of keys at Ian. "You and Katie head in. I'll follow with the first-aid kit and the bags."

Ian caught the plastic key tag and examined the number. Then he scanned the line of rooms until his gaze alighted on the correct door.

"Come on," he said to Katie, though he was careful not to touch her or act too aggressively.

She hesitated only a slight moment before she turned and followed him.

The room was musty and stale and it was nearly as chilly

inside as it was outside. Ian yanked at the yellowed drapes to obscure the view and then turned on the heater under the window.

Katie sat on the edge of the bed, her body language ill at ease. The heater lurched and started to hum, and the smell of exhaust filtered into the room.

Braden stepped inside and tossed a couple of duffel bags on the bed. Katie's backpack landed next to her, and she grabbed it, yanking open the zipper. She poured out the few changes of clothes and rifled through the contents until she came to a wad of cash and her bankcard.

She fingered the bills and looked up first at Braden and then Ian in confusion.

"Did you think we ripped you off?" Ian asked dryly.

"What was I supposed to think?" she said. "I wake up tied to you in my bed, and my money and bankcard are gone from my pocket."

"Not that I don't love watching you two butt heads, but Katie, you need to jump in the shower and wash all the blood and dirt off, and then we need to tend to your wounds," Braden said.

Her posture immediately became defensive. "I can manage on my own."

"He didn't offer you a choice," Ian pointed out. "Get in the shower or I'll do it for you. That's all the choice I'm giving you. When you get out, we're going to take care of those cuts and bruises."

Even as he issued the edict, his loins tightened at the idea of being in the shower with her, his hands running over her wet body. He turned away before she could witness his arousal. He was losing his mind. Not to mention his control.

He heard her quick intake of breath. Did her thoughts coincide with his? He glanced down at his fist, held so tight that the skin stretched painfully across his knuckles. With a quick flex, he released his fingers then turned back around.

Katie disappeared into the bathroom and closed the door quietly behind her.

"You okay, man?" Braden asked.

"No, I'm not okay," Ian bit out. "Where's the inhibitor? Carry it on you from now on. It does us no good stashed in a bag. I could have hurt you and Katie."

Braden flopped down on the bed and lay back, his eyes closing in fatigue. "I'm not so sure the inhibitor would have worked, Ian. You shifted really fast."

Ian grimaced and pinched the bridge of his nose between his fingers. Desperation was a constant companion, working in tandem with his pulse, with his every breath, every heartbeat.

"We can't go on like this, Braden."

He hated the helplessness, the weakness in his voice. He sounded like a goddamn fatalistic pussy. But they couldn't continue living like this. Unpredictable. Changing to wild animals in an instant.

What if he killed his brother?

It was the question that haunted him the most. It was easy to isolate himself from the rest of the world. He and Braden had always been loners. But he couldn't walk away from Braden. Not when his brother needed him. But if he stayed, would he be responsible for someday attacking the one person in the world who mattered to him?

"What the hell is your problem?"

Ian looked down to see Braden staring at him. He shook his head, and Braden made a sound of exasperation.

"Things could be worse." Braden tucked his hands behind his head and stared up at the ceiling. "I mean there are worse things than having a naked woman a room away."

Some of the tension eased from his chest, and he looked at his brother in mock disgust. "That naked woman would like nothing better than to play with your nuts and not in a fun way."

Braden grunted. "I'd be willing to let her. I've always had a slight masochistic streak."

Ian laughed and was surprised by how good it felt. Maybe some of Braden's irreverence was rubbing off on him. Or maybe he was too slaphappy to have any goddamn sense.

"Ian?"

"Yeah, man."

"It might be better if you handled Katie's, uh, injuries. I'm tired, and I get this weird vibe around her, like I'm about to crawl out of my skin. I don't want to risk any, uh, complications."

Ian cursed under his breath. He didn't trust himself around Katie any more than Braden apparently trusted himself. What was wrong with them? They hadn't reacted to Tyana or any other woman they'd come into contact with like this. Was it merely the thrill of the chase? A track-and-capture element? Something ingrained deep in their animal psyche?

"We both need to do it," Ian said grimly. "A system of checks and balances. We'll have the inhibitor and a large dose of the sedative on hand just in case."

He paused for a moment as he saw the bleakness enter Braden's eyes.

"Braden, you have to promise me something."

Braden cocked his head forward to look at Ian. "What's that?"

"If I ever try to go after you, you have to swear to take me out."

Chapter Eleven

Eli probably thought they'd all lost their minds. Tyana leaned back against the bar, a joint in one hand, a drink in the other, and watched in amusement as Mad Dog and Jonah sparred in the middle of the game room.

If anyone thought the two men were merely joking around, they obviously hadn't been witness to past practice sessions. Before it was over, there would be blood, cuts and bruises, and both would, of course, claim victory.

To Tyana's side, Damiano stood and watched with a grin on his face. He was on his fourth drink and had even rolled one of Mad Dog's joints. He wasn't as brooding or distant tonight, and that gave Tyana more hope than she'd had in a long time.

He caught her gaze and smiled warmly. He turned and set his drink down then ambled over to stand beside her. One arm looped around her shoulders as they watched Mad Dog and Jonah trade punches.

"How long you think it'll be before they get tired of pounding on each other and invite Eli to join in so they have fresh meat?" D asked with dark amusement.

Tyana turned to stare at Eli who was across the room sprawled in a chair holding a beer while he looked on with a bored expression.

"I don't think he likes our entertainment," she said.

D shrugged. "He'd probably be having a lot better time if Ian and Braden had checked in. It's been several days since we heard from them."

Tyana frowned. It was hard for her to put herself in Eli's position because the people most important to her were right here. But D was right. Eli was a fish out of water in this environment. He was the new guy playing by new rules not set by him, and his team was on a mission without him.

"How are you feeling tonight?" she asked D. She didn't really want to get into an analysis of all that Eli was giving up. For her. Because then she'd wonder why the hell he bothered with a woman who'd gone to Jonah in an effort to get him out of her hair for a few days.

"I'm good," D said. "Stop worrying so much, Ty." He glanced at her with reproach in his eyes. "You and I have no control over what happens to me. What will be will be."

She ground her teeth in frustration. She wanted to scream at him and then shake him senseless. No, she wanted to kick his ass and tell him to stop spouting philosophical nonsense. Fate was what you made it, not the other way around.

She took another long drag of the joint to steady her rage and exhaled in a long, steady plume. Across the room, Eli's eyebrow went up as he watched her. She wasn't entirely sure he approved of her new brand of poison, but he'd never said anything. He knew better than to think she'd give it up just because he didn't like it.

D straightened and leaned against the bar, his elbows propped behind him. "Do you remember the tiger?"

It was a general question, one that would confuse many people in its simplicity, but she knew immediately what he was talking about. When they were much younger, alone on the streets of Prague, they'd freed a tiger from a street vendor. The result had been chaos, but to two children dreaming of their own brand of freedom, it had been symbolic.

"I remember," she said softly.

"I dream of him often," D said.

She cocked her head sideways to stare at her brother. "Why?"

He shrugged. "I don't know. I feel a kinship with him, I suppose. And maybe I'm waiting for someone to come and free me."

She turned, awkward as her cast bumped into D's leg. He was quick to help her, but she pushed him away.

"Don't wait, D," she said. "Don't wait for someone to come

along and save you. You have to save yourself. Do you understand me?"

"Relax, little sister, I'm not throwing in the towel. I meant it more in a metaphorical sense than anything. I forget how black and white you are," he said in a teasing tone.

"I am when it comes to you."

"Yeah, I know. I'm going to be fine, Ty. Believe that, okay?"

She reached down and caught his hand, squeezing it tight. "I won't allow you to be anything else, D."

Mad Dog and Jonah had evidently had enough. Jonah shoved at Mad Dog before heading over to the bar. He poured a generous amount of liquor into a glass while Mad Dog forewent the cup and reached for the bottle.

They performed a mock toast and downed the liquid.

"Your boyfriend looks bored," Mad Dog said in Ty's direction. "Shouldn't you be keeping him company?"

Tyana glanced over at Eli, irked by Mad Dog's statement. "Give me a push," she muttered.

D smiled but helped her forward while Mad Dog shoved her crutches at her. She'd just gotten them under her arms when the door opened and one of the Falcon secondary stuck his head in. He looked first at Eli and then Jonah.

Eli sat up, his bored look gone. Jonah also started forward, ignoring the annoyed scowl that flickered across Eli's face.

"Must be Ian and Braden checking in," D murmured.

Tyana itched to go after them, but hell, by the time she made it the conversation would be over. Still, it rankled that she was relegated to the sidelines while the action went on around her.

She took a step forward and grimaced when pain shot up her leg. No amount of alcohol or marijuana managed to take the edge off her discomfort.

Mad Dog was quick to take notice, and he grasped her elbow, all but forcing her to lean on him.

"I've got her," D said calmly as he appeared at her other side. "Go get her pain medication."

Mad Dog frowned as he looked around at the empty room but nodded and headed for the door.

"I'll be back in a second," he said.

"Where you want to sit?" D asked after Mad Dog had left.

"Couch is fine," she said in a disgruntled tone.

She glanced sharply up at D when his hand trembled around her elbow.

"Are you okay?" she demanded.

He wiped shakily at his brow and refocused his attention on her. "Yeah, just too much weed, I think. Don't know what you and Mad Dog see in the shit."

"Yeah, well I don't either," she muttered.

She thumped with her crutches while D walked by her side. They were almost to the couch when his hand fell away from her arm and he turned abruptly from her.

"D?" she asked hesitantly as she saw the muscles in his back ripple and spasm.

"Get away from me."

Fear rocketed through her. She dropped her crutches and twisted, her hands reaching for him. As soon as she touched him, he flinched and bolted away.

He hit the bar, his back still to her, his palms braced on the counter, his entire body heaving with exertion.

Tyana hobbled forward, wincing when her injured leg took the brunt of her weight. But she had to get to the inhibitor that was out in plain sight on the countertop.

Her eyes locked on D as she limped heavily. To her horror, his body contorted and lost its shape. It rippled like some movie special effect. Flashes of orange and fur. A low hiss and then a growl.

Dear God, she wasn't going to be able to get to him in time. She yelled hoarsely as she lunged the remaining distance for the inhibitor. Pain nearly paralyzed her. Her hand glanced off the bar top, but she caught herself and hauled herself upright, only to find herself staring into the eyes of a Bengal tiger.

Holy fuck.

She licked her lips and backed nervously away. Her leg tangled with the barstool, and she went down with a thump. The tiger growled and closed in on her.

She extended her arm, reaching for her crutch, anything. Something she could defend herself with. This was no longer D. She was eyeball to eyeball with one pissed-off predator.

Ignoring the searing pain and the awkwardness of her cast, she pulled herself along the floor. Just as her fingertips touched the cool metal of the crutch, the tiger leaped.

She yanked the crutch in front of her and jammed it into the cat's jaws when his mouth would have closed over her throat. The tiger's upper body landed on her chest, knocking the breath from her.

She shoved the crutch deeper into his jaws, refusing to let go. If she did it would mean her death.

Where the fuck was Mad Dog? The Falcon secondary?

She heard a commotion outside and realized they were coming. What seemed an eternity to her had in reality been a few seconds.

The cat shook his head and growled his displeasure, but Tyana refused to budge. She held onto the crutch for dear life, matching the cat's movements with her own. Anything to keep those teeth from her flesh.

"D, come back to me," she pleaded.

"What the fuck?"

Mad Dog's voice exploded into the room. The cat never looked up, too locked in his battle with Tyana. With a toss of his head, he managed to rip the crutch from Tyana's grasp. It went sailing across the room, landing with a clatter.

Tyana shoved her hands into the cat's face, knowing she was now in deep shit.

More voices, more shouts, more pounding of feet. Tyana dimly registered it, but she was focused solely on the tiger and staying alive.

A thin plume of smoke wrapped around the tiger's neck, twining and twining again. Eli. It whispered through the fur and into the cat's nostrils.

"No!" she cried. "Eli, don't kill him."

The cat snarled and shook his head, forgetting Tyana for a moment as he fought with his invisible assailant.

Then the tiger let out a yelp and his huge body jerked.

Tyana looked down to see two syringes protruding from his haunch. Mad Dog and Jonah both tackled the cat, rolling him off her in a tangle of bodies and paws.

She tried to scramble up, but the damn cast made her as helpless as a beached whale. Cursing, she righted herself and crawled upward with her one good leg.

The cat roared in rage as Mad Dog, Jonah and Eli fought to subdue him. More of the Falcon secondary rushed in. Two high-powered rifles were up and trained on the tiger, ready to take a clear shot. She screamed at them to put the guns down.

Two more syringes stabbed into the cat's fur. A final one in his neck finally made him go limp. His heavy body lolled to the side, and Jonah and Mad Dog cautiously inched away.

Eli came back to form beside Tyana as she pulled herself painfully across the floor toward D.

His arms came around her, and he tugged her to him as he examined every inch of her skin.

"Are you all right?" His hands framed her face, touching and reassuring himself.

"D," she choked out.

The tiger's eyes glazed as his head flopped to the floor under the power of the sedative. Already the Falcon secondary swarmed the room, their rifles all pointed at the helpless cat.

She tried to crawl toward the cat as he lay panting.

"Keep her away," Jonah barked.

Eli hauled her back against his chest.

"Not now, sugar," he murmured. "D will be all right. Let them take care of him."

"I want this room secured," Jonah ordered as he stood. He stalked over to where Tyana lay in Eli's arms and squatted down in front of her. "Are you all right?"

She nodded shakily.

"Get her out of here. I'm locking this room down until he shifts back," Jonah told Eli.

It was useless for her to argue. For once, she knew there wasn't anything she could do, no argument she could wage. D had finally slipped beyond control. Tears clogged her throat, squeezing, relentless. Grief welled, sharp, like a blade. Always,

always she'd been there to comfort him, to shield him as he'd shielded her. Only now, they would be separated. Jonah would never leave them alone after what happened today.

Chapter Twelve

Katie huddled under the steaming hot spray of the shower and let it pelt her skin until it was pink and raw. Even after she'd lathered her hair twice and soaped her body repeatedly, she stood still as the water cascaded over her.

She didn't want to move. Ever.

But she had a strong suspicion if she didn't get out soon, one of them would come haul her out.

With a regretful sigh, she turned off the water and stepped out, reaching for a towel. She dried briskly, taking care around the more tender parts. When she looked at herself in the mirror, she grimaced. Then she pulled the towel away and let her gaze trail down her body.

Her shoulders slid downward, and her eyes crossed with fatigue. She was starting to have some serious fantasies involving a pillow and a bed. Blankets were completely optional.

An irritated sigh escaped when she realized she'd neglected to bring clothes into the bathroom with her. And there was no way she was putting the nasty stuff she'd taken off back on.

She wrapped the towel around her and kept her arms pressed against the fabric so it had no chance of slipping down. Then she stuck her head out the door before exiting.

Braden was lying on the bed, eyes closed, and Ian was perched on the edge of the mattress, his expression brooding. Ian looked up at her, his eyes shuttered.

"I, uhm, just need to get some clothes," she said in a low voice.

Ian stood. "Not yet."

He walked toward her, and she blinked in surprise. His hand cupped her elbow, his touch gentle as he urged her toward the bed.

"You can keep the towel wrapped around you for now," he said gruffly. "I need to tend to that cut on your foot, and then I'll take a look at your arm."

Braden opened his eyes and rolled to the edge of the bed before putting his feet down with a thud. He rubbed his face in a tired gesture then rose to stand beside her.

"Get the kit," Ian told Braden.

Ian urged her down, and she sat awkwardly, keeping her gaze on her knees, bared just below the edge of the towel.

"Lay back and let me see your foot," Ian directed.

She eyed him for a moment but did as he said. Her head bounced softly on the mattress as she settled down, and she focused on the ceiling.

Gentle hands covered the top of her foot and tilted it back as he examined the instep. His fingers were firm and warm against her skin.

Braden leaned over and took her arm, lifting as he examined the bruising and swelling.

How long had it been since she'd simply enjoyed the touch of another? Close proximity, the feeling of not being so terribly alone?

It was overwhelming and yet so deeply pleasurable that she couldn't ask them to stop. She didn't want them to stop.

These were concerned touches. Caring and light. There was no desperate mark of possession, no shouted words, no deep-seated insecurity.

She shivered even as she craved more.

Ian felt her tremble beneath his fingers. He saw raw vulnerability behind a flash of sudden tears, and it tore at his gut. Here was a woman unused to any sort of tenderness. She expected the worst, and it seemed she usually got it.

What the hell kind of life had she led, and why had Gabe left her to fend for herself?

Trying not to let himself be too affected, he put antiseptic on her cut and quickly bandaged it. Braden was carefully manipulating her arm, but other than a few winces, she didn't seem too bothered by it.

He thrust the small bottle at Braden along with fresh bandages. "For her hand."

Braden took the stuff from him and settled next to Katie, his hip close to her shoulder. Her fingers shook against Braden's as he carefully pried them apart.

Ian eased down on her other side. "I need to look at your ribs, Katie," he said in a low, soothing voice.

Color flooded into her cheeks, and her eyes flickered away, her gaze focusing on the wall.

Braden touched her cheek, running a finger down her delicate jawline. "Don't be afraid," he said quietly. "We just want to make sure you're okay. I swear to you we won't hurt you."

She closed her eyes and slowly nodded.

Ian arranged the towel so that it hung loosely over her waist. He couldn't cover her breasts *and* her pelvis and felt she'd probably be the least embarrassed to have them staring at her breasts.

Bruises were scattered along her ribcage, some the size of a fist, others smaller, purple fingerprints against pale skin. When he saw the dark smudges close to her nipples, his jaw tightened in rage.

"Did they rape you?" he demanded bluntly.

Braden yanked his startled gaze to his brother, and his brows drew together in admonishment.

Katie's eyes flew open, and she too stared at Ian in shock.

"N-no," she stammered.

"Did he try?" Ian pressed, not sure why it was so important that he know the depths of Ricardo de la Cruz's depravity.

A dark flush stained her cheeks, and her eyes glittered with anger.

"I doubt he'll be able to use that part of his anatomy for a long while," she said darkly.

A grin flirted with the edges of Braden's mouth. Ian relaxed, unaware of just how tense he'd been until some of the edginess left him.

"Okay, so what exactly did he do?" Ian asked as he tended to a cut just below her left breast.

She let out a sigh. "Does it matter? I have no plans to get caught by him again. I wouldn't have this time if you two hadn't slowed me down."

Braden winced. "We were only trying to help."

She turned to look at Braden for a long while. "I'd like to believe that. Really, I would. But I still don't know why you're here. You say Gabe sent you. Why? You hint that someone else is after me, but I've spent all my time running from Ricardo."

Ian absorbed that latest piece of information. He and Braden exchanged glances, and then Braden cleared his throat.

"Why don't you get dressed, Katie. Then we can have that conversation we talked about."

Ian raised one eyebrow in question.

"We worked out a trade," Braden explained. "While you were...sleeping. She gives us information, and we give her the same."

Katie wrapped the towel around her body and struggled to sit up. Ian put his hand behind her neck and helped her forward. His fingers lingered at her nape, drawn to the softness of her skin. Tiny little goose bumps prickled and raced across her flesh, and her muscles quivered beneath his palm.

She wasn't immune to him any more than he was immune to her.

Unsure what to do with that realization, he pulled his hand away and let her get up from the bed. For a brief moment, she hesitated and looked back at him, her eyes wide with equal parts confusion and uncertainty.

Then she clutched the ends of the towel tighter around her and grabbed her bag before heading to the bathroom.

"I get the distinct impression that we're not going to like what we hear," Braden murmured. "What could she possibly have done to make a man treat her like he has?"

"Sometimes a woman doesn't have to *do* anything," Ian said with a growl. "Maybe he just couldn't take no for an answer. Whatever the case, we need to get her the hell out of the country."

"So *we* can use her," Braden said in a low, dissatisfied voice.

"Do you see another way?" Ian kept his voice as low as Braden's. "Hell, Braden, I don't like it either. She's obviously had a shitty time, and God knows why Gabe left her alone, but do you really want to stay like this for the rest of your life? Half man, half wild animal with no control, no *choice*?"

He cupped his hand to the back of his head and rubbed up and down to the base of his neck in agitation.

"At least we'll keep her safe. Hell, when was the last time you think she ate? Did you see how slim she is? She had, what, two hundred dollars on her? Yeah, we need her to draw out Esteban, but that doesn't mean we're going to throw her under the bus."

Braden stared back at him, brief uncertainty flashing in his eyes before his lips drew together in a fine line. "No, I don't want to be this way forever. But maybe...maybe we need to be realistic. There might not be a way to fix this, Ian."

Chapter Thirteen

Katie took her time dressing as she pondered just how much to tell Ian and Braden. Of course how much she told them was solely dependent on what they told *her*. She still wasn't convinced they weren't full of shit.

Logic told her, not that she could be accused of being logical, that whoever they were, they weren't involved with Ricardo. If so they would have hand-delivered her back into Ricardo's hands when she'd escaped his house.

Instead they'd risked their lives to save her.

She frowned. No one did anything without reason, so what was theirs? What did they want with her? She didn't buy that they were here simply because Gabe had sent them.

As much as she'd avoided the details surrounding Gabe's death, she realized she needed to know. Somehow, as much it pained her, her wellbeing was inexorably tied to Ian and Braden.

With a quick frown, she shoved her still-damp hair behind her ears and smoothed her hands down her T-shirt. For good measure, she pulled on the zip-up hoodie and left it open in front. It gave her added warmth, and she didn't feel quite as exposed.

She squared her shoulders, took a deep breath and opened the bathroom door. As she stepped out, she glanced over to the bed to see Braden still sprawled out, his long legs dangling off the end.

When he saw her, he rose up on one elbow and glanced at Ian who was standing by the window. Then he patted the space on the bed beside him.

She ignored the summons and took refuge in the only part of the room where she didn't feel overwhelmed by their presence. She stopped a foot in front of the door, careful to keep it easily accessible.

"We'll just go after you, Katie," Ian said calmly.

She fidgeted nervously and refused to meet his gaze. Instead she focused on Braden. "Talk," she said huskily. "Why did Gabe send you? What happened to him?"

"I'm not talking to you when you're standing there looking the world like you're going to run the minute we say something you don't like," Braden said. "We can sit down and discuss this without resorting to violence."

She stood unmoving for several seconds before she grudgingly relented and walked over to the bed. She sat on the corner opposite Braden and still a decent distance from Ian. To her utter irritation, they closed in on her, flanking her on both sides.

"How often was Gabe in contact with you?" Ian asked.

She pressed her hands into her lap. "I asked you a question first."

Braden grunted. "There are some not very nice people who are looking for you."

"What was your first clue?" she asked snidely.

"These people make Ricardo de la Cruz look like a kindergartner," Ian said.

Fear fluttered in her chest and ran circles around her throat. "Why?" she croaked. "What people?"

Ian's face darkened. "The people Gabe sold us out to."

Katie shot to her feet.

"Ian, what the fuck?" Braden's angry voice rose over the red haze circling Katie's mind.

"She wanted the truth. She's getting it."

"You're a liar," she spat. "Gabe is intensely loyal. He wouldn't betray his team."

"For you he would," Ian said calmly. "Sit down, Katie. You wanted to hear everything and I'm telling you."

She stood there paralyzed by the utter conviction in Ian's

voice. *For you he would.* What did it mean?

She sank back onto the bed.

"Tell me," she said hoarsely.

"Gabe sacrificed himself for us," Braden said gently. "For Ian and I."

She turned to stare at Braden. "But Ian just said he betrayed you."

Braden grimaced. "He did. It's complicated. There were threats...against you. Gabe was trying to protect you. In the end it didn't matter because they were going after you anyway."

"They used *me* to make Gabe betray you?" she asked in bewilderment. "How did they know anything about me?"

"We didn't even know about you," Ian said. "Why is that, Katie? Why were you such a big secret?"

A dark flush heated her cheeks. "Because of Ricardo," she murmured.

"Ah yes, Ricardo. Why is he after you? Why does he want you so badly? Is it simply a case of obsession and unrequited love?"

Her temper flared, and like so many times in the past, she let her mouth get ahead of her brain.

"I think it has more to do with the fact that I killed his brother than me refusing his sexual advances, though neither won me any points with him."

As soon as the words flew out she clamped her mouth shut in disgust. Bad judgment and rampant stupidity clung to her like stink on shit. After so long of playing it safe, of finally making smart decisions, of keeping horrible secrets and taking charge of her life, she'd risked it all by letting a man rattle her.

"You killed his brother?" Braden asked in disbelief. "Damn, Ian, I think I'm in love."

She bolted off the bed and whirled around, rage choking her, closing off her airway like a giant fist had seized her neck. Tears of pure fury burned her eyes. "You think it's a joke?"

The grin disappeared from his face about the time her fist connected with his mouth. His head snapped back, and he had to plant his hand into the mattress to keep from falling.

She was instantly on guard and yanked around to check

Ian's position. He held up his hands defensively.

"Don't look at me. Have at it. The dumbass deserved it."

She turned back to Braden to see him rubbing his jaw, a scowl darkening his face.

"So much for not resorting to violence," he grumbled. "Don't have much of a sense of humor, do you."

"Braden, stop it," Ian barked. "You're upsetting her."

Braden's expression softened. "Sorry. I've never been accused of having tact."

Katie backed away. She just wanted to be gone. She bumped into Ian, and his arms came around her to steady her. His cheek rested against her hair, and his breath blew lightly over her ear.

Warm. It was her first thought. He felt warm and solid. She waited for the panic to hit, but all she registered was the ripple of awareness deep in her belly.

She found herself being turned around in Ian's arms. He gripped her shoulders loosely and stared intently into her eyes.

"Level with me, Katie. Why did you kill Ricardo's brother, and do we need to be worried about the police being on our asses in addition to de la Cruz?"

She shook her head resolutely and drew her lips into a compressed line.

"We deserve to know what we're up against," he said.

"You're not up against anything," she said quietly. "I am."

Ian shook his head. "Afraid not. We became involved when Gabe took a bullet meant for us and with his dying breath made us promise to protect you. Now you may not like it, and I'm sorry for that, but you don't have a choice in the matter."

She swallowed and then swallowed again, determined not to let emotion overrun her control. Gabe was still trying to look out for her even in death.

"Talk to me," Ian whispered. "I'm not here to judge you. If he was anything like his bastard brother, I can see why you'd kill him."

Her eyes watered and stung. She retreated, the backs of her knees bumping into the bed. Her hands flew to her face to cover the surge of tears as she slowly sank down.

"I've made so many mistakes," she whispered.

A gentle hand crept over her shoulder, and she realized it was Braden. He'd scooted up beside her and sat mere inches away.

"We've all made mistakes, Katie."

"And what if trusting you is yet another mistake?" she asked. "My instincts never lead me right."

"And what are your instincts saying about us?" Ian prompted.

She glanced up to see him towering over her. "Not to trust you."

"Well then if you can't trust your instincts, and they're telling you not to trust us, then I'd say maybe you need to do just that."

"That's twisted," she muttered.

"Yeah, it is," Braden agreed. "I like it."

"Look at us as the lesser of two evils then," Ian said patiently. "Whether you trust us or not, we need the whole story, Katie. You owe us that much at least."

She went back and forth, the panic of her decision buzzing in her head like bees on speed. She swallowed back the edge of fear and took a deep breath.

"You didn't know about me—no one knew about me—because Gabe didn't know about me until I was a teenager. We had different fathers, and our mother wasn't stellar parent material. She ditched Gabe when he was young. She ditched me when I was ten.

"I got into trouble when I was sixteen, and the cops tracked Gabe down. I'm still not sure how. He was just about to enter the service, so he didn't have a whole hell of a lot of time to play big brother or try to straighten my ass out.

"He took me home, told me I could stay or leave but he wouldn't be around to drag me back or bail me out of jail."

"Sounds like Gabe," Braden said dryly. "Not a very warm and fuzzy guy."

"He was fine," she said fiercely. "I didn't need or want warm and fuzzy."

"So he joined up. What then?" Ian asked impatiently.

"I stuck around his apartment. He arranged for the bills to be paid and left just enough money that I could eat, and not enough that I could get into trouble.

"We spent his leave together when he could get back. He didn't pressure me or make demands. Just gave me a place to live and a way to survive. When I was twenty, I met Paulo de la Cruz and fell madly in love as only someone that young and stupid does."

Braden made a sound that resembled a cross between a snort and a guffaw.

"You're not very hard on yourself, are you?" Ian said.

"I'm aware of my faults."

She rolled one shoulder as she prepared for the rest of the sorry tale.

"I was high on love and lust. Paulo was wealthy and came from a good family. He was everything I'd spent my life dreaming about. Roots. A big family. Security.

"When he took me to meet his family, Ricardo immediately put the moves on me. He made it clear he thought I was a whore for the taking. When I turned him down, it pissed him off. From then on out, he took every opportunity to convince Paulo that I was unfaithful.

"Paulo grew increasingly unstable. He got angry and started knocking me around. No matter what I said or did to prove my innocence, it only pissed him off more.

"And one night I fought back," she said quietly.

"So you killed him in self-defense," Braden said.

"I meant to kill him. I had a chance to escape after fending him off. I chose not to," she said with steel in her voice.

"If you're looking for reproach, you're not going to find it here," Ian said. "Bastard deserved what he got."

Katie didn't respond, but she expelled a sigh of relief. Somehow it felt good not to be judged. Ricardo had judged her a whore and then a murderer.

"I panicked and called Gabe. He got there a day later and helped me clean up the mess."

Braden lifted an eyebrow. "Mess? You make it sound so domestic."

"The body," she said dully. "Gabe helped me get rid of the body."

Ian whistled. "Why on earth didn't you go to the police?"

Katie trembled and twisted her hands in front of her. "I know how stupid it sounds, but I'm not an idiot. I knew damn well that Ricardo had half the police department in his back pocket. I knew that just from things Paulo had said. I couldn't risk going to them and having a fifty-fifty chance of picking the wrong cop to confide in. When I told Gabe everything, he agreed the best thing to do was get rid of the evidence and for me to haul ass out of there and start over somewhere else."

"So how did Ricardo figure out you killed his brother?" Braden asked.

Katie sighed. "He doesn't know for sure. What I mean by that is he didn't see a body or anything, but he's not stupid. He knew Paulo was knocking me around, and he also knows Gabe showed up, and I disappeared right after. He caught up to me in Vegas a year ago, and I didn't deny it. Paulo would never disappear off the face of the earth. He was too tied to Ricardo's will and completely under his thumb."

"So back up to the part where Gabe helped you dispose of the body," Ian said grimly. "He just took off afterward and left you to fend for yourself?"

Katie furrowed her brow. "He made sure I was safe, and he taught me how to take care of myself and how to always look over my shoulder. What else was he supposed to do? He couldn't go AWOL, he damn sure couldn't quit because his sister murdered someone, and he couldn't just start hanging out with me either. Together we attracted a hell of a lot more attention than me by myself."

"She has a point," Braden conceded.

Ian scowled. "I fail to see how Gabe is the good guy here. He left her by herself with a deranged asshole who wanted her blood. He had other options, and he damn sure didn't use them." He looked hard at Braden. "If she was your sister would you have left her behind like that?"

Braden pursed his lips, then glanced at Katie. Finally he shook his head. "No, I wouldn't."

"It doesn't matter now," Katie said firmly. She wasn't about to let them rag on Gabe's decision. He'd kept her alive, and that's all she cared about.

"You're right, it doesn't," Ian said with a nod. "What does matter is that we get the hell out of the country before crazy-ass de la Cruz catches up with us."

She cocked her head and stared up at Ian. "Why out of the country, and where are we going?"

"Can you think of a better place?" he asked calmly. "Or maybe you want to hang around and let Ricardo play target practice with our asses?"

She shook her head. "But I don't have a passport. Right now I don't have much beyond a driver's license."

"We can handle that," Braden said. "We'll worry about it when we've put an ocean between us and Ricardo."

She nodded shortly then stared between the two brothers. "Now it's your turn. Who are these people supposedly after me? You said Gabe sold you out but in the next breath, you say he took a bullet for you. So which is it? Is he a hero or a traitor?"

Chapter Fourteen

Braden grimaced. "He's both."

Katie stared up at him, pain and confusion brimming in her eyes. After hearing what she'd endured at the hands of the de la Cruz brothers, he had no desire to cause her more distress.

"He betrayed you for me? I'm to blame for his death?"

Ian cursed and backed away from the bed, his fists clenched tight at his sides. "You're not to blame for the choices Gabe made, Katie. Gabe was a big boy. He didn't have to do things the way he did. He could have come to us or to Eli. We've been out of the service for a while now. There was no reason to keep you a secret any longer."

She blinked in shock. "What? He wasn't enlisted anymore?"

Braden blew out his breath. Gabe was causing way more trouble dead than he'd ever caused alive. It was too bad he wasn't around because Braden would be tempted to kick his ass for the way he'd *taken care* of Katie.

Hell, she'd been little more than a kid. Completely alone save a few visits when Gabe was on leave. The rest of the time she was left to fend for herself. Instead of doing the right thing when she was forced to kill a man in self-defense, Gabe only ensured that she'd spend the rest of her life running after he covered up the deed. Damn fool. He could have asked his team for help. They would have gladly given it.

And here she was, grateful for whatever morsels Gabe had doled out. Yeah, maybe he'd taught her to survive in a tough world, but he damn well should have been protecting her from predators like de la Cruz.

"No, he wasn't enlisted any longer. None of us are, Katie. It's why he damn sure should have come clean about you. We could have helped. We certainly could have gotten you the hell out of the country where you'd be safe."

She twisted her hands in her lap and stared down at her fingers. "He talked about taking me to Argentina. But that was a while ago. Right after that he got weird. More distant and...paranoid. It went beyond the stuff with Ricardo."

Braden exchanged glances with Ian. It was obvious that Gabe hadn't told her shit about what had gone on during their mission to Adharji or the consequences. Which meant she didn't know of her brother's ability to become invisible or of Braden's and Ian's unstable shifts to big cats.

Ian cleared his throat and shook his head in warning at Braden.

A peculiar expression crossed Katie's face followed by the slow downturn of her mouth. "If he wasn't enlisted, why didn't he come home? What have you been doing all this time? Or was this recent? Why did he keep so much from me?"

If she only knew just how much he'd kept from her.

Braden threw Ian another desperate look. Ian ran a hand over his head then settled on Katie's other side.

"Look, Katie. I don't know why Gabe did half the shit he did," Ian said. "I can only tell you what I do know. He sold us out because there were threats against you. But in the end, he stepped in front of a bullet meant for us."

"And he asked you to find me?"

"He wanted us to make sure you were safe," Braden said gently.

She leaned forward and buried her face in her hands. She rubbed tiredly then dragged her fingers through her still-damp hair. "Okay, so you swoop in and save me from the bad guys. What then? You say we're leaving the country. That's all well and good but I've got to come back sometime. What about these people you say are after me?"

Braden slid a hand over her shoulder comfortingly. An alarming prickle skirted up his spine and squeezed his nape. He snatched his hand away and cupped the back of his neck.

Ian shot him a sharp look, and Braden looked away,

closing his eyes wearily.

"One thing at a time, Katie," Ian said as he stepped closer. Was it an attempt to get between Braden and Katie? The man appreciated the idea that Ian was ready to step in. The beast growled deep within.

Shit. Shit, shit, shit.

He sucked in deep breaths through his nose, his nostrils flaring with the effort.

"We'll eliminate the threats as they present themselves," Ian said calmly. "You won't be alone anymore."

Braden lost Ian's voice as a dull roar began in his ears. He jerked up from the bed like a puppet and staggered toward the door, his only purpose to escape. Instead, from the void, he heard Ian's harsh command for Katie to get out and stay out. Before he could protest, Ian tackled him.

They went down in a tangle on the floor, Ian's heavy body sprawled over his. He struggled weakly, and then a cool blast of aerosol hit him in the face. Seconds later, the jab of a needle made him flinch. His body went lax and fatigue swarmed over him with the speed of a bullet.

He was dimly aware of the battle between the man and the cat. For a few moments, he felt what the cat felt, saw what it saw, smelled what it smelled. And then the beast retreated with a low snarl.

For the moment he'd won.

Ian's low curses registered in the distance.

"Braden, talk to me, man."

Braden groaned and tried to open his eyes but the sedative Ian had injected was too powerful. His body jerked as Ian hauled him to his feet, and he stumbled. He went down like falling timber, hitting the bed with a thump.

Ian looked down at his brother and swore. Then he swiveled and saw Katie staring from across the room. She was backed against the wall in a defensive posture, and her gaze was locked warily on Braden.

"What's wrong with him?" she demanded. "What's wrong with both of you? Do you have some sort of seizure disorder?"

Ian latched gratefully onto the opening she unwittingly

offered, because he sure as hell had no intention of telling her just how close she'd come to being cat food.

"Something like that," he muttered. "Look, we need to get on the road. We're sitting ducks. Let's get everything into the truck and then you need to help me get Braden out of here."

She froze, her body stiff against the wall.

His eyes narrowed as he stared impatiently at her. "You're not still holding on to the stupid idea of going it alone are you?"

A hysterical-sounding laugh escaped her lips. "You're asking me to trust two ex-military guys with some funky seizure disorder who've done nothing but fuck things up for me ever since they walked into my life. Yeah, real hard choice here."

"Sarcasm doesn't become you," Ian said. "Get your things and head out to the truck or I'll stuff you in the back myself."

Rage flared in her eyes, and to his surprise, she stalked over and got into his face. Oh hell, did she have to get that close? He was already having a devil of a time keeping the cat from rearing its head. One whiff of her, and he'd be shit out of luck. Braden wouldn't be able to help him this time.

"What you can do is back the fuck off," she snarled as she rose up on tiptoe to get a better angle into his eyes. "I am tired of men with more brawn than brains. I'm tired of being manhandled and pushed around. You touch me, and so help me God, I'll castrate you."

"I don't have time for your tantrum," Ian said in a bored tone. "If you want to stick around and let Ricardo's men grab you so you can be his plaything then knock yourself out. Braden and I are out of here."

It was chancy, calling her bluff, because he had a feeling she'd tell him to fuck off and head out on her own. That wasn't something he could let her do, not when she represented their best chance at drawing Esteban out.

Indecision flickered in Katie's eyes as she glanced between him and Braden. For a moment he caught a glimpse of her bone-deep fatigue and the worry she tried so hard to conceal. Against his will, he softened.

With a brief shake of her head, she squared her shoulders and went over to grab one of the bags. She didn't say a word as she left the room. Ian smiled slightly and turned back to

Braden.

He was hoisting Braden up from the bed when Katie returned. All vestiges of vulnerability were gone, replaced by a hard shell. Her *don't-fuck-with-me* look was back in spades.

"I'm not going to be a whole hell of a lot of help," she muttered as she surveyed Braden's sagging body.

"Just get underneath his other arm and make sure he doesn't fall," Ian said. "I'll bear most of his weight."

She shrugged and then wiggled under Braden's other shoulder. She wrapped one arm around his waist and gripped his wrist with her other.

Ian headed for the door, dragging Braden's considerable weight with him. Katie struggled but bore up well. They stumbled into the sunshine, and Ian squinted as he scanned the area. Things were quiet, and only the sounds of distant traffic permeated the air.

"Let's go," he muttered.

They managed to shove Braden into the backseat and shut the door.

"Want me to drive?" Katie offered. "I have the most rest of any of us."

Ian shook his head sharply. "Get in. Let's go."

She said something unintelligible under her breath but walked around to the passenger side. As she settled in, Ian remembered that they still hadn't gotten food, and Katie had to be hungry. It wasn't like she could afford to miss many more meals.

As soon as he had the thought, he shrugged it off. She wouldn't starve, and right now, safety was more important than food.

He gunned the engine and drove back onto the highway. They still had several hours to go until they hit their rendezvous point, and the sooner they were in the air, the less antsy he'd feel.

"How uncontrolled is yours and Braden's condition?" Katie asked.

He glanced over in surprise until he remembered the whole bit about the seizures. She sure didn't pull any punches.

"We manage," he said shortly.

"Look, I have a right to know what I'm dealing with," she said. "You're offering me protection. Well, you can't very well protect me if you're constantly freaking out and having to be medicated to the point of passing out. What the hell am I supposed to do if both of you freak out on me at the same time?"

"You shoot whoever's after you," Ian said calmly.

She snorted. "With what? You haven't exactly been generous with contributing to my own self-preservation."

"That's because I can't be sure you won't shoot me or Braden," Ian muttered.

"At least tell me what the hell I'm supposed to give you if you wig out," she said.

Ian sighed. "There are syringes already filled in the back. Give us one of those and get the fuck away from us. The guns are back there too," he said after a brief hesitation.

It was true she deserved to know what she was dealing with, particularly since she needed to stay away from them if they shifted. They could kill her in shifted form. But if he told her that now, she'd not only think he lost his mind, but she'd never agree to leave the country with them. Better to fill her in on the kitty details in the air.

Every once in a while he caught Katie glancing over her seat to check on Braden. It amused him only because she went to such pains to make sure it didn't look like she was concerned.

"He'll be fine," Ian said. "He'll sleep it off and wake up a little muzzy-headed."

She scowled and focused her attention out her window.

For an hour, they drove in silence. A few of the roads they took were barely ribbons snaking through the rough terrain. Ian flexed his hands around the steering wheel and worked his head back and forth to stretch his neck.

"You sure you don't want me to drive?" she asked as she stared balefully at him from across the seat.

"Nah, I'm—"

The world went crazy around him. A sickening crunch. A

jolt so severe that his hands left the steering wheel as his body backlashed. He vaguely registered that they'd been hit. Broadside. Before he could react, regain control of the steering wheel as they careened sideways, they were hit again.

Glass shattered and sparkled in his vision like rain. They rolled and then rolled again. The SUV came to a shuddering stop and bounced hard as it righted itself. They had spun completely around and were angled in the ditch with the driver's side mashed against the ground.

Katie moved slowly, reaching groggily for her seatbelt.

"No," Ian said harshly. "Stay where you are."

Before she could respond, her door was wrenched violently open. A large man loomed over her. He glanced briefly down at Ian, but apparently discounted him as a threat. He slashed at Katie's seatbelt with a knife and then grabbed a handful of her hair. She cried out in pain when he yanked her from the truck.

A pulse of adrenaline rocketed through Ian's system, making him forget about his possible injuries or the pain that ricocheted through his head just moments ago.

He had to get to Katie.

He tried to move his legs and swore when he realized the dash was caved in around him. He wiggled his toes and was relieved that he didn't seem to suffer any pain or loss of motion, but he couldn't get free.

Goddamn it.

He twisted and tried to maneuver his upper body along the seat to get a different angle with his legs, but they didn't budge.

A low snarl simmered through his throat. Feral. Animalistic. His breaths came in short bursts. Pants. His vision blurred, and pain began deep in his bones as they started reshaping.

For once he didn't fight. He didn't concern himself with what might be because if he didn't make it to Katie, they'd kill her anyway. She'd have a better chance against the cat.

So he let go and surrendered to the intoxicating power surging through his veins. Warm and heady. The pain diminished as soon as he relinquished control.

"Braden!" he cried out with the last vestiges of humanity.

Where a moment before a man had lain trapped, a great cat arose and scented the air. Another growl rippled from his throat as he leaped from the vehicle.

Chapter Fifteen

Though every part of Katie shrieked in outrage, she forced herself to go limp until she could mentally examine herself for injuries. Her feet hit the ground with a resounding thump as one of Ricardo's henchmen yanked her out of the vehicle. He obviously wasn't concerned over potential injuries, which just told her she was going to die at Ricardo's hands shortly.

Could things get any worse? Braden was unconscious in the backseat, and as far as she could tell, Ian was trapped in the driver's seat. Which meant she was SOL when it came to any help from them.

Story of her life.

Her captor shoved her toward a waiting Ricardo who stood outside his untouched sports car, his expression furious. He backhanded her to the ground in one swift motion. She stayed down, nursing her throbbing cheek, knowing he wanted her to get up so he could go at her again.

Think, Katie, think. How on earth was she going to get herself out of this one?

A hand tangled in her hair and yanked her upright.

"Enough with the hair already," she growled as she tried to shake free.

Instead of letting her go, the man tightened his grip and shoved her closer to Ricardo. This time when Ricardo hit her in the face, the man holding her prevented her from falling. Warm blood trickled down her chin, but she glared defiantly at Ricardo.

"Quite a man, aren't you," she jeered. "Have to have another man hold me so you can beat up on me? Are you afraid of me, Ricardo?" She let her gaze fall to his groin. "How's the equipment, by the way?"

"Bitch," he said through clenched teeth. "I'm finished toying with you." He withdrew a switchblade from his pocket and flipped the blade in front of her face in a series of fancy motions.

"I'm going to gut you like a pig and leave you on the side of the road to die."

She bared her teeth and then spit at him, mimicking the time he'd done the same to her. It landed on his face, and his eyes widened in affronted shock.

He wiped the spittle from his cheek and stared at the back of his hand as if not believing she'd dared to insult him. She steeled herself for his retaliation even while she frantically searched for a way to escape.

The glint of metal flashed, and searing pain tore through her belly. She looked down to see the bright red bloom of blood spread across her abdomen. He'd slashed the knife across her skin instead of plunging the blade deep.

Painful and effective but not life threatening.

He raised the knife again but a ferocious growl rippled through the air. It sounded so primitive, so vicious, that it raised the hairs at Katie's nape.

Ricardo's hand stopped in midair, and his eyes went wide with fear. The hold on Katie's hair loosened, and the man holding her suddenly bolted away. She turned in time to see a big-ass cat leap from the interior of the SUV.

Before she could run, piss on herself or curl into a ball in a feeble attempt to protect herself, the cat streaked by her and launched itself at Ricardo.

Ricardo's screams rent the air before a mouth closed around his throat, effectively silencing him. It was over so fast that Katie barely had time to register that she wasn't having some bizarre hallucination.

Ricardo was sprawled on the ground under the weight of the animal, his eyes glassy and locked into a lifeless stare as his throat lay open and bleeding beneath the cat's mouth.

Holy fuck. The cat. Ian. Braden.

Her mind couldn't even catch up in its frenzy to understand what she'd just seen. Not waiting to see if she'd be the jaguar's next meal, she bolted toward the SUV. Only to find the driver's side empty.

Seizure disorder, my ass.

A quick look in the back told her Braden was either still unconscious or dead. She couldn't be sure which, and she wasn't going to hang around and find out. Hell, he'd probably turn into a damn...well she didn't know, but again, she didn't want to find out. Her brain simply couldn't comprehend what she'd witnessed.

She turned to see the cat shaking Ricardo like a rag doll. The other men had scattered like screaming girls, but they'd likely return.

She ran to the back of the SUV and prayed the door would open. It took some pulling, but she managed to crack it just enough to haul one of the assault rifles out.

Her stomach was bleeding heavily, and she spared only enough time to shove a balled-up T-shirt over it before she took off in the opposite direction. And then she heard gunfire.

Don't turn around. Don't do it. Get the fuck out of here. Save your ass and don't worry about the damn cat that's currently having Ricardo for lunch.

She turned around, her gun up against her shoulder. Ricardo's men were holed up behind their banged-up SUV. One dumbass had apparently shot at the jaguar and missed, and now the cat was stalking them.

Shit. If the cat was really Ian—and at this point, unless she believed in spontaneous combustion, she couldn't come up with a better explanation—then the least she could do was keep the gunmen off his ass, or hide, or whatever the hell you called a cat's skin.

She started to take cover behind the SUV but then realized that Braden was still inside, life status unknown, and if she started shooting at the bad guys they were going to shoot back, and if Braden wasn't already dead, he'd soon be. The idea of either man dying did odd things to her. They'd done their damndest to protect her, and she could do nothing less than return the favor.

"You're turning into a complete girl," she muttered.

She dropped the bloody T-shirt and jumped the ravine the SUV had tumbled into. She scrambled up the incline and dove behind a clump of trees. On her belly, she slithered painfully forward, her blood mixing with the soil. Maybe if she got enough dirt packed in there, it would stop the bleeding.

Taking careful aim, she focused on the scene below her. Her first priority was to take out the lead gunman. The other two were pussies, and if she could nail the first guy, the others would probably tuck tail and run. Thank God for all the time she and Gabe had spent at the shooting range.

As soon as he stuck his head above the truck, she squeezed off a round. Blood arced through the air, splattering the metal hood as he fell. To his right, curses rang out as the other two men scrambled for cover like rats abandoning ship.

One made the mistake of running into the open. She nailed him before he took two steps. And darn, it wasn't a clean shot, which meant the slimy little bastard would have to suffer for a while.

The other ran for Ricardo's sports car. She clipped him in the leg, but he staggered on, diving into the interior. He peeled away in a cloud of dust, tires squalling as they made contact with the road.

Satisfied that she'd put an end to any immediate threat, she turned her attention to getting out fast. No way in hell was she going to stick around to see what plans the jaguar had, nor was she inclined to learn what wild animal Braden could turn into.

Seizures. Just what kind of a moron did they take her for?

As she darted through the trees, the reality of what she'd just witnessed hit her like a ton of bricks. A fucking jaguar. What in the holy hell? People didn't just turn into animals. Was she losing her grip on sanity?

She pressed on, ignoring the searing pain in her abdomen and the warm rush of blood coating her skin. And then she remembered the tracking device.

She reached up to her neck, barely slowing in the process. When she felt the slight protrusion, she yanked with her fingers. The sliver came free, and she tossed it on the ground.

Her energy was fast fading, but she couldn't stop. Not now. She had to find a place to hide and regroup. Preferably where she was safe from a predator like a jaguar.

The image of the cat's jaws around Ricardo's throat flashed back to mind. Not that the jackass didn't deserve what he'd gotten, but Katie had no desire to be the cat's next meal. She had no doubt that as humans neither man would hurt her. She wasn't sure when she had embraced that knowledge, but it was there, irrefutable. But as wild animals? She'd seen the way Ian had taken Ricardo out, and she knew in that moment he was capable of horrific violence.

God have mercy, had Gabe known what Ian and Braden were?

Fatigue swept over her, swift and unmerciful. She'd lost too much blood, spent too much adrenaline. She was going to crash and burn.

She spun around, looking for a direction, someplace to hide. Shelter. Picking an old deer trail, she barreled through the underbrush, determined to ride the well of her strength until she went bust.

She crossed over what looked to be an old logging road or an ATV trail, and she stopped in the middle to stare down either side. She couldn't afford to remain in plain sight, so she headed into the woods on the other side. The brush enveloped her, and a chill raced across her skin in the absence of the sun.

For two hours, she pushed herself relentlessly, until she was beyond simple endurance. Nearly unconscious, she staggered over a rise and fell to her knees. She jammed the stock of the rifle into the ground to give her leverage as she hauled herself to her feet once more.

Ahead she saw a thick shroud of snarly bushes, and she focused single-mindedly on it. In the end, she didn't even remember crawling those last feet. She dove into the brambles, wincing as the branches tore at her skin. She struggled to the middle and hollowed out a spot where she could rest. Gripping the gun tightly to her chest, she curled into a tight ball and closed her eyes.

Chapter Sixteen

Tyana stared dully over the ocean as the sun's first rays peeked over the horizon. The sky was bathed in soft lavender, a beautiful contrast to the dark rolling sea. The sea fit her mood. The beauty of the sunrise mocked her.

Her foot was propped on a pillow but there was no comfort for her. Inside, Jonah and Mad Dog were determining D's fate while Tyana grew sicker at heart by the moment.

He can't stay, Ty.

He's a danger to you. To himself. To everyone.

He'll be better off.

It's better this way.

She closed her eyes against the statements that had been flung during the long night. No one had slept. No one had rested. They kept watch over the unconscious tiger until finally, an hour before dawn, the tiger had slowly given way and D's naked, weakened body had appeared on the floor of the game room.

The glass doors opened. She looked up to see Eli file out followed by Mad Dog, Marcus, the team physician, and finally Jonah. Her chest tightened with dread. They'd come to deliver their edict.

"Are you all right, Ty?" Jonah asked in a gruff voice.

She nodded, her throat too knotted to speak. She glanced expectantly at Marcus. He stared back at her, apology in his eyes.

"He has to go," Mad Dog said quietly.

"No," she choked out.

Eli sat down next to her, his fingers curling around her nape and massaging.

Marcus nodded even as she shook her head in denial.

"It's time, Tyana," he said. "I've done all that can be medically done. It's time to pursue other means. It's our only hope. He grows more unstable all the time. His shift last night was so fast that you didn't even have time to react before it was done."

She closed her eyes. "I won't leave him alone."

"He won't be alone," Jonah said. "Marcus is going with him."

"Where?" Her voice cracked and shattered like glass.

"I want him to try alternatives to medicine," Marcus said. "As I said before, I think the key is psychological. His DNA has been altered, and there is no cure for that. I can bandage it, but it won't fix the problem. I firmly believe..." He glanced around at D's family. "There is no cure right now. As much as we want there to be one. Damiano is going to have to learn to control his abilities or they'll kill him. There's no way to soften that truth."

"Where are you taking him?" Tyana demanded hoarsely. "Why can't I stay with him?"

"He has to do this alone," Marcus said. "It's best if you don't know where. I want him to take on a regimen of meditation and spiritual honing. Mind over matter. He needs discipline."

Tyana's mouth twisted. "It sounds like a bunch of bullshit."

"He's going, Ty," Jonah said.

Panic and grief crashed over her like a wave. "When?"

Mad Dog's expression drew into a grimace. "As soon as the chopper gets here."

Eli's grip tightened around her, but she didn't want comfort. Not when Damiano was going to be alone. Without his family. Without her.

"Where is he now?" she demanded.

"He's resting under guard," Jonah said.

"I want to see him. To say goodbye."

Jonah nodded. "Of course. As we all do."

"Does he know?" she asked.

"He knows," Mad Dog said quietly.

She closed her eyes against the sudden tears. She and D had been together since they were children, never separated for longer than a few days. He needed her now more than ever, and he would be alone. She'd sworn he'd never be without her. And now she was forced to break her promise.

Gently, Eli helped her to her feet. The agony caused by the tiger's attack was nothing compared to the pain lashing at her soul. Ignoring the crutches and the hands that reached to help, she dragged her casted leg behind her as she hobbled to the door.

When she walked inside, she saw D sitting on the couch, his face in his hands. Four of the Falcon secondary stood guard around him.

Slowly, painfully, she made her way toward him. When she was but a few feet away, he looked up. The anguish in his eyes was her undoing. She dropped heavily to the floor, her hands clutching at him as he reached to hug her.

"I'm sorry, Ty. I'm so sorry."

His voice was muffled in her hair. She hung onto him, her tears seeping into the material of his shirt.

She pulled slowly away and touched her hand to his cheek. "Don't be sorry, D. I'm the one who's sorry. I've failed you. I swore to find a cure."

He shook his head. "I could have killed you. Marcus is right to take me away."

She shook her head harder. But he stilled her motion with a finger to her lips.

"I have to do this, Ty. For me and for you. I won't stay where I might hurt you. It's already happened once before. I could have killed you this time."

"I love you," she whispered.

He cupped her cheek in a loving gesture, and with his other hand, he stroked her hair. "I love you more."

He glanced up at Eli who hovered protectively over Tyana. "Keep her safe for me."

Eli nodded. "You know I will."

D's gaze went to Jonah and Mad Dog. He swallowed as though he didn't know what to say. And then he stood, letting his hand fall from Tyana's face. Eli helped her to her feet so that she was beside her brother.

"You take care, little brother," Mad Dog said gruffly as he enfolded D in his beefy embrace.

Then it was only D and Jonah, standing face to face. Dark emotion, so uncharacteristic of Jonah, clouded his face. His eyes flashed with pain, and Tyana felt guilty for all the times she'd thrown such nasty accusations at him.

"You'll beat this, D," Jonah said. "You'll beat it and you'll come back to us. Your family. We'll always be here for you."

He hugged D tightly, stiffly, his face a mask of sorrow.

"The chopper is two minutes out."

The statement came from behind Jonah, from one of the secondary standing guard. Tyana stifled the urge to scream. She turned into D's arms and held on tight.

D stroked her hair in his quiet, generous way. God, it should be her offering him comfort, but as always, he took care of her.

"Come back to me, D. Swear it."

He pulled away and brushed his lips across her forehead, his words whisper soft. "I'll always be wherever you are."

Chapter Seventeen

Braden dragged his eyelids open but couldn't for the life of him get them to stay that way. It felt like bricks were sitting on his eyes, and his head pounded like someone was taking a jackhammer to it.

He moved his hand, surprised to feel the roughness of carpet under his palm. He blinked and then blinked again as he became aware that he was on the floorboard of the SUV, his nose pressed against a floor mat.

What the ever-loving fuck?

His nerves were jittery and jumping around, but not like what happened right before a shift. This was different. And damn, he hurt from head to toe. What had Ian given him? And why was he on the floor?

He shoved himself upward. He realized several things at once. The truck wasn't moving. They'd had one hell of a wreck. Ian and Katie were both missing.

Adrenaline surged, liquid and edgy. The cobwebs cleared from his brain as he leaned forward to examine the damage to the front seat.

The dash was caved in on the driver's side. No way Ian could have gotten out by himself. He had to have been trapped. Had Katie managed to get him out? Or were they both dead?

An icy chill cooled some of the adrenaline rush. He reached for the door only to find it wouldn't budge. He leaned back and kicked at it, hammering it repeatedly until it gave way.

He crawled from the interior and nearly fell out onto the ground. Struggling upward, he leaned a hand against the truck as he surveyed the immediate area.

It looked like a damn war zone.

There wasn't much that he hadn't seen—certainly not much that would shock him—but seeing Ricardo de la Cruz laid out with his neck gaping open, blood spattered in a three-foot radius around him and one of his henchmen on the ground several yards away with half his head blown off was so bizarrely surreal, he wondered if he was dreaming the entire thing.

A sound to his right shook him from his stupor, and he charged over, half afraid he'd find Ian or Katie in a bad way. He saw another of Ricardo's goons slithering along the ground leaving a thick blood trail. Dark, almost black. Braden shuddered. Gut shot. Painful, messy way to die.

Braden kicked the man's shoulder with the toe of his boot to turn him over. The man stared up at him with frosted-over eyes that told Braden he wasn't long for this world.

Braden bent down and gathered his shirt, yanking him a foot off the ground.

"What the fuck happened?" he growled.

The man's lips flapped up and down, but nothing would come out. He was obviously scared shitless.

"C-cat. Big c-cat," he sputtered.

Oh fuck. Ian had freaked out and shifted.

"The girl. Where is the girl?"

"Don't know," the man gasped. "She escaped...when the cat...when it attacked...Ricardo. She s-shot me...and the others."

"Good girl," Braden murmured.

He let go of the man and gently returned his shoulders to the ground. His breath caught and stuttered, and for a moment his eyes widened in panic. Then air escaped softly, and he deflated. His head lolled back until his stare was locked sideways, focused on something distant. At least the bastard wasn't suffering any longer.

Braden got up and stalked back to the SUV. He needed to get the fuck out of here before the cops showed up. He had no idea how long it had been since things had gone to shit, but it couldn't be that long judging by the fresh blood and the guy who'd only just died from his wounds.

He surveyed the damage to their vehicle with a grimace. It was toast. He glanced over at the SUVs driven by Ricardo's following. There were two. One with extensive front-end damage. The other had a few bullet holes but was otherwise intact.

Only taking time to haul out the gear from the back of the truck, he transferred it to the other SUV and climbed behind the wheel. He'd have to stash the vehicle and backtrack to find Ian. And Katie.

He peeled away and looked for a path into the wooded area. A few minutes later, he dove off the road onto a faint, overgrown trail. He barreled through the woods, tree limbs slapping the windshield.

Christ, but they didn't have time for this. The last thing he wanted to do was have to call Eli to come bail their asses out. He remembered with abashed clarity that he'd snidely decided if they couldn't handle one slip of a woman he and Ian needed to fucking quit.

Yeah, real smooth.

He broke into a short clearing as the road widened, and the trees fell away. And he almost ran over the body lying in the pathway. With a vicious curse, he wrenched the wheel sideways and tumbled into the trees. He came to an abrupt halt mere inches from a huge-ass pine. Not exactly what he wanted to pick a fight with.

He bolted from the truck and ran back to where he'd seen Ian—or at least who he thought was Ian. He didn't think there'd be too many other naked men in the vicinity.

He wasn't dead. Braden wouldn't contemplate that something had gone horribly wrong. Okay, scratch that. Something had indeed gone terribly wrong. The bloodbath he'd left behind was evidence enough. But as long as it was Ricardo's thugs and not Ian or Katie who'd taken the heat, he could deal.

He dropped to his knees over Ian's sprawled body. Ian was facedown in the road, one arm tucked underneath him and the other over his head. His body glistened with sweat, but Braden couldn't see any blood.

Hesitantly, he reached for his brother, touching the warm,

113

damp skin of his back. The muscles twitched and quivered under his fingers, and Braden expelled a huge sigh of relief. Ian was alive.

"Ian. *Ian*," he said louder. He shook Ian's shoulder.

Ian moaned softly but didn't move.

"Come on, man. We don't have any time to waste, and I can't carry your ass."

Ian's head turned and he stared at Braden with unfocused eyes. "You're alive," he rasped.

"Funny, that was my reaction when I found you," Braden said. "What the hell happened? When I came to, the SUV was toast, there were dead bodies everywhere, and you and Katie were gone."

Ian shook his head. His brow wrinkled in confusion. "Katie?" he said hoarsely. "Is she okay?" His expression became more intense as he pushed himself unsteadily to his feet.

Braden reached out to steady Ian, but his brother shook him off.

"What happened, Braden? Where's Katie?"

"Get in the truck," Braden said firmly. "We'll talk there. We've got to get the hell out of here. Katie has the tracking device on her. We'll find her."

Ian drew up short when he saw the SUV. Before he could form the inevitable question, Braden shoved him into the seat.

Seconds later, Braden climbed behind the wheel and looked over at Ian. Then he reached into the backseat for one of the duffel bags and dragged it into the front.

"At the rate you're running through clothing, we're both going to be butt-assed naked."

Ian cracked a small grin, and Braden relaxed. If Ian could smile then things weren't too bad.

As he awkwardly started pulling on his clothing in the confined space of the SUV, Braden started the engine.

"We don't have much time so we need to talk fast and piece together what the hell happened back there."

Ian pulled a T-shirt over his head and stared at Braden with haunted eyes. "I was driving and talking to Katie and then *wham.* Out of nowhere we got broadsided. Before I could react we got hit again. I was pinned under the dash."

He absently rubbed at his legs as he spoke, and Braden, remembering the crushed front end, could understand why. It was a miracle his legs hadn't been broken.

"Some guy, I'm assuming one of Ricardo's men, yanked Katie out of her door. I tried to get free, and I remember thinking that shifting was my best hope. After that I don't know."

"You killed Ricardo," Braden said grimly. "He had his throat torn out. No human did that to him."

Ian's jaw tightened. "I can't say I regret it. Bastard deserved to die. But what about Katie?"

Braden shook his head. "I don't know, man. Get the satellite out and see if she shows up. No way she could have gone more than three hundred miles, so she'll be in our radius. I'd say no more than half an hour has passed since the wreck. One of the guys was still alive when I found him. Took a bullet to the gut."

Ian's gaze sharpened. "But how?"

"Katie. That's how. Another guy had his gray matter smeared all over the truck. I'm telling you, some crazy shit went down out there."

"So, Ricardo is dead along with at least two other guys. If I killed Ricardo, then that means Katie got to the others. And if that's the case, where the fuck is she now?"

Braden gestured toward the bag. "You track, I'll drive."

Ian fumbled with the equipment while Braden drove deeper into the woods searching for an outlet that didn't lead right back to the road littered with dead bodies.

Braden glanced over to see Ian's expression darken and his jaw tighten.

"What's eating you, man?"

Ian gave a quick negative shake of his head as he opened the small unit and powered it up. Then he dragged a hand though his hair and turned to Braden, consternation and loathing in his eyes.

"I don't regret taking Ricardo apart, Braden, but what if it had been someone else? What if it had been you? Or Katie."

"It wasn't," Braden said simply. And really, what else could he say? He didn't have the answers, and he wasn't going to spout some bullshit about how Ian would never hurt him, because shit, what the jag did was completely independent of Ian.

Ian sighed.

"Are you hurt from the crash?" Braden asked.

Ian shook his head. "Sore, but I don't know if it's from the wreck or the shift. You?"

"Yeah, I'm good. Head hurts like a bitch but then I've had a headache since the day I laid eyes on Katie Buchanan."

"I hope to hell I got to Ricardo before he hurt her," Ian said softly.

"You got a bead on her yet?"

Ian glanced back down at the handheld unit then frowned. "Yeah. Close." He looked up and out the window. "Maybe a mile. She's not moving."

Braden cursed. "Steer me. Where am I going?"

"We need to head due east."

Braden slammed on the brakes and surveyed the landscape. No way they were going to make it in the truck. Hell. With a sigh he opened the door and got out.

He grabbed two rifles and tossed one over the hood at Ian. Ian was moving slow, but if turtles had guns no one would bitch about their speed.

They took off into the woods, moving in the direction of the tracking device. According to Ian, she hadn't budged since he'd locked on to her location, which couldn't be good given her propensity for running like a scalded cat.

Two hundred yards in, Ian pulled up sharply and turned in a circle, his gaze raking over the area.

"Here," he said. "It says she's here."

Braden shook his head. "She ditched the device, man. We're flying blind now."

"Maybe not," Ian muttered as he squatted down and touched his finger to a leaf. He pulled it back up and held it out to Braden.

Blood. Fresh blood. Shit.

Ian stood, shoved the locator in his pocket and hauled his gun up. Head down, he followed the blood trail further into the woods. Braden took off after him, his gut tight as he noticed just how much blood was spattered on the ground.

Chapter Eighteen

The longer it took to follow Katie's blood trail, or what he assumed was her blood, the edgier Ian got. From what Braden said, the road, even as out of the way as it was, was littered with dead bodies, which meant getting to the airport in Chama was going to be a bitch. As soon as the cops closed in, going anywhere would be damn near impossible.

Was Katie all right or would they find her dead? And worse, who had caused the injuries that bled so heavily? Dread closed in, suffocating and hot despite the chill in the air. She knew what he was now. Getting her to go anywhere with him and Braden was going to be impossible.

"There, Ian." Braden pointed to an area on the ground a few feet in front of where they stood.

Ian followed the direction of Braden's hand and saw a larger amount of blood, and ahead the ground and dirt looked like something had been dragged over it.

"She went down here." Braden looked up, following the line into a heavy growth area.

Ian burst past him, his focus on the brush that was slightly disturbed. Someone or something had gone in there. He tossed his gun at Braden and crawled on hands and knees into the thick tangle.

Brambles slapped him in the face and caught at his clothing, but the blood was heavier here. She'd been here and had been moving much slower.

He parted a particularly thick tangle and stopped cold. A small, bare foot lay in the dirt. He followed it up to a jeans-covered leg. The denim was dirty, tattered and covered in blood.

With angry slashing motions, he shoved aside the branches until he stared down at Katie's pale face. She lay on her side, an assault rifle tucked close to her chest, the other hand cupping her blood-smeared abdomen.

He fumbled at her neck, tilting her until he could press his fingers into her supple flesh. Her pulse beat reassuringly, and he breathed a sigh of relief.

"I've got her," he called back.

"Then let's get the hell out of here," Braden bit out.

Ian picked up the gun and gently pried it from her grip. She never stirred which worried him. She'd run hard, and that combined with the blood loss couldn't be good.

After calling back a quick warning, he tossed the gun at Braden and then returned his attention to Katie. Rolling her carefully so he could get a look at her injuries, he pushed aside her torn shirt to see a four-inch gash starting at her side and snaking just underneath her breast.

Son of a bitch had cut her.

The blood had slowed to a trickle, but when he hoisted her into his arms, it seeped faster. Backtracking the way he'd come was a bitch when he couldn't use his arms to clear the path. He finally shouted for Braden to get the hell in and help him out.

Between the two of them, they finally managed to free themselves from the tangle, and Ian stood unsteadily with Katie in his arms.

"I'll take her. You get the guns," Braden said as he reached for her.

Ian gripped her tighter and shook his head. "I'm fine. Let's go."

Braden regarded him skeptically but then shrugged, bent down and collected the rifles and started out ahead of Ian. They moved at a fast clip, and though Ian was tiring, he forged ahead, determined to get back to the truck so they could get the hell to the airport.

When they got to where the SUV was parked, Ian headed for the backseat.

"Put the seat down and you drive," he instructed Braden. "I need to see how bad she's hurt, and we can't afford to waste any more time."

Braden quickly collapsed the backseat and then climbed up front. Ian laid Katie down and got in after her.

"It's going to be bumpy getting out," Braden warned.

Ian nodded and positioned himself so Katie wouldn't roll to the floor.

After examining the filthy wound, he decided it wasn't as bad as it looked. It needed stitches. Several. She'd lost a lot of blood but it was nothing that would kill her.

Her face had taken another beating. Her lip was split and swollen, and a dark bruise shadowed her cheek. He was thankful the jaguar attacked Ricardo and not Katie. He only wished he'd been cognizant of making the kill. He would have relished every second.

In an odd gesture of tenderness, he trailed a finger softly over her cheek and to the bloodied cut at her lip. And then, realizing that he was wasting valuable time, he cursed and yanked his hand away.

He reached for one of the bags in the back and hoped he still had enough shit to get the cut cleaned and bandaged. He paused when he found one of the syringes with the sedative.

Her remaining unconscious until they got on the plane served several purposes. She wouldn't cause further trouble, and she'd also not feel anything when he cleaned the wound.

After injecting her, he waited a few moments before pulling out a bottle of water and several bandages. He meticulously cleaned all the dirt and debris from the cut. After swabbing the fresh rush of blood, he carefully pushed the edges of the cut together and added small strips of medical tape to keep it closed.

He applied a clean bandage and secured it. If she didn't move much, it shouldn't start bleeding again.

"She all right?" Braden asked.

Ian looked up to see Braden watching in the rearview mirror. He offered a short nod.

"I've sedated her so she should be out until we get on the plane. I cleaned the wound. It needs stitching. I'll call Eli before we take off and make sure he has a doc lined up when we land."

"Let's just hope we get to the plane in one piece," Braden muttered.

Chapter Nineteen

Tyana watched as Eli finished shoving his clothes into a duffel bag and then tossed it onto the bed. Afterwards, he methodically performed a weapons check, going over each gun, each piece of electronic equipment.

She was jealous as hell.

D had left with Marcus hours before, and now Eli prepared to rendezvous with Tits before they headed to Austria.

She was itching to go. She wanted Esteban, and she wanted him badly. Wanted to make him pay for D's pain and suffering.

"You look like you just swallowed a really nasty-tasting bug, sugar," Eli drawled.

She blinked and then glared at Eli. "I hate being left behind," she muttered.

He grinned and dropped a kiss on her upturned lips. "Yeah, I know you do. I'd rather you come along because I hate leaving you, but until that cast comes off, you're stuck here."

"Get him for me, Eli," she said softly. "Promise me you'll take him down for D. For what he tried to do to you."

Eli's expression turned serious. "I know how much D means to you, Tyana. I know how much it's hurting you to be separated from him. I'm going to do everything I can to help you both. I have a personal stake in this, remember? Ian and Braden aren't far behind D. They're deteriorating more each day."

She grimaced. "I don't mean to leave them out of the equation, Eli. It's just that for so long it's been just me and D.

It's hard for me to get used to the idea that we aren't alone anymore."

Eli brushed her hair behind her ear. "No, sugar, you aren't alone. You'll have me for as long as you want me."

Though the words were meant to comfort her, she saw the flash of uncertainty. Was he so unsure of her feelings? How could he not know how much she wanted him, how much she needed him?

Because you've never told him, dumbass.

The idea of laying bare her soul made her lightheaded. But he'd already given up so much for her. To give him the words seemed like so little. If only it didn't feel like she was stabbing an ice pick through her eyeball.

Queasiness attacked her stomach, and she was sure she was turning green.

"Tyana? Are you okay?"

Eli's concerned voice reached through the haze, and she focused on his face. On the earring that glittered in his ear. On the strands of dark hair that hung to his shoulders.

"I love you," she blurted out.

Mortified by the brash way it tumbled out of her mouth, she closed her eyes and prayed he hadn't heard.

"Tyana," he said in a quiet voice.

She opened one eye to peek at him. In that moment she wanted to throw her arms around him and kiss him senseless. He seemed to understand how difficult it had been for her. He didn't demand she say it again. Didn't make a huge deal out of it. But she could see the stark relief in his eyes, and in that moment, she'd tell him a hundred times over if it meant he'd never look at her with insecurity again.

"I love you too."

"I'm sorry I haven't told you before now," she went on in a rush. "I assumed you knew, I mean—"

He hushed her with a kiss. Long and slow. Gentle yet demanding. She emitted a little sigh as she melted into his arms.

"I do know," he said as he pulled away. "But it's damned nice to hear."

"Eli, chopper's here," Mad Dog called from the other side of the door.

"Be right out."

He glanced back at Tyana as he made a grab for his bags on the bed.

"Well, that's my ride, sugar. I'll see you in a few days. Try not to drive Mad Dog and Jonah too crazy, okay?"

She smiled but thought it was a rather weak attempt. He slung a backpack over his shoulder then leaned in to give her a quick kiss before he threw open the door and hurried out.

As she watched him go, she was struck by the thought that a few days ago she'd wanted this reprieve. Wanted room to breathe. And now, suddenly, the two people she loved most in the world were gone.

Hollow achiness invaded, stretching and invading her veins like poison. Alone. She was alone. And it felt horrible.

Chapter Twenty

"What the hell do you mean, they changed safe houses on us?"

The furious words swarmed in Katie's ears even as she couldn't quite force her eyes open. There wasn't a muscle in her body listening to what her brain was telling it, and so she continued to lay there like a limp noodle. Wherever *there* was.

"No, I don't like it, Eli. CHR still has places for us to crash. Why are we relying so heavily on Falcon?"

Ian. Ian was talking to someone, and he was pissed. He made a rude noise before continuing on.

"We need a doctor as soon as we hit the ground. Katie's hurt. No, it's not too serious, but she needs stitches."

Vaguely, other sounds began to register. The low hum vibrating her body. The whir of an engine. A jet?

Shit. She was on a goddamn plane.

And then the events of the day, or yesterday, because who the hell knew how long she'd been out, stormed through her bruised mind.

She was on a plane with a bunch of wild animals.

She lurched upward and nearly passed out when pain ripped across her abdomen. Almost as quickly, a big hand planted itself over her chest, the palm a little too close to her breast for her liking. She found herself shoved back down on the couch. Couch? On a plane?

Her head was about to explode with confusion.

Braden loomed over her, his expression grim. "Stay your ass down. You trying to open up your wound again? You've

125

already bled like a stuck pig."

When she didn't immediately respond, his expression tightened, and his eyes glittered with challenge. He pulled a syringe out of his pocket and held it where she could see it.

"You've got two choices, sister. You can stay down or I can knock your ass out. Makes no difference to me, and quite frankly, you're less of a pain in my ass when you're out cold."

She forced herself to relax, and slowly he took his hand off her body and stood to his full height.

"Where are we?" she asked, her voice cracking. God, she was thirsty. And so damn hungry her stomach was going to start eating itself.

"We're landing in Austria in about an hour and a half," he said.

"Austria? What the fuck?" She started to raise her head, but he gave her a warning look and hovered menacingly.

"Yeah, well, it wasn't our first choice either," Braden muttered.

"How is she?" Ian asked as he shoved his way past Braden.

Katie stared at him and shrank back against the seat. How could he look so normal? Had what happened been the product of her twisted mind? Had she finally lost her grip?

Ian's eyes flashed and then he spun around and stalked out of her vision.

"You deal with her," he tossed back to Braden. "Apparently she's not afraid of you."

"Bullshit," Katie refuted.

Braden raised an eyebrow. "What the hell did I do?"

"So what's your little trick?" she demanded. "Lion? Wolf? Hyena?"

"Very funny," he growled.

"I wasn't joking," she said, her voice deadly quiet. "What the fuck are you? All that bullshit about a seizure disorder. Is that a code word for turning into wild animals?"

Again his eyebrow went up and his eyes twinkled with amusement. "Seizures?" He turned in the direction Ian had walked. "You know anything about seizures, Ian?"

Ian muttered something unintelligible.

"Can I get up?" she asked. "I don't like lying down where I can't see. I want to be able to defend myself if the need arises."

Braden's gaze narrowed. "Defend yourself from who?"

"You," she said evenly.

He shrugged and bent down to help her up. "We can eat you sitting up just as well as lying down."

She went to slug him, but he caught her fist in his firm grip. He stared levelly at her. "You're starting to get predictable."

He picked her up, and even though he was extremely gentle, she let out a low moan.

"Sorry," he muttered as he set her in one of the larger chairs independent of the couch.

She sucked in several breaths and waited for the fire to subside in her gut. She glanced down to see that all the blood was gone, she was wearing a fresh T-shirt way too large for her, and she was still barefooted. For some reason that amused her.

When she let out a shaky laugh, Braden shot her a concerned look.

"What's so funny?"

"My feet."

"Your feet?"

"Yeah. No shoes. I've run across God knows how many states with no shoes."

She said it almost mournfully which was stupid. To be hung up on shoes when she was damn lucky to be alive at this point was absurd.

"We'll get you shoes when we land," Braden said gruffly. "You need to rest."

"I'm starving," she said. "And thirsty. I'd kill for about a gallon of water."

He froze for a moment, and then he let out a rush of scorching expletives. Then he turned. "Hey Ian, do we have anything to eat on this damn thing? Katie still hasn't eaten. Hell, *I* haven't eaten."

Ian reappeared a few moments later with a handful of

snacks and some bottled water. "Sorry," he said as he thrust them at her. "It's all we've got."

She latched onto them gratefully. First she ripped off the top to one of the water bottles and slugged the liquid down like an alcoholic falling off the wagon.

"Slow down. You're going to make yourself sick," Braden said gently.

She managed to slow herself just as she drained the last of the first bottle. Then she turned her attention to the array of food she'd dropped on her lap. There was a box of crackers, a bag of chips, a couple of cereal bars and some sort of fruit shit.

She opened the chips and the crackers then ripped open a cereal bar.

"And she calls us wild animals," Braden said with an amused snort.

Both Katie and Ian glared at Braden who simply shrugged with a distinct *I-don't-give-a-fuck* air.

As she devoured a cereal bar, she glanced up at Ian who hadn't yet retreated. She tried to see a glimpse of the jaguar, and then she wondered at the sheer idiocy of her thoughts. People couldn't change into animals. They just couldn't.

"Eat first, Katie," Ian said in a low, stiff voice. "We'll talk afterward."

She stopped chewing, frozen as she stared back at him. Finally she nodded and resumed eating.

She polished off the cereal bar, scarfed the bag of chips and ate half the crackers before she even considered slowing down. The other cereal bar she held was tempting even though she felt the urge to puke.

Only the idea of having to barf and the agony it would cause her because of her injury made her put it away with regret. She contented herself with another full bottle of water and finally leaned back with a sigh. She couldn't even remember the last time she'd eaten. Ricardo hadn't concerned himself with making sure she was fed and those days were a big blur anyway.

Through it all, she watched Braden and Ian suspiciously, looking for any of the erratic behavior they'd displayed before. Ian's lips were tight, but Braden stood in a defiant posture, clearly inviting her to fuck off.

"What are you?" she demanded.

Ian's lips curled in irritation while Braden continued to stare her down, his eyes as unfriendly as his posture.

"Don't look at me like I'm some kind of pond scum," she burst out. "I'm not the problem here."

Braden snorted, and she glared heatedly at him.

"You came after me," she pointed out. "Things have been bizarre since the day you kidnapped and drugged me. You act strange, like you're hanging on to control by a thread. The next thing I know, Ian turns into some kind of damn big-ass cat and tears Ricardo's throat out. And then you want to get snotty when I run like hell and act worried about the fact that I'm trapped thirty thousand feet in the air with two wild animals?"

Ian lost some of his surliness. He dragged a hand through his hair and walked over to flop into the chair across from Katie.

Braden remained standing, but he turned to include Ian in his view. The two brothers exchanged what could only be described as looks of resignation. There was more there. A deep sorrow. Katie's chest tightened even as she damned herself for feeling anything for these two men.

"Did Gabe ever tell you anything about our mission to Adharji?" Ian asked.

Her brow puckered, and her eyes narrowed in confusion.

"I'll take that as a no," he said dryly.

She shook her head.

"We were on a hostage recovery mission when we got gassed. We were captured behind enemy lines and were prisoners until we escaped several days later."

"Gassed? What kind of gas?"

"That's just it. We don't know. But whatever it was turned us into a bunch of shifters. In my case a jaguar, as you've seen." He gestured toward Braden. "He turns into a panther. Eli is more elemental. He can turn into shit like vapor, or smoke, steam, funky shit."

"And Gabe? Was he affected?" she asked hesitantly.

Ian nodded.

"Wow, he never said—I mean he never told me." She twisted her hands nervously in her lap. She'd always thought she and Gabe were close, but now she wondered how much of his interaction with her was solely based on obligation. "What was wrong with him?" she asked as she looked back up at Ian. "I don't understand how this happened. It's like something out of science fiction."

"Gabe could become invisible," Braden said.

"Invisible? Why something so different? That doesn't make sense. The rest of you change physical forms, become something else entirely and he merely became invisible?"

"None of it makes sense," Ian said tersely. "We were some scientific experiment gone wrong. Or at least Braden and I were. There was one other guy, our guide, and apparently he fared the worst. While Eli and Gabe were stable, the rest of us have no control over when and how we shift, and we retain no human cognizance when we're in animal form."

"Shit," she breathed.

"Yeah, tell me about it," Braden muttered.

"So Gabe could become invisible at will? And you and Ian have no control?"

She couldn't hold back the surge of fear at being at the mercy of unstable shifters. She'd seen what Ian could do in jaguar form. He'd gone for the kill with no hesitation, and it hadn't been pretty.

"We carry an inhibitor," Ian said. "It's in aerosol form. Most of the time it works to prevent shifting. Lately though..."

"Since we met you it isn't as effective," Braden said bluntly.

"Me?" She reared her head in surprise. "What do I have to do with anything?"

"Braden," Ian growled in warning. "There's no point."

Braden ignored him. "I have no idea, sister. I'd love the answer to that. All I know is that ever since we got around you, our shifts have been more erratic, and the only thing that's worked has been knocking ourselves out."

"Seems like it would be a damn good idea to stay away from me," she said sweetly. "Funny I suggested that from the beginning, but you didn't seem to listen."

"Look, Katie, I know it has to freak you out," Ian said. "If it makes you feel better, we'll give you the inhibitor so you can keep it on you at all times, and we'll give you preloaded syringes with a sedative that would knock an elephant out. Worse comes to worst, you stick that in our ass and run like hell. Believe me when I say we're not any happier about this situation than you are."

"Is there nothing you can do? No cure? Who gassed you? And why?"

"You don't ask the hard questions, do you?" Braden said mockingly. "If we knew all that, neither of us would be feeling the urge for scratching posts and kitty litter."

"You're not funny," Ian snarled.

Despite herself, Katie burst out laughing. She wiped at the corners of her eyes as tears gathered. She sucked in a breath and kept laughing.

"Apparently Katie thinks so," Braden said smugly.

She swiped at her eyes again and wheezed as she tried to regain her composure. When she looked up, though, she saw a glimmer of amusement in Ian's eyes. She relaxed a bit in her seat and then groaned when the movement sent a fresh wave of pain through her gut.

"You okay?" Braden asked gently.

She closed her eyes briefly as she ran her hand over the thick bandage covering her wound. "It hurts like a bitch."

"You need stitches," Ian said. "There'll be a doctor to see you when we land. It's a pretty bad cut."

"You dressed it?" she asked.

"Yeah, it was full of dirt. Needed to be cleaned or you'd get one hell of an infection."

She glanced down. The whole reason her wound had been so nasty was because she'd run fast and hard. Neither man had said anything about the fact she'd taken off again, but what else was she supposed to do when faced with a bloodthirsty predator? Still she felt guilty—for what, not trusting them? The funny thing was she did—well, when they weren't snarling cats.

"I'd like the inhibitor and the sedative," she said quietly.

"I'm not as keen to give it to you as Ian is," Braden said

131

dryly. "I want some assurances before we just hand that shit over."

Her gaze jerked back up to his. "Assurances? What kind of assurances do you want? You sure as hell can't offer me the one I need most, mainly that you won't turn into kitty cats on steroids and make dinner out of me."

"How 'bout that you don't use the sedative unless it's a last resort," Braden said. "Seems to me we'll be handing you the perfect weapon for you to escape whether we shift or not. I think we've proven that we have your best interests in mind here. I want your word this crap is going to stop."

"And you'd accept my word? That's pretty stupid," she taunted. "I'd lie in a heartbeat to protect my interests." Why, oh why couldn't she just shut up? She was fully prepared to offer them something—an olive branch? But she just couldn't keep her fear, her insecurity, from surging up, and then she became a defensive, surly bitch on wheels.

"Thanks for the warning," Ian said.

She moved her gaze to him, searching his expression, for what she wasn't certain. Earlier, her fear of him seemed to bother him, and even now his eyes were guarded. Had she hurt him? It seemed odd that she'd have that kind of power. Did she like this man? Did she trust him? Before he'd changed into a freaking jaguar, she'd found herself softening toward him, and yet by shifting, he'd saved her. He hadn't come after her. His ire had been directed at Ricardo. Coincidence? She couldn't decide.

"What were you saying about a safe house a while ago? And now that you've got me out of the country, what next?"

"Just a change in plans," Ian replied. "We had a place set up in France but we're going to Austria instead. As for what's next, we go there and lay low until Eli and Falcon nail Esteban."

"Esteban is the man after me?" she asked.

He nodded. "He's the one responsible for the chemical agent that turned us into shifters."

Her eyes narrowed. "Why does he want me? What could he possibly want with me now that Gabe is dead and he can't use me against him?"

"That's a good question," Braden interjected. "We don't have any idea. But we promised Gabe we'd make sure you were safe."

"And what then?" she asked. "What happens when there is no longer a threat to me? I can't go back and pick up where I left off. I may have gotten away with killing Paulo, but now there is a vehicle with my fingerprints all over it and several dead bodies that I'm sure the police wouldn't have to work hard to pin on me."

"We'll figure it out, Katie," Ian said quietly. "We aren't going to let you go down for that scumbag de la Cruz."

She leaned her head back against the seat and closed her eyes. It was tempting as hell to take that promise and hold it close, but she couldn't afford to be such a moron. No matter that Ian and Braden wanted to *look out* for her, she'd be a damn fool to place her trust so implicitly. But hadn't she already? The whole saying about leaving the barn door open came readily to mind. The fact was, she did trust them. She didn't want to. She thought she was dumb to, but it didn't alter the fact that deep inside, she knew, she just *knew* that they weren't out to screw her. Did that make her an even bigger dumbass?

A warm hand slid over her cheek, startling her into opening her eyes. She found Braden leaning down, his fingers stroking over her bruised cheekbone.

"I know you don't trust us, Katie, but we aren't going to hurt you."

His voice was warm and vibrant and slid over her skin like the softest of blankets. She wanted to wrap herself in those words and hold them tight, like a talisman. She *wanted* to tell him that she did trust him. But she wanted a lot of things, and it didn't mean they were good for her. And she was uncomfortable giving them that kind of power over her.

To her immense shock, he leaned further in and brushed his lips across the cut at the corner of her mouth. Though it was the lightest of kisses, it was as if he'd branded her with a hot coal. She jumped at the slight contact, but before she could yank away, his tongue flicked out and lapped gently at the small wound.

She reared back but had nowhere to go. He had her trapped between him and the chair. Her hands flew up and made contact with his muscular chest. She shoved, but he caught both her wrists with his hands and held them against his shirt.

His warm tongue swept over her abused flesh once more, soothing and sweet. Then he coaxed her lips, forming them into a moue with his own as he first nipped and then molded his mouth to hers.

What started gentle turned hot and urgent as he devoured her mouth. Hungry and restless. He stole her breath and returned it in stuttered gasps.

He tasted...male, and she was hungry. So hungry.

Finally he pulled away so that she could see the heated glitter in his eyes. "I've wanted to do that every single time you piss me off," he said huskily.

She swallowed and opened her mouth to tell him precisely what she thought about keeping his damn tongue in his mouth, but nothing came out. The she remembered Ian, and for some reason, guilt crept over her shoulders at the idea that Braden had been kissing her in front of him. Only when she looked over to where he sat, she saw he was gone.

Chapter Twenty-One

"What were you doing kissing her, for God's sake?" Ian demanded as Braden walked into the front cabin of the plane.

Ian stood with his fists curled at his sides, surprised by just how angry it had made him when Braden had kissed Katie. He felt juvenile and rash, not to mention like a giant, stupid fuck.

Braden gave him a *what-the-hell* look and sauntered past to snag one of the bottles of water from the galley area.

"What do you care if I kissed her?" Braden asked calmly, after he'd taken a long swig from the bottle. He recapped it and gave Ian a curious glance.

Ian looked past Braden to where Katie lay curled on the couch all but passed out. They were already making their descent, but she was clearly still exhausted and in pain.

"Ah, I get it. You've got a thing for her," he said before Ian could respond.

"I don't fucking have a *thing* for her," Ian snarled.

Braden shrugged. "Not like you to get hyped up because I made a move on a woman you were interested in."

Ian sucked in a breath. No, it wasn't like him at all. Women flocked to Braden. Ian wasn't the jealous type, and it wasn't as though they didn't regularly fuck the same woman. At the same time. What was unusual was for one of them to actually have sex with a woman solo.

Boy, did that sound screwed up.

"Just forget I said anything," Ian mumbled.

"Hey, if you want me to back off, I will," Braden said. He

lifted his hands in a gesture of surrender. "I'm not going to lie and say I'm not hella attracted to her. There's something about her that makes me crazy, but at the same time, she lights my fires like no other woman ever has." He grinned and rubbed his chin as if remembering. "Every time she slugs me, I get a hard-on from hell."

Ian rolled his eyes, but he couldn't help the chuckle that escaped. Braden had a way of diffusing even the tensest situation.

"So what's the deal, man?" Braden said. "You got a thing for her or what?"

Ian sighed and flopped into the seat. "Do you have any idea how ridiculous it is for either of us to even consider getting tangled up with her?"

Braden sat down across from Ian and tilted the bottle to drain the last of his water. "You didn't answer the question."

"I think reminding you how stupid it is for either of us to get involved with her is a damn good answer to your question."

"My head may know that, but the rest of me ain't cooperating," Braden said with a grunt. "There's something about her, man. She makes me nuts but at the same time I have the strongest urge to protect her." He paused and looked down at his water bottle in disgust. "It's not just sexual attraction. I wish to hell it was. I don't know what the fuck is going on, but I don't like it."

Ian laughed. At least in this he could relate. He didn't like his attraction to Katie any more than Braden did, apparently. The problem was, there was something primitive about his reaction to her. Something that spoke to the beast locked within him. It wasn't something he could control, and he didn't like it a damn bit.

"I take it you don't think fucking her brains out is the way to get her out of our systems," Braden grumbled.

"I can think of about a dozen reasons why it would be a bad idea," Ian said.

"Yeah, well, I can come up with at least one reason why we should."

"I'm not even going to ask."

"You can't tell me that you don't know she would rock our

damn world," Braden said with a grin. "Violent chicks make the best lovers."

Pure unadulterated lust streaked through his groin as Ian imagined fucking her mouth while Braden took her from behind. Yeah, she'd probably eat them both alive, but just because they'd be assured of mind-blowing sex, didn't mean they should do it.

"Why don't you jerk off in the shower and get some rest instead. It won't get you into near as much trouble."

"Gee thanks, man. You're all heart," Braden drawled.

"You know this makes us assholes," Ian said. "She's injured, exhausted, bloody and bruised, and all we're thinking about is how good in the sack she'd be."

Braden chuckled. "Yeah, well, so we'll never win any sensitivity awards. But glad you've finally admitted you want her."

"I didn't do any such thing."

"Goddamn liar. And hey, I'd be gentle with her. I'd be more worried about how rough she'd be with *me*."

Ian shook his head but cracked up at the hopeful look on Braden's face. Yeah, he wanted her. As much if not more than Braden did, but unlike his brother, he didn't plan to do anything about it.

They landed at a remote airstrip in the mountains of Austria an hour before dawn. Ian descended the steps carrying Katie who was still out cold, whether from exhaustion or pain he wasn't sure.

Braden ambled down after him, carrying their bags. A shadow emerged from the darkness, and Ian tensed. A large black man with arms and legs the size of tree trunks stared, unflinching, at him. His bald head gleamed in the glare of the lights from the plane.

Braden stepped in front of Ian and Katie, his stance belligerent. Then he relaxed when Eli Chance stepped out beside the big dude, a grin cracking his lips.

"What's up?" Eli asked as he closed the distance between them.

"Damn good to see you," Braden said as he bumped fists with Eli.

Eli looked beyond him to where Ian held Katie. "You kill her?" he asked in a tone that was half serious.

Braden looked over his shoulder then back at Eli. "You're kidding, right? That hellcat? We're lucky she hasn't killed *us.*"

The man beside Eli chuckled, the low sound rumbling into the night. "She has nice tits."

Eli laughed. "Gentlemen, meet Tits."

This was Tits? Ian shifted Katie in his arms as he stared at the mountain in front of them.

"I thought you'd be bigger," Braden said.

Tits laughed again and stuck his beefy hand out to Braden. "I get that a lot."

Braden snorted and slapped his hand against Tits' to shake it. "Damn glad to meet you finally. You do good work."

"That I do," Tits said immodestly. He glanced beyond Braden to where Ian stood. "Want me to take her?"

Ian tensed and then shook his head. That annoying tingle, the prickle of alarm, skated up his spine, raising the hairs at his nape.

Braden looked cautiously at his brother and then put a hand out to stop Tits' advance. "Not a good idea, man. I'll explain everything later. For now, let's get the hell out of here. We've had all the damn excitement we can take."

Tits sent a curious look at Ian but retreated. Ian immediately relaxed and looked down at the still-unconscious Katie.

Her cheek rested against his chest. The position implied trust, even though Ian wasn't stupid enough to think she had any idea how she was positioned. Or that she trusted him.

If she truly had any inkling of how vulnerable she looked nestled in his arms, she'd be fighting him tooth and nail.

"How is Tyana?" Ian asked Eli as they headed for a Range Rover parked on the helipad a few feet away.

"Tyana is Tyana," Eli said enigmatically. "More worried about D than her own recovery."

"He's just mad because Ty Baby wanted him out of her hair which is why he's here playing babysitter to you guys," Tits said, his teeth flashing in amusement.

Eli grunted. "Fuck you."

Tits slid into the driver's seat while Eli got into the front. Braden hopped into the backseat on the opposite side while Ian carefully got in holding Katie.

"And how is D?" Braden asked quietly.

Eli grimaced as he looked back at Braden. "Not good."

Ian and Braden exchanged uneasy glances when Eli didn't elaborate. Braden slumped further down in his seat, and for the first time, Ian saw defeat in his brother's demeanor.

"Marcus is at the house," Eli said. "He wants to take a look at both of you after he checks Katie out."

"You're not planning to stay, are you?" Ian directed his question at both Tits and Eli.

Tits glanced in the rearview mirror, his earring glinting briefly. "There a reason we shouldn't?"

"Yeah, two reasons. A jaguar and a panther," Braden said. "We're getting worse, man. The shifts...they're even more unpredictable."

He glanced over at Ian as if weighing his decision to say anything further. Ian tensed but didn't call Braden down. He looked away though, not out of guilt or shame, because he truly didn't regret killing Ricardo. All he regretted was the fact that he had no control over when he shifted or his apparent victim.

"Ian killed someone after a shift," Braden said.

His statement fell like a bomb in the small interior. Tits yanked his head to stare over his shoulder into the back while Eli turned completely around, his eyes flaring in the darkness.

"Bastard deserved it," Ian said calmly. He tightened his hold on Katie as he said it.

"Did you realize what you were doing? Did you go after him purposely?" Eli asked. "Think, Ian. This could be a huge breakthrough."

Ian flinched at the hope in his teammate's voice. He shook

his head grimly while Braden expelled a weary breath.

"I don't remember any of it," Ian said tonelessly. "He was after Katie. I can only remember the moment right before I shifted. I came to later with Braden over me, and he had to tell me what happened. Apparently I ripped the guy's throat out."

"Righteous," Tits said with an approving nod of his head.

"Esteban's man?" Eli asked in confusion. "Why haven't we heard of any of this?"

"It's a long story."

"You got time," Tits said.

Ian repositioned Katie on his lap then glanced over at Braden who shrugged.

With a sigh, Ian filled them in on everything that had happened since the moment he and Braden had returned to the States to find Katie.

When he finished, Tits gave a low whistle, and Eli shook his head.

"Trust Gabe to make things goddamn complicated," he said in disgust. "What the fuck was he thinking keeping something like this under wraps? How the hell did he think he was going to protect Katie half a world away?"

"He didn't win any points with me either," Braden said. "But Katie doesn't see the problem with it."

"Of course she doesn't," Eli said. "She was too busy trying to stay ahead of Ricardo and company while being grateful to big brother for his generosity."

Sarcasm dripped from Eli's voice as he shook his head.

"So what are you going to do with the little girl then?" Tits asked.

Braden snorted. "Little? I'll let you call her that, Tits. You may be a big motherfucker, but my money is on her in a throw-down."

"She ain't but a little thang. Besides, fighting ain't what I'd want to do with her."

A low growl trembled and welled from Ian's throat.

"Uh, about that," Braden said quickly as he looked over at Ian. "I know you're joking and all, but it might be better to just leave Katie out of your conversation. That is unless you want to take on one pissed-off jag."

"I think I'll pass." Tits glanced nervously back at Ian in the rearview mirror. "Her tits aren't big enough anyway."

"Thought you said they were nice," Eli said.

Tits grinned as he looked over at Eli. "Well, they're bigger than Ty's. That's all I meant."

"You can stop looking at Tyana's breasts any time," Eli said mildly.

"What fun would that be?"

Ian relaxed and rested his cheek on the top of Katie's head. He was starting to worry about her prolonged state of unconsciousness, but he reminded himself that she was absolutely spent. The last week had been hell for her, and if anyone deserved rest, it was her. He'd just be glad when Marcus could take a look at her and give her something for pain.

"Glad you guys are back." Eli looked at Ian and Braden. "It was a mistake to let you go back to the States on your own."

Braden gave a disgruntled snort. "It wasn't anything we couldn't handle."

"Still, you're lucky you didn't end up a permanent guest of the judicial system there," Eli returned.

"I don't know. It could have been fun," Tits said with a wide grin. "I've always fantasized about staging a jailbreak."

"We won't be going back," Ian said firmly.

Eli looked down at Katie's sleeping form. "And her? Will she be going back?"

Braden and Ian exchanged glances. "No," they said together.

"And does she know that?" Tits asked in amusement. "From all you've told us about her, I can't see her taking that too well."

"What the hell is she going to go back to?" Braden demanded. "She's killed three men. She has no family, no life, no way to support herself. Gabe left her in a hell of a position. Besides, until Esteban is taken care of, nowhere is safe for her."

"Except with us," Ian said.

Braden nodded. "Except with us."

Eli flashed them a strange look. "You aren't forgetting what our goal is, are you?"

"Goal? Our goal is to take Esteban down," Braden said. "And hopefully figure out a cure somewhere in there."

"Yeah, and we're using her as bait." Eli jabbed a thumb in Katie's direction.

Ian stiffened. He knew what they were doing. But it didn't mean they were going to throw her to the wolves.

"We'll make damn sure she's safe," Ian said gruffly.

"Yeah, we can do that," Tits said in a casual tone. "Not a problem, man."

"Is she even alive?" Eli asked as he stared over at her.

Ian felt her soft breathing against the shelter of his body. She was alive. He could feel every twitch, every movement, no matter how slight, hear every soft sigh when she shifted the tiniest bit.

"She'll be just fine," Ian said tightly. "Marcus can stitch her up and give her something for pain. She's experienced way too much hurt in the past few days."

Eli nodded then gave Tits a long, hard look before turning back around in his seat.

"Sit back and relax," Tits offered as he accelerated up the mountain road. "We'll be there in half an hour."

Chapter Twenty-Two

Ian and Braden hovered over Marcus while he finished stitching Katie's wound. Marcus had given her a sedative to ensure she'd remain asleep while he worked.

When he finished, he started to arrange Katie's shirt back over her, but Braden stepped in and took over. Marcus stood and glanced up at Ian, while Braden tucked her into the bed.

Marcus moved closer to Ian. "I'd like to draw some more blood from you and Braden," he said in a low voice. "I can't stay long. We moved Damiano off the island, and I'll need to be with him in the coming days."

Ian regarded him warily. "What do you mean you took him off the island?"

"He's getting worse. He shifted to a tiger and attacked Tyana."

"Shit," Ian muttered. "It must be getting bad if he turned on her."

Marcus nodded. "We thought it best to remove him from the possibility of harming her or the other members of Falcon."

He glanced up at Ian, and Ian could see the reluctance in his eyes.

"What is it, Marcus?" he asked, though he didn't really want the answer.

Marcus sighed. "I'm not convinced a cure can be found, that even if Esteban manufactured one, it would be successful. Damiano's DNA has been altered. There's no spontaneous changing back."

Ice-cold dread trickled down Ian's spine. "So you're saying

Braden and I are screwed?"

"No, I'm not saying that," Marcus said quietly. "I just think our approach has to change. I'm going to be working with Damiano. Hopefully I'll see progress."

"How so?"

"Meditation. Spiritual guidance. Mind control. More and more I think the key is going to be in mental fortitude. The ability to control, not eliminate, the shifts."

Eerie calm descended over Ian. "So we learn to live with it," he said tonelessly.

"Yes," Marcus said softly.

Ian cursed and dragged a hand through his hair. "Then why are we even after Esteban? What's the point?"

"Because we need to know what he did," Marcus said. "We need the chemical compound that was responsible for changing you into shifters. My ideas are only that. Ideas. I don't have proof to substantiate them. I would have said it was impossible to create a chemical that could so radically change your make-up, but Esteban did. If there is a chance he has a way to reverse the process, then we need to find it."

"He'll die for what he's done," Ian vowed.

Braden walked over, his gaze questioning. "What's going on, Ian? You look pissed."

"I'll tell you about it later," Ian said. "Marcus needs our blood before he leaves."

"He's turning into a regular bloodsucker," Braden muttered.

Marcus smiled. "Why do you think I only come out at night now?"

Ian put his hand on Braden's shoulder and squeezed. He wasn't sure just who he was comforting, Braden or himself. Braden shot him a curious stare, but Ian looked away before following Marcus out of the room.

Katie opened her eyes and wondered why everything felt so

numb. Then she wondered why she was so comfortable. And then she realized she was in a bed. A very nice, comfy bed with pillows and sheets.

She was dead. That was the only explanation. And she was okay with that as long as she didn't have to move.

Her hand appeared in front of her face, and she blinked since she recognized it as her hand, but hell if she remembered her brain telling her hand to move. For that matter, she knew it was her hand but it didn't *feel* like her hand.

"They gave you some good shit, huh."

She yanked her head sideways to see a large black man standing a few feet away in the shadows. His expression was indecipherable, and because of that, she couldn't figure out whether he was one of the good guys or the bad.

And then she reminded herself there were no good guys.

He chuckled. "No need to get all uptight. You're as helpless as a kitten right now so there's no need to entertain fantasies about me."

She looked at him in disgust. "If I had a knife, I'd stab you."

"And if you had bigger tits, I'd fuck you."

She almost laughed as she looked down at her chest. "No one's ever complained that my tits were too small."

"I didn't say they were too small. Just that they'd have to be bigger. I have a big dick. I need plenty of cleavage to slide it between."

She did laugh this time and then groaned when the wound in her abdomen protested. She reached down only to find thick bandages covering the area. Cautiously she looked back up at the man still standing against the wall.

"Uh, you weren't the one who tended my cut, were you?"

White teeth flashed in a grin. "Nope. That would be Marcus, the team doc. He got the pleasure of seeing you naked. Although I got a peek, and I have to say, not bad, girl. Not bad at all. I can see why Ian and Braden are so growly when it comes to you."

She flipped him the bird. "Fuck off."

He chuckled and walked forward. Lord but he was big.

"Did nobody ever tell you that steroid use will shrink your

145

penis?" she asked calmly.

He threw back his head and laughed. "You know what, I like you, Katie. I like you a lot." He held out his hand as he drew closer to the bed. "Name's Tits."

"For the love of God," she muttered. "Tits? No way your mama named you that."

He grimaced. "No, she named me Theodore, but if you ever tell anyone, I'll have to cut your throat."

"What the hell are you doing, Tits?" Ian demanded from the door.

Tits rolled his eyes and jerked his thumb in Ian's direction. "See what I mean about growly?"

"She needs to be resting," Ian said gruffly as he walked closer to the bed.

"Doc done with you?" Tits asked.

"Obviously."

Tits shrugged. "I just need to know because I've got to fly the man out of here."

"Yeah, we're done. He's waiting for you."

Tits turned to Katie and flashed her a grin. "I guess I'll see you later, Miss Katie." He blew her a kiss then sauntered toward the door and past a scowling Ian.

After Ian watched Tits go, he turned back around to stare at Katie. There was something in his gaze that discomfited her. Or maybe it was the fact that she'd kissed his brother—correction, he'd kissed *her*. Was it absurd that while she'd enjoyed Braden's kiss very much that she'd wondered what it would be like to kiss his brother? To have him touch her?

It made things more awkward than they already were, and that was the last thing she needed.

He sat on the edge of the bed at her side. "How are you feeling?"

"Kinda freaky," she admitted. "Did you give me some weird drugs?"

"Marcus gave you a sedative so he could stitch you up, and then he gave you pain medication so you wouldn't hurt when you woke up."

"That would explain the inability to recognize my limbs," she said ruefully.

"It's good that you aren't in pain." He touched her cheek tentatively, as though he expected her to protest. "You've had far too much pain in the last little while."

She wasn't sure what was weirder. The fact that Braden had kissed her and Ian was treating her as though he harbored attraction for her, or that she welcomed his attentions even as the memory of Braden's kiss simmered in the back of her mind.

Could just be the drugs.

She liked that explanation, and it absolved her of the need to analyze the weird chemistry between the three of them.

"Where are we? Besides somewhere in Austria."

"Innsbruck is the closest city, but we're holed up in the mountains. We're a short hop from Italy, Switzerland and Germany, so we have options."

She raised an eyebrow. "Options? Are we going to need them?"

He pushed her hair from her forehead and continued to run his fingers through the short strands. She wondered if he even realized what he was doing. For that matter, she wondered why she was lying here so docilely, allowing him to touch her and worse, enjoying it.

It was definitely the drugs. Or maybe she just really wanted him to touch her.

"It's always good to have options. Escape routes."

She nodded, yawning so big her jaw nearly caved in. He smiled and ran a finger down the jaw she'd almost cracked.

"You need to get some more rest."

"It's the drugs," she said. "You could lay down with me. You look as tired as I feel."

They stared at each other, and she wasn't sure who was more stunned by the invitation, her or him.

"Drugs," she muttered. Definitely the drugs. *Liar.*

"Give me a minute and I'll take you up on that," he said.

Oh hell, he wasn't supposed to accept. But then she didn't exactly withdraw the offer either. He gave her a long look before slowly rising from his perch on the edge of the bed. Was he aware of what she was offering? Was she?

"Get comfortable. I'll be back as soon as I see Tits and Eli off."

Yeah, he was aware. His eyes positively simmered with sexual awareness as he turned to leave the room. Which left the question of whether she was. Despite the dullness of her limbs due to the drugs, there was still a tingling excitement. She wanted Ian to touch her. As for what to do about Braden, she wasn't sure. She wanted to explore her attraction to Ian, but she knew damn well there was explosive chemistry between her and Braden.

Chapter Twenty-Three

"We're going, but we won't be far," Eli said. "According to Tits' intel, Esteban could be heading this way. We don't know because he hasn't shown his face yet. He's laid low ever since we busted out of his compound in Switzerland. For now, his attention has shifted from me and anything to do with Falcon or CHR. His henchmen are on the move, and they're looking for Katie. We're going to make sure he knows where she is, so be on your toes. The Falcon secondary is moving into place as we speak, so you won't be alone. Keep us posted, and we'll do the same."

Braden nodded and bumped fists with Tits and then Eli.

"You sure you two going to be okay?" Tits asked.

"Yeah, we'll be fine," Ian said. "If Esteban rears his head, we'll roll out the welcome mat for him."

Eli grinned. "I'd like to see that."

"Let's do this," Tits said as he headed for the door. "Check you boys later."

Eli followed, leaving Ian and Braden standing alone in the small entryway of the mountain cottage. Braden started to walk toward the kitchen when Ian put a hand out to stop him.

"I need a favor, man."

Braden stopped and looked curiously at him.

Ian ran a hand through his hair as his stomach knotted. God, this was awkward as hell. He hadn't felt this dumb since he and Braden were foster kids flipping a coin to see who got to ask Tracy Hawkins to the school dance.

"Look, uh, I need you to stick around. With me and Katie,

that is. Not directly, but I could shift, and I don't want to hurt her."

Braden looked incredulously at him. "You're planning to have sex with her? Now? After I kissed her? After giving me shit about kissing her?"

Ian's cheeks tightened.

"And you want me to watch?"

"Christ," Ian mumbled. "I knew it would all come out wrong. You know damn well I'm not asking you to watch. Okay, maybe I am. Goddamn it. I'm not trying to turn this into a kink-fest. I just want to be with her for a while and not worry about turning into a damn jaguar and ripping her throat out."

"Dude, do you forget that Marcus just put about ten stitches in her gut? Or that I kissed her?"

Ian sighed. "First of all, I'm not going to hurt her. I'm aware of her injuries. I don't need a lecture like I'm some kind of goddamn kid. Second, are you telling me you have a problem with this?"

Braden stared at him for a long moment. "Would it matter if I did?"

Ian hesitated a little too long.

"Yeah, that's what I thought."

"*Do* you have a problem?" Ian asked again.

"Maybe? I don't know. I guess I would have taken it a lot better if you'd have said, 'Hey, Braden, let's go make love to Katie'. But it came out more like, 'Hey bro, I'm going to go have sex with Katie and I want you to watch to make sure I don't flake'."

"I guess this time I don't want a threesome," Ian said in a low voice.

"She's attracted to us both, Ian. You know that."

"Yeah, I know. And I'm okay with it. I just don't want my first time with her to be...hell, I don't know."

"You got condoms?"

Ian's head came up. The abrupt change in subject damn near gave him whiplash. "Fuck me. No, I don't have goddamn condoms."

Braden grinned. "Aren't you glad at least one of us has sex on the brain all the time?"

Ian sighed in relief, more over the fact that Braden didn't seem pissed than the fact that he had condoms. Although the condoms didn't hurt.

Braden went to his bag and pulled out a couple of packets then tossed them one at a time in Ian's direction. Ian caught them and shoved them into his pocket.

"I doubt she's going to like me watching," Braden said.

"If it's done right, I don't think she'll object. As you said, she's attracted to both of us. I guess the sooner she's used to both of us being around, the sooner she'll accept having sex with us both at the same time."

Braden cocked his head and studied Ian. "And is that going to happen, Ian? Because I see you being mighty possessive when it comes to her. If I ask the same thing of you tomorrow, as in you back off while I make love to her, how are you going to react?"

Ian shoved a hand through his hair and blew out his breath in frustration. "Look, can we get into this another time? Preferably before Katie changes her mind about inviting me into her bed?"

"No, we can't," Braden said simply. "Because you aren't going in there unless we've reached an understanding."

Ian's eyes widened in surprise. "So it's like that."

Braden nodded. "You damn right it is. I kissed her, remember? I've been attracted to her from the beginning. The only reason I'm cool with this is because she's attracted to us both and because a woman has never been a problem between us in the past. Now you need to tell me if Katie is going to be that problem."

Ian shook his head. "No. She's not going to be a problem, Braden. But what if it's a problem for *her*?"

"Then we let her decide on her own," Braden said softly. "But fair warning, Ian. If she can't accept both of us, then I don't plan to sit back and let you take her from me."

Ian stared at his brother in astonishment. When had they decided to stake a claim? Hell, all he wanted was sex. Wasn't it? And if it *was* just sex then why would he care what Braden did afterward? And why did the idea of Katie not accepting both of them and choosing Braden instead leave a very bad taste in his mouth?

He glanced toward the bedroom where Katie was. Part of him wondered if the smartest thing would be to just leave her alone and not open the door to a whole host of potential problems. The other part of him knew if he didn't make love to her soon, he was going to turn himself inside out.

Then he looked back at Braden who surveyed him with brooding intensity. Was it fair for him to ask his brother to watch over him and Katie when Braden so obviously wanted to make love to her too?

"Go, Ian," Braden said quietly. "I'll make sure Katie stays safe from you."

Katie lay staring at the ceiling, wondering how much of her stupidity she could blame on the drugs. Or maybe she just needed to take more.

She'd invited him to come lie down with her. She nearly snorted. Who the fuck was she kidding? She'd invited him to screw her senseless. No wonder he'd looked at her so oddly. He was probably in the next room hoping to give her enough time to pass out.

Her gaze flickered lazily toward the door when she heard a sound. Warmth and longing flooded her when she saw Ian standing there, one arm propped on the doorframe as he watched her.

Her pulse quickened. Adrenaline shot up her spine and rebounded off the base of her skull.

Then he moved. He awkwardly shuffled forward, his feet making dragging sounds on the floor. As he'd done before, he settled on the edge of her bed at her hip. She held her breath, wondering what he'd say. What he'd do.

"I need to know how much of your invitation was the drugs and how much of it was you knowing what the hell you were saying."

Her blood stirred and rushed just a little faster, heating her skin and bringing a flush to her cheeks. They stared at each other, not like two potential lovers, but two people who might just devour each other before the night was over.

"It's been a long time for me," she said evenly.

One part of her recognized that she was stalling, while the other part wondered why she was babbling like an idiot.

"Paulo was my last lover."

"Was he any good?" Ian asked bluntly.

She turned her head and studied him. Such a strange conversation to be having.

"Yes, he was," she said. "Very good. It was for that reason that I had such an easy time turning Ricardo down when he showed interest. I was young and starry-eyed. The older brother would have been the better choice since I wanted security and family. I wasn't the choosiest of women back then. I was more interested in the trappings than the actual man."

"If that were true, you would have dropped Paulo with no compunction," Ian pointed out.

She shrugged. "Paulo was actually very good to me in the beginning. I'm not defending him. He turned into quite the asshat, but for a while we were happy. For a while I actually hoped that I'd fit in. That I'd have the things I wanted."

"And what do you want right now?" he asked, bringing them back to the two of them. In this room. Right now.

"I want you," she said softly.

"Is that the drugs talking?"

She smiled. "I won't lie and say I'm not a bit loopy. I won't even lie and say that I might not regret it tomorrow. All I can tell you is that tonight, it's what I want more than anything. Can you accept that?"

His breathing sped up, and his eyes glittered with lust. "Yeah, I can accept that. As long as you realize that tomorrow, when you may or may not regret it? Too damn bad. Because once won't be enough."

Her hand went automatically to her stomach and the thick bandage. Excitement rocketed through her body at his words. This was supposed to be on her terms. She called the shots.

But she had the distinct feeling that once they made love, she was going to be giving a much larger piece of herself than she planned.

"I won't hurt you, Katie," he said softly.

His fingers curled around her wrist, and he moved her hand gently away from her wound. She watched with shocked arousal as he leaned down and pressed his lips to her belly. So soft, she nearly didn't feel the slight brush of his mouth.

Carefully he pushed at her shirt until it rode high on her belly, baring the skin and the bandage to his gaze. And his lips.

She shivered when he kissed her navel then trailed his tongue around the indention. The stubble of his jaw scraped delicately against her skin. Then he slipped her shirt higher until it gathered at her neck.

Free of constraint, her nipples puckered and stood erect. He palmed one breast, molding it in his hand. His thumb rubbed across the tip and then back again. Her breath caught when he pinched it slightly between his fingers.

Her gaze moved beyond Ian to the doorway where she was stunned to see Braden leaning against the wall. She stiffened as she locked stares with him.

Ian's head turned to follow her line of vision, and then he looked back at her, his expression odd and unreadable.

"Why is he there?" she said in a low voice.

Braden heard, though. He straightened his stance and stared at her with hungry eyes. She looked back at him, remembering his kiss. Hungry was an apt term. He'd devoured her. There was nothing gentle in his approach. Not patient as Ian was being.

Desire burned low in her belly, spreading like a fire she had no control over. She wanted them both. Wanted what they could both give her, or what she thought they could.

"He's here to protect you...from me," Ian said. "Can you forget his presence, or is it going to be a problem?"

Her gaze slid to Braden once more. He stared back challengingly, a slight smirk on his face as though he dared her to go the route of the prude and put on some hysterical fit because he was watching.

"Maybe I don't want to forget his presence."

Braden smiled. A slow, arrogant smile that was a tad triumphant. She wondered then what had gone on between the two men outside of her room. The last thing she wanted was another pissing match between brothers. Been there done that, had the dead bodies to prove it.

"Do me a favor then and try not to forget about *me*," Ian said dryly.

She glanced back and gave him a small smile. "If you're good enough, you won't have to worry about that."

Ian's eyes narrowed, and Braden snickered from across the room. Then Ian braced both hands on either side of her and leaned in until he hovered over her, his face inches from hers.

"That, little wench, was a challenge, and I never back down from a challenge."

Chapter Twenty-Four

Katie reached up to wrap her arms around Ian's neck. "Kiss me," she whispered.

He lowered his mouth until their noses touched, and then he angled to the side, his lips so close that hers trembled in reaction.

"Tell me something, Katie. Tell me you want me and that it's not the drugs talking. I think I know, but I want to hear it again. If I really thought you were impaired, I'd be out of this bed so fast it would make your head spin."

Her eyes widened fractionally as she stared up at him.

"I think you'd like to use the drugs as an excuse to give yourself permission to want me, to have sex with me, but then I also don't have you pegged as a coward."

She stroked the muscles in his back, enjoying the feel of her palms against his flesh. Firm. Toned.

"I take full responsibility for my decision, and if I beat anyone over the head about it, it'll be me, not you."

"Christ, you two are going to talk each other to death," Braden muttered.

Ian turned fiercely and scowled at his brother. Katie had to bite her lip to keep from laughing. The entire situation was beyond absurd. She'd agreed—no—she'd *instigated* sex with a man who could well turn into a jaguar on her. A man who for the most part irritated the living piss out of her. And his brother, a man who'd kissed her senseless just hours before, was standing by, prepared to watch them have sex, all so he could protect her if Ian freaked out and shifted.

Sex had become more complicated than it was worth.

Curious, now that Ian seemed distracted by Braden's presence, she slid her hand down his firm abdomen and between his legs to cup him intimately.

"The question is, do you want *me*?" she murmured.

He surged against her hand, immediately filling it as his jeans tightened. His erection pushed impatiently at her fingers, straining to be free of constriction.

"Hell yes," he growled. "If I don't have you, I'm going to go nuts."

"Hmm, and how do you feel about that?"

"It wasn't my first choice," he said honestly.

She laughed, and he seemed relieved that she wasn't pissed by his bluntness. "How about we dispense with the recriminations and get on with it?"

"Hallelujah," Braden muttered. "I at least want to see her naked."

Katie grinned. She couldn't bring herself to be self-conscious over the fact that Braden was watching. Instead it made her feel naughty and desirable. She licked her lips, remembering his kiss. Hard. Bruising. Like he couldn't wait to get at her. It had been a long time since she'd felt those things in a man's arms. She was ready to get back to that.

She let her hands fall away from Ian's neck and pulled her shirt away from her throat.

He pressed his lips to the valley between her breasts. "Let me."

He worked the shirt over her head, and she extended her arms upward so he could take it off.

"You have beautiful breasts," he said as he stared down at her. "Perfect."

"Not big enough according to Tits."

"Tits is a damn fool. Yours are gorgeous. Full and plump." He licked one taut point, eliciting a deep spasm from her chest. She moaned softly and arched up, wanting more. Wanting his mouth, his tongue, his teeth.

"Careful," he warned. "Lie still so you don't open your stitches."

She made a frustrated sound through her teeth. How could she remain still when her skin was alive and itchy with want and need?

"I'll do all the work," he purred against her ear. "You just enjoy the ride."

She sighed. Oh hell, she loved that in a man. Before Paulo lost his mind, he was an extremely attentive lover. He spoiled her, and she wanted that again. Without the obsession and insanity, preferably.

Ian—and Braden—had afforded her the first real possibility of any sort of intimacy with a man since she'd run from the reality of what she'd done to Paulo. She craved a stolen moment. Just one. She wanted a strong man's arms around her, and if that made her weak, she'd just have to deal.

Warm, sensual lips stirred along her skin, lighting a heated path from below her ear to her collarbone and down to the swell of her breast. His dark head bent to capture one nipple, holding it against his tongue with his lips.

She twisted her hands in his hair, urging him closer, hoping she could convey her need with the sharpness of her fingers. His teeth grazed the rigid, puckered flesh. Ahh. God, yes, that was what she needed. Only more. She wanted that edge of pain. She didn't want soft and sweet.

He nipped again, and she rewarded him with a moan and a gentle caress at his nape. Then he moved to her other breast, plumping the swollen mound with one hand while he sucked at her nipple. Hungry, like he couldn't get enough.

She stirred restlessly beneath him as need powered through her body.

"Slow down, baby," Ian whispered against her skin. "I'll give you what you want."

His sensual promise sent shivers of absolute delight racing down her spine.

For a long while he played and toyed with her breasts, tweaking the nipples between his long fingers and nibbling with alternating gentleness and sharpness. He was careful around her wound, kissing a circular pattern around the bandage.

He licked at her bruises, his warm tongue abrading the sensitive skin. When he got to her navel, he dug his fingers into the band of her pants and tugged until it curled down her hips.

She sucked in her breath when he pressed his mouth to the tender expanse of flesh just above her mound. Her pussy tightened, wanting, little twinges of excitement stirring and exploding. Her clit swelled, aching. She closed her eyes, imagining his mouth on her, his tongue delving deep to her innermost sanctum.

And then her underwear inched downward under his coaxing fingers. He rose and leaned back on his heels, carefully bent her legs and freed them from the confines of the panties. Then he settled her thighs on either side of his hips and spread them wide.

He stared down at her, his hands wrapped around her ankles, a look of deep satisfaction on his face. Her gaze never left his as she reached down with her hand to part the folds of her pussy. Her fingers caressed the softness and then delved deeper into the wetness.

His eyes flared, and she saw his groin bulge and tighten when she fingered her clit in a slow up-and-down motion.

"Kiss me...there," she whispered.

Ian lowered himself until his shoulders nudged at her thighs. "Spread yourself for me, Katie."

Cool air blew over her clit as she complied with his dictate. Then she felt the warmth of his breath. She shivered in anticipation before finally his mouth touched her. Slightly. Just a gentle press. A kiss that didn't end.

Her other hand snaked down to thread into his short hair. She gripped his scalp, holding him against her as she worked her fingers in unison with his mouth.

His tongue laved through her folds, sparking electric currents. She moved her fingers to give him better access to her erect clit. Her legs trembled uncontrollably as he licked and sucked. She wanted to move, to buck, but he gripped her hips to keep her still while he worshipped her with his tongue.

Her head fell to the side, and she looked at Braden with glazed eyes. He watched her with glittering intensity, his eyes bright and feral. The decadence of having him watch, of him being a passive participant, thrilled her and heightened her arousal. She began to imagine what it would be like to have both men touching her, kissing her, their mouths and hands sweeping over her body as though they owned it.

As she stared at Braden, his hand slid over his hip to the bulge between his legs. He rubbed and massaged while he watched Ian's head move over her pussy.

Ian quietly lapped between her legs, each stroke so intensely pleasurable that she closed her eyes against the agony of such sweet bliss.

Her knees shook. Her orgasm welled. Each touch of his tongue brought her closer to the edge. And then he moved his arm and slid a finger inside her entrance, touching the tip against the swollen passage.

"Ian, please," she gasped. "I need you inside me."

His head slowly came up, and he locked eyes with her. He shifted forward and kissed her belly. As he continued to move up her body, he pressed gentle kisses over her skin until he reached her neck.

She arched her throat upward, baring the expanse of flesh to his mouth. She wanted him to bite her and bite hard, to mark her.

"You're beautiful," he rasped as he tugged at her hair to expose her neck further.

He bent and sucked hard, his teeth nipping sharply at the column of her neck. He latched onto her skin and suckled, a steady rhythm that had her nipples and pussy tightening in unison.

His jeans abraded the insides of her thighs, and she impatiently reached down, tugging at the waist, wanting to be rid of the barrier.

He laughed softly against her neck. He kissed just below her ear one more time before pulling away. The bed dipped and swayed as he crawled carefully off her. For a moment, he obscured her view of Braden as he quickly shucked his jeans.

Her gaze was riveted to the white briefs and the bulging outline of his dick, straining against the thin material. And then with one shove, the underwear slid down, revealing the thick, ruddy erection.

Surrounded by dark hair, it jutted upward, the swollen, distended length rippled with a heavy vein on the underside.

Moisture beaded at the tip, just one clear drop of fluid clinging to the head.

She licked her lips, and an agonized groan echoed across the room.

"You're killing me, woman."

"Take me," she said in a sultry, entreating voice. "Please, Ian. Don't make me wait."

He bent and scooped at his jeans, his hand delving into one of the pockets. He yanked out a condom and tore the wrapper with shaky hands.

She watched with rapt attention as he slowly rolled the latex over his cock. His thick, heavy erection strained at the transparent covering, and she wondered if it would hold.

Excitement scuttled at the back of her throat as he stalked forward, closing the distance between them once more. Placing one hand on the mattress at her side, he got onto the bed and settled between her splayed legs.

"Are you ready for me, Katie?" He slid one hand fluttering past the curls at her apex and into the softness beyond.

She flinched when he found her swollen nub. With calculated roughness, he spread her and slid one finger deep, testing her slickness. When he pulled it out again, she could see her fluids glisten on his knuckle.

He put it to his mouth and licked it clean. Then he lowered himself to her, taking care not to put his weight on her belly. He propped himself up on his arms and flexed his hips. The movement sent his cock over her clit and lower to her waiting pussy. She moved frantically, trying to sheathe him, but he stilled her with his thighs.

He reached down and positioned himself. Her breath caught in her throat as she nearly came apart at the first touch of his crown rimming her entrance. He put his arm back at her side and then rolled his hips forward, sinking into her with excruciating precision.

She closed her eyes and expelled the pent-up breath in long, painful bursts.

"Am I hurting you?" Ian panted.

She opened her eyes to stare up at him. "You aren't hurting

me nearly enough. Take me, Ian. Hard. I want you."

He surged against her. She could feel him swollen and stiff deep in her pussy.

"You destroy me," he whispered.

He began to stroke, back and forth, deep, hard, foregoing the gentleness he'd been so careful to exert. Even so, he was careful not to brush against her wound.

She wanted so much. She wanted to wrap herself around him so tight that he'd never let go. She wanted to roll him over and ride him hard and unrelenting. She wanted him to ride *her* mercilessly.

"Fuck me," she panted. "Let go, Ian. Stop trying not to hurt me and let go, damn it."

A snarl rolled off his lips, and he slammed against her, rocking her up the bed. Oh God, yes. Finally.

"Harder," she urged. "Make me feel it, Ian."

He swooped down and ravaged her lips in a hot, open-mouthed kiss that was as carnal as she'd ever experienced. He breathed into her, for her, with her. He rammed into her, forcing himself harder and deeper.

Pain speared her abdomen, but she didn't care. She wanted it, needed it, craved it like an addict craved a fix.

His thighs slapped against hers, and he reached down to pry her legs further apart. He looped them over his arms and shoved upward, forcing her into a position of greater vulnerability.

"Yes," she whispered. "Yes!"

His balls pounded the curve of her ass, the crisp hairs tickling her anus as he wedged himself deeper into her pussy.

"Come, damn it, I'm close," he grated out.

"Don't stop," she demanded. "Please, please don't stop. Oh…I'm going to come, Ian, please don't stop."

Her pleas came out as half uttered, brainless sobs. He gave an agonized groan and then ripped into her, his hips driving with ruthless intensity.

Her orgasm stabbed, sharp and edgy, suddenly exploding like a short fuse on a stick of dynamite. She heard him shout, felt him pummel into her one last time before he stayed there, deep and straining, pushing himself as though he couldn't get far enough into her.

He leaned into her, burrowing his hands underneath her body so he could gather her close. For a long moment, he heaved against her, his breaths exploding in the silence. Her pussy pulsed around his cock, sending aftershocks floating through her belly.

It had been way too long since she had such a magnificent orgasm. Man, she missed good sex.

Unfortunately she was going to pay for this. Pain ripped through her belly, fierce and edgy. A whimper escaped her lips before she could call it back.

Ian rolled off her immediately, his eyes flashing with concern. "Goddamn it, I knew I'd end up hurting you."

She shushed him before he got too absorbed in his self-condemnation. "I don't regret a minute of it, and so help me, if you don't shut up, I'll castrate you. But yeah, it hurts like a bitch about now."

He slammed his lips together, and she could tell it was killing him to remain silent. He scrambled off the bed, and it was then she noticed that Braden had left. She didn't spare a lot of thought as to why he bolted, because frankly she was too busy sucking wind as waves of pain assaulted her.

"This was stupid of me," Ian muttered as he yanked on his jeans. She nearly laughed when the pants met his cock—his still-condom-covered cock. He swore then yanked it off and aimed it at a nearby garbage can. He shoved his semi-erect cock into his pants and then fastened the fly.

"Don't move. I'll be back with something for pain."

"Sure..." She trailed off as he turned and stalked out of the room.

So much for post-coital glow.

Chapter Twenty-Five

Braden looked up in surprise from the darkness of the small kitchen when Ian charged out of the bedroom. He fumbled with the light switch, and Braden shoved his hand up to shield the sudden flood of light.

"Sorry," Ian mumbled as he poked around the cabinets with no clear direction.

"Something wrong?" Braden asked calmly.

Ian stopped and grimaced as he swung his head back and forth, surveying the countertops. "I hurt her, man. I was too fucking rough. You seen the pain shit that Marcus left?"

Braden almost laughed. He would have if Ian wasn't so intense. Ian wouldn't take his irreverence in this moment. He'd probably try to take his head off.

"She wanted it, Ian. Wanted it pretty damn bad, I'd say."

"There's no excuse," Ian said.

"Dude, I was there, remember? She didn't exactly give you a choice. As long as she didn't bust any of her stitches, she'll be fine."

He reached over and snagged the package that was right in front of Ian's nose. He held it out, and Ian made a sound of disgust. Then he stared up at Braden.

"You go in and make sure she's all right. I need to...get cleaned up."

Braden rolled his eyes. Big, bad Ian was scared of a woman. Katie had knocked him for a loop, and his nuts were so twisted that he didn't know his head from his ass. It was pretty damn funny.

"So you get to have great sex, and I get stuck with the cuddling afterward? Hardly sounds fair to me."

Ian yanked his head around, ready to jump down Braden's throat until he saw Braden's grin. Braden held up his hands. "Chill, man. You're way too uptight for someone who just had bone-melting sex."

Ian leaned heavily against the counter and ran a hand through his hair. "Yeah, well, you sound like a jealous bitch."

Braden laughed. "Maybe I won't be jealous for long." He grabbed a bottle of water and sauntered past Ian.

Ian caught his arm. "Don't mess with her now, Braden. She's hurting pretty bad."

Irritation seized Braden, and he looked pointedly down at Ian's hand. Ian let it fall away. "I didn't tell you how to handle your dick when you were with Katie. I don't need you telling me what to do with mine, okay?"

Ian muttered under his breath and turned away. Braden headed toward the bedroom. He paused at the door and looked in to see Katie curled in the covers, her hand clutching her side.

Shaking his head, he strode toward the bed. When she heard him, she looked up and then did a double-take. No doubt she was expecting Ian.

He stopped at the edge and then sat down at her hip. As he shook out her medicine, she looked at him in amusement.

"Ian afraid I'm going to insist on a preacher and a ring?"

Braden grinned and choked back his laughter. Yeah, he liked this woman. A lot.

"He's more worried about the fact that he hurt you. Here, open up," he said as he shoved a pill at her lips.

She opened her mouth and then took the bottle of water he handed her. As she tilted her head back and swallowed, her gaze settled on his face.

He took the bottle back when she was done, and she wiped her mouth with the back of her hand.

"You enjoy the show?" she asked bluntly.

Willing himself not to flinch or act like her question caught him off guard, he calmly regarded her. "I'd have enjoyed it a hell of a lot more if I was participating instead of watching."

Let her make what she wanted of that statement. At least he'd get a good read on whether she'd ever be down with both him and Ian at the same time.

She didn't so much as blink. "So why didn't you?"

"Join in?" he asked, surprised by her seeming acceptance.

She nodded.

"I don't think Ian would have appreciated it," Braden said with a small smile.

"And yet you kissed me before he ever touched me. Some might say you had more to be unappreciative about."

"Are you saying you wanted me to join?"

"Maybe."

"There's no maybe about it, sweetheart," he drawled. "Either you wanted me there or you didn't. An extra person doesn't just show up for sex without some preplanning."

"Oh, I don't know about that," she said thoughtfully. "Some of the best sex is rather spontaneous, wouldn't you say?"

As soon as she'd delivered that cryptic remark, she closed her eyes, her face creased with pain.

"Damn," he murmured. "Ian was right. You totally overdid it."

"If you knew how long it had been since I had sex, you wouldn't have begrudged me," she muttered.

He laughed and touched her face in a tender gesture. Her eyelids fluttered open, and she stared back at him with wide blue eyes.

"Want me to stick around and do the post-sex cuddling thing since Ian bailed?"

Amusement glittered deeply in her eyes. The corner of her mouth quirked up in a grin. And then her expression grew serious.

"Hey, what's that for?" he asked.

As he waited for her answer, he stood and pulled his shirt over his head. She watched while he kicked off his boots and then began undoing his pants. When he was down to his underwear, he crawled back onto the bed and eased close to her body.

With a contented sigh, she spooned back against him, nestling her pert little ass to his aching groin. Hell, he should have jerked off before attempting this shit.

Still, she felt good against him, all limp and contented, even if he wasn't the reason she was all limp and contented. He slid his hand down the curve of her body and settled it on her hip.

"So what was the look for?" he asked when she still hadn't responded.

He felt her grimace. "Just an observation," she murmured. "A nice one. I was going to say that it was cool that you and Ian were so relaxed about women. And sex. Paulo and Ricardo were psychotic. Both were jealous. Insanely so. It was what destroyed them. And nearly me," she added softly.

Braden's arm tightened around her, though he was careful to stay away from her wound. Her fingers found his and trembled as they cautiously slid over his palm. He twined his with hers and rested them comfortably over her middle.

"Ricardo was an egotistical ass," Braden said darkly. "And Paulo sounded like an immature pussy."

She shook against him then groaned when her laughter caused her pain. "Yeah, but he was good in the sack."

Braden growled close to her ear. "I'll show you good in the sack, woman."

"Promises, promises," she whispered as he grazed her ear with his teeth.

His entire groin tightened. Nice, *sensitive* Braden was saying: *She's exhausted, in pain and in no shape to be rode long and hard again.* The Braden with blue balls was shouting: *Flip her ass over and fuck her senseless.*

"What I can promise is that when I make love to you, you won't be thinking about how good Paulo de la Cruz was in bed."

"Mmmm, I'd like to take you up on that challenge."

"It wasn't a challenge, sister. It was a promise."

"Braden?"

He frowned at the thready sound of her voice. "Yeah."

"Can we go to sleep now?"

She sounded faint, like she was already ninety percent there.

He nuzzled against her neck, his lips finding the softness against her hairline. She sighed in contentment and scooted back further against him until you couldn't fit a hair between them.

"Yeah, baby. Go to sleep."

"You won't go anywhere, will you?" she asked sleepily.

He kissed her behind the ear, inhaling her sweet scent. "I'll be right here, Katie. I'm not going anywhere."

Chapter Twenty-Six

Braden awoke with Katie sprawled across him like she owned him. Half her body was draped across his chest, her cheek pressed tight against his skin and her mouth open.

There was nothing maidenly or shy about her.

For a long time he lay there, quiet, studying her while she slept. Her hair was tousled, the strands teasing his skin. He toyed with the uneven locks, twirling them around the tips of his fingers.

She stirred against him, a restless little move that sent her soft body seeking further into his. His cock stood up and paid attention, much to his dismay.

She went still, and he felt the catch in her breath. Then she raised her head and looked up at him with sleepy, drugged eyes.

"You got a condom?"

He blinked in surprise. Of all the things he thought she might say, that wasn't it. His chest shook with laughter, but he kept his lips tight to prevent any sound from escaping.

Her eyes narrowed, but he caught a glint of amusement sparkling in their depths.

"If you tell me that's just your usual morning hard-on and that I have nothing to do with it, I'm going to be deeply offended."

"Oh, it's all you," he said. "And yeah, I have a condom. Give me a sec to go get it."

He carefully extricated himself from her body and strode out of the room. He found Ian asleep on the couch in the living room, and a distinct chill in the air. Damn, but it was cold.

Sparing his brother only a quick glance and a whispered directive for him to sleep a while longer, he dug into his pack for one of the condoms and then headed back to the bedroom.

He paused inside the doorway to shed his underwear. Katie watched from the bed, her eyes tracking his every movement. His hand curled around his heavy erection, and he worked up and down in a slow, steady motion.

Hunger flashed in her eyes, and a bolt of awareness sizzled through his groin. He walked over to the bed, tossed the condom onto the pillow and then climbed back onto the mattress. She covered him immediately, her body warm and supple. She fit. So damn perfect.

She reached for the condom and rapidly tore the wrapper off. With deft fingers, she rolled it over his dick, and he nearly groaned at the restriction.

"You don't want foreplay?" he asked with a raised eyebrow as she moved to straddle him.

"What I want is to fuck you," she said in a voice tight with desire.

"Oh hell, I think I just fell in love," he murmured.

He helped her by spanning her waist with his big hands and positioning her so she didn't hurt herself. Then he allowed his fingers to wander up her lush body to cup her breasts.

She leaned up, did a tight little fidget and then sheathed him.

They both groaned. His entire body tightened and spazzed out. He felt like he was going to twitch right out of his skin.

"You have to move, baby," he said as he lifted her hips. "Oh, yeah, like that. Just like that." He expelled all of his breath in one long sigh.

She rolled forward and then back, undulating her pelvis so that her pussy rippled over every inch of his cock.

"Kiss me," he said huskily as he urged her on with his hands. He couldn't wait to taste her again. He'd thought of nothing else ever since kissing her on the plane.

Her lips melted over his, sweet like syrup and soft. So deliciously soft. His hands skated up her sides to cup her breasts, and he brushed his thumbs across her nipples. She shivered delicately against his hands as their tongues met and dueled for supremacy.

He let her win that particular battle, enjoying how she took control of the kiss.

She tasted him, swept her tongue over his and deep into his mouth. She pulled away and then nipped sharply at his bottom lip. She followed it with a soothing lap of her tongue and then she sucked it back into her mouth to nibble erotically.

He'd never been kissed so thoroughly by a woman. There was nothing inhibited about her, and he found it extremely arousing.

One hand left her breast and glided downward until he cupped the bandage over her wound. He held her gently to protect the area as she continued to ride him, but she wasn't having it.

She grasped his wrist and dragged his hand back to her breast, moaning when his fingers stumbled over her nipple. Remembering the night before when she'd urged Ian to bite her, he gathered the taut point and pinched, lightly at first and then with more pressure.

She went liquid around his cock. Oh hell yeah, she liked the pain, needed it.

"Harder," she panted.

He stared up at the hot-as-hell image she posed, head thrown back as she rode him with abandon, her breasts spilling into his hands as he worked her nipples with his fingers.

He pinned them both with his thumbs and forefingers and squeezed as she shuddered around his dick.

"I hope you're close," she said in a strained voice. "Because I'm so ready to come."

"Then get there," he ordered, his statement spilling out raw and demanding. His release was a razor's edge, sharp and sliding closer.

He arched his hips, pounding into her as she fell to meet his thrusts. Her thighs gripped him as her hands came down to grasp at his shoulders.

He pulled mercilessly at her nipples, leaving them red with

his fingerprints. A harsh cry of pleasure tore from her mouth and then her body seized. Her pussy rippled and contracted, spasming around his cock like molten lava.

"Yeah, baby, like that. Come for me, Katie."

His ass left the bed as he bowed and arched wildly. He exploded like a canon just as she dissolved around him. She fell, and he caught her, gentle even amidst their animalistic mating.

This time...this time *he* was the reason for her soft, sated sounds, and the sweet lethargy of her body. Pleasure that had nothing to do with the mind-blowing orgasm he'd just experienced rippled through his body.

She lay across his chest, limp and unresisting as he stroked her back.

"Should I get you drugs?" he asked wryly. "You're hell on stitches, woman."

She trembled slightly, and he couldn't be sure if it was pleasure or pain making her shake. And he was loath to move enough to see. His fingers made slow circles on her back and shoulders. He slid them to her nape where he gently massaged.

"I'm hungry," she said. "And cold."

"It is pretty frigid in here. Either we don't have a heater, or no one bothered to turn it on. There's a fireplace in the living room. If you feel up to it we can go in there. I'll build a fire and see about cooking up some grub."

"Where's Ian?" she asked as she pushed herself gingerly off his chest.

"Asleep on the couch."

She glanced down to where their bodies were still joined. "Is this going to bother him?"

He curled a hand behind her neck and kissed her hard. When he pulled away, her eyes were slightly unfocused.

"I can't answer that. But I can guarantee he won't go off the deep end like your previous lover. One, he'd never hurt a woman, and two, he's well aware that I'm as attracted to you as he is."

"Guess we'll go find out," she whispered.

Chapter Twenty-Seven

Katie showered with Braden, more in an effort to use their body heat to keep from freezing than a need for intimacy. The temperature had continued to drop in the cabin, which told her that there was probably heat at one time, and now there wasn't.

Figured.

She stepped shivering from the tiny shower cubicle, hugging herself in an effort to get warm. Braden stepped out beside her and wrapped his big body around hers while he dried them both with his towel.

"Get dressed. I'll go build a fire and then get started on the cooking," he said as he arranged his towel over her shoulders.

She watched as he walked naked from the bathroom. She absolutely loved his pale ass. His tan line stopped at his waist, and only a fine dusting of hair disturbed the lighter skin of his behind.

She'd have been disappointed if he turned out to be a pretty boy who sunbathed nude out of vanity. Of course Braden didn't strike her as the type to sunbathe at all. And he certainly lacked the smooth, polished good looks of pretty boys like Paulo and Ricardo. Braden and Ian both were rugged. Not good-looking in a classical sense or even drop-dead GQ gorgeous. But she positively shivered each time she looked at them, even when they annoyed the piss out of her. They wore power like it was the most natural thing in the world, and they had an *I-don't-give-a-fuck* look that she found enormously appealing. Maybe it was because it was a sentiment she echoed.

She searched for clothes, and to her surprise discovered several pairs of jeans and sweaters in her size. Or close, anyway. And then she found a pair of boots just half a size larger than what she wore, and she nearly cried. Stupid to get so emotional over boots, but after going so long barefooted, she wanted to kiss the worn leather.

She pulled on heavy wool socks, delighting in the warmth they offered her freezing feet. Then she put on jeans and a sweater. For a moment, she considered the boots just for the luxury of having shoes, but she put them back down and padded out to the living room in her sock feet.

Ian was awake, though he didn't look like he'd been that way for long. He sat on the couch a few feet away from the roaring fire, his hair rumpled, and a sleepy, disgruntled look on his face.

She glanced toward the kitchen to see Braden clanging around, putting a skillet on the stove and poking in the small refrigerator.

Ideally, she'd feel at ease with either man, after all she'd fucked them both. But something about Ian still made her nervous. Or maybe she just wasn't as sure of herself around him. Or...maybe he meant more to her than she'd like to admit.

Braden, on the other hand...she felt confident with, but only because she knew he was in it for the sex. Ian...well she had no idea what he was in it for.

When she would have gone into the kitchen, Ian looked up and locked gazes with her. She shivered under the intensity of those eyes, and it wasn't because she was cold.

"Come here," he said softly and held out a hand to her.

She hesitated for a moment before crossing the room. She didn't reach for his hand but got close enough that he could touch her. He laced his arm around her waist and pulled her down onto his lap.

Before she could react, he reclined her until her head rested on the couch and her back was laid across his legs. He pushed her sweater up and put tentative fingers to her wound.

He looked over at her and frowned. "This needs to be bandaged."

"I took it off to shower," she said with a shrug.

"Stay put. I'll get Braden to bring me the stuff to cover it again."

She stopped short of rolling her eyes. Barely. He called over his shoulder to Braden who came ambling out a few seconds later, medical supplies in hand.

He winked at Katie who had brought her arms behind her head in an effort to get comfortable.

Ian didn't miss the exchange, and he gazed curiously at Katie. Okay, he wasn't stupid. Surely he hadn't slept through her and Braden's rather loud bout of sex this morning. Or had he?

She shot Braden a quick questioning look, and he shrugged and headed back toward the kitchen. And then she shook her head, pissed that she'd spare any guilt over Ian's feelings. It was sex. Good sex but just sex all the same.

"What are you frowning about?" Ian asked as he carefully applied a strip of gauze to her stitched wound.

"I don't care if you're pissed that I had sex with Braden."

He raised one eyebrow and cast her a sideways glance. "Who says I'm pissed?"

"You're not?"

"Should I be?"

She frowned again as he finished taping the gauze. "So you're not?"

"Do you want me to be?"

She growled in frustration. She wasn't sure whether she wanted to beat him or fuck him senseless. Both held a certain appeal at the moment.

A small smile quirked one corner of his mouth. "No, Katie, I'm not pissed. I was the one who asked my brother to watch while I had sex with you, for Christ's sake."

"Anyone ever tell you how weird you are?"

He shrugged. "Plenty of times."

"I see how bothered you are by that," she said with a grin.

He pulled her to an upright position and then moved her to his side. She leaned back against the couch, content to absorb his warmth.

A few minutes later, Braden brought two plates and thrust them at her and Ian. He returned shortly with his own plate and plopped down in a threadbare armchair close to the fireplace.

Breakfast food. Not her favorite, but she was so hungry, she'd eat shoe leather.

For several minutes, she contented herself with stuffing food into her mouth. Then she became aware that both men were staring at her, their own food forgotten.

"What?" she asked around a full mouth.

Braden shook his head. "God almighty, I thought the first time we fed you was merely an aberration. I've never seen a woman put away food like that. It's sorta scary and sexy all at the same time."

She choked on a laugh and then coughed when part of her food went down the wrong way. "Sorry," she mumbled as she finally managed to get her breath. "It's been a long time since I got a chance to eat good food."

Ian gave her a look of horror. "Hell, you must really have fallen on desperate times if you consider Braden's cooking good food."

"Hey, fuck off," Braden said good-naturedly.

She grinned. It was amazing to her that she was so relaxed. Sex and a full belly certainly helped. More than that, though, she felt safe with Ian and Braden despite their less-than-stellar beginning.

She trusted them.

It was easy to forget what was at stake. That they were in the wilds of Austria because supposedly some goon was after her.

And then it hit her. Truly hit her with the force of an avalanche. Ricardo would never be a threat to her again.

Sure, she knew he was dead. She'd even taken a moment, albeit a brief one, to contemplate what his death meant. But things had moved so quickly. It was all such a blur that she hadn't really had time to think about what her life might be like without Ricardo breathing down her neck.

She put the fork down when it became obvious that her hand was shaking like the last leaf on a tree facing winter.

"What's wrong?" Ian asked sharply. He touched her cheek,

and she slowly looked up to meet his gaze.

"Nothing. I was just thinking. Realizing, I guess."

"Realizing what?" Braden asked.

She glanced over to see him studying her as intently as Ian was.

"Just that I don't have to worry about Ricardo anymore," she said with a nonchalant shrug that belied just how much she wanted to shout her joy and relief. "It hadn't really sunk in until now. I've been running from him for so long. I mean he's been the entire focus of my life in a twisted sort of way. My every waking moment has been spent staying a step ahead of him and trying to determine his next move."

Ian's hand curled around the back of her neck, cupping it possessively. He stared hard at her, his green eyes flashing with anger and determination.

"You don't ever have to worry about anything again, Katie. Braden and I are going to see to that."

Her brow instantly furrowed at the oddity and finality of his statement. How could he make that kind of guarantee? They were nothing to each other. There was no permanence, no relationship. Until a week ago, she'd never known they existed.

"I appreciate the sentiment, but I'm afraid I'm the only person who can make sure I don't have men like Ricardo to worry about." She added a reassuring smile for emphasis. "It was sweet of you to say, though."

"Sweet, my ass," Braden bit out. "You aren't alone anymore, Katie. You may not be used to it, but you damn well better get that way. We aren't going away."

She blinked at his ferocity. His entire body was taut like a bowstring, and determination was locked into his face. She let her gaze flicker to Ian only to see the same steely resolve reflected in his eyes.

Not knowing how to respond to that little outburst, she calmly picked her fork back up and resumed eating. After several long, awkward minutes, she gripped her now-empty plate and started to get off the couch.

Ian circled her wrist and tugged her back down. "I'll get it, Katie. You sit."

No escape. It nearly made her giggle. It seemed her life revolved around escape and capture. Granted she was convinced that Ian and Braden were the good guys here. So, she'd exchanged an unsavory prison for a much better one. It was still a prison all the same. Freedom was an elusive creature indeed.

But was freedom really what she wanted? Did she want to be away from these two men? She could lie to herself—she'd certainly been less than honest with herself in the past—but the truth was she trusted these two men as much as it galled her to admit, and more than that, she wanted them. Wanted to be close to them, wanted intimacy, and it went beyond just sex, no matter that she'd damn near beaten herself over the head trying to convince herself otherwise.

The fire had warmed the room or at least taken away the bitter chill. She awkwardly positioned herself so she could curl her feet underneath her as she turned in the direction of the fireplace.

Braden watched her, and she peeked at him from underneath her lashes.

"What now, Braden?" she asked. "Do we stay here forever? Wait for the boogeyman to come get us? What are we doing, exactly?"

To her surprise he looked briefly away. She was used to his bluntness, counted on it. While Ian usually tried to couch things and be more diplomatic, Braden tended to say it like it was without deference to her feelings. She liked that.

There was a hint of unease in his expression when he turned his eyes back to her. "Eli and Tits along with the Falcon secondary are hunting Esteban. We stay here until it's safe to leave."

"And?" Surely there had to be more to their plan than that.

"And nothing. When we get word that Esteban is no longer a threat to you then we take things from there."

She continued to stare at him in silence. He probably didn't understand her worries or concerns. He had a place in the world. He and Ian were part of this Falcon team. They had friends, jobs, each other. She had no one. No home to return to, no life to get on with.

It was a daunting thought and something she had to do a lot of thinking about, because when it was all over with, she would be solidly on her own again. And for the first time in a long time, that scared the hell out of her.

Chapter Twenty-Eight

Katie stood at the window watching the snow drift steadily downward. She raised the cup of cocoa framed in her palms and took a cautious sip. A flood of sweet, warm chocolate filled her mouth and trailed down her throat.

A few days of rest and plenty to eat had damn near made a new woman out of her. She felt stronger. And she wasn't afraid. Despite the unknown danger, a danger that only Ian and Braden seemed aware of, she still felt safe. It had been so long since she'd known anything but the paralyzing fear that gripped her every time she went out, walked down the street or tried to sleep at night.

She liked the quiet of the snow. The peace. It was clean and beautiful. A clean slate. She'd like one of those. Redemption. Freedom from mistakes.

Forgiveness.

No. She didn't want forgiveness. Forgiveness implied a guilty conscience in need of soothing. She only regretted her own personal choices.

For the first time in so long, she was...happy. It sounded ludicrous, that here, on the run, shacked up in a remote cabin with men determined to protect her, she could be so content. She'd relaxed her guard willingly and allowed herself to become immersed in the fantasy of being taken care of by two men who took her breath away.

She didn't want it to end. Esteban was a world away, not a reality to her, and she wanted it to remain so. No intrusions, no awakening to the real world.

Never before had she felt cherished, like she mattered. Here in Braden and Ian's arms, she'd found... She swallowed, refusing to say it, to think it. *Home.* Even she couldn't become that delusional.

She bowed her head, tearing her gaze from the snow-blanketed ground to stare into the mug she held. Firm hands gripped her shoulders, squeezing lightly as lips nuzzled her neck. She smiled and closed her eyes, leaning into Braden's strong chest.

"Hi," he murmured.

She set the mug on the windowsill and then turned to face him. His hands settled on her hips, and he pulled her to his body until she was flush against him.

"Hey yourself."

He knuckled her chin up and kissed her lingeringly. "Want breakfast?"

"Mmm, does this mean I have to go wake Ian up?"

Braden chuckled. "Yeah, you drew short straw. I'd rather have KP duty."

"Give me twenty minutes," she murmured as she reached up on tiptoe to give him another quick kiss.

She stepped around him and headed for the bedroom. She paused inside the doorway and took in Ian's sprawled body. He was lying on his stomach, one arm tucked underneath his pillow and the other flung over the other pillow at his head.

Quietly, she walked further, not wanting to disturb him even though she'd come to wake him. She eased onto the bed, her gaze sliding up his muscular form.

The past days had been satisfying even if odd. The three had formed an easy camaraderie, and both men took every opportunity to make love to her. Separately. It was as though she enjoyed a relationship with both men simultaneously, and they were okay with it.

She caught the looks they exchanged, usually about the time one of them put the moves on her. There was an understanding between them. *She* was an understanding between them. And yet they hadn't attempted to have a threesome with her.

Based on previous conversations, she knew they'd gone

that road in the past, and she also knew from innuendo laced into their flirting that they were certainly open to fucking her at the same time. Which begged the question: Why hadn't they?

Unless...they were waiting for her to make the move.

Considering she'd made the first move the first time with both men, it wasn't too hard to believe that they could very well be letting her call the shots.

She placed her hand at the small of Ian's back and slid it upward, enjoying the feel of his skin, the roll of his muscles under her palm. She leaned in and put her lips to his shoulder.

He tensed against her lips, and she heard the change of his breathing, signaling his break from sleep. And then he rolled, snagging her with his arm and hauling her against his chest.

She came willingly, landing against him with a slight jolt. Her mouth was inches from his lips, and she didn't shy away. She took them in a hungry movement, sucking his bottom lip between her teeth. She nipped and then licked and swallowed his growl.

He was usually slow to awaken, and when he did, he was surly and grumpy. She and Braden spent the first hour of Ian's day avoiding him and the rest of the time giving him a hard time about what a grouch he was. This morning, however, he went from a dead sleep to instant alert.

His cock bulged in his underwear. It was rigid against her side, hot and thick as his body worked against hers. He was aroused and ready, and a dark thrill singed through her veins when his hands tore impatiently at her shirt.

"Good morning," she murmured.

"Shut up," he growled as his lips slammed against hers in a kiss that drove the breath from her chest.

Oh hell yeah, she liked waking the beast.

She tried to get her hands into his underwear, but he yanked her arms back, pinning them behind her. Then he rolled her over so that he straddled her body and stared down at her with glittering eyes.

She was at a distinct disadvantage, and while it would usually irritate the living hell out of her, she found herself liking it. Liking it very much.

As soon as his hands touched her breasts, a shudder worked through her body. He cupped them roughly, massaging and kneading the plump mounds. Then he pulled at both nipples, elongating them. He gave each a sharp pinch. A long hiss escaped her clenched teeth.

His engorged cock, still encased in his underwear, rested on her belly. His knees dug into the bed at her sides, and then he rubbed his groin up and down her pelvis until she moaned and twisted restlessly.

"You know what they say about not starting something unless you can finish it," he said in a voice thick with desire.

She spread her hands in a gesture of helpless innocence. "All I did was wake you for breakfast."

"And if I plan on having you for breakfast?"

"I try never to interfere with a man and his appetite," she murmured.

"I guess neither of you will be making it to the table," Braden said dryly.

Katie turned her head to see Braden leaning against the door, his gaze raking up and down her naked body. She stared boldly in return and then looked back up at Ian to gauge his mood. Would it be as simple as telling them both she wanted them? Together?

She glanced back at Braden. For a moment, indecision wavered in her mind. She didn't want to screw up what she had. Sex with both men was fantastic. Even as good as she knew it would be with both of them together, she could certainly live with their current arrangement. For as long as it lasted.

"Say what's on your mind, Katie," Braden drawled.

"We're not mind readers," Ian said.

"I want you...both," she said simply.

Braden shoved off the doorframe and stalked toward her, all sense of easygoing teasing gone. There a hint of darkness to his face that sent prickles of excitement dancing over her skin.

She peeked back up at Ian who had the same smoldering intensity lurking in his eyes. What the hell had she just done?

Braden leaned down, his fingers caressing her cheek. "Be sure about this, Katie. Be damn sure. We've played things your way, but if you want us both, it's going to be our way. Can you handle giving up that kind of control?"

Holy hell. It was suddenly all sorts of hard to breathe.

"In bed," she said coolly. As coolly as she could under the circumstances. "It doesn't go any further than in bed. As long as we're clear on that."

Ian chuckled. "We don't expect you to undergo a complete lobotomy." He twisted her nipple between his fingers, sharply enough to send a spark of pain racing through her breast.

She closed her eyes. She craved the darkness she saw lurking in their eyes. Wanted it, needed it with a dangerous appetite. The bite of pain, the heat of raw, uncontrolled passion.

They knew her secrets, and now they were going to wrest control from her hands and give her everything she most desired.

She emitted a low growl. A primal sound of a woman greeting her mate. Her submission and her acquiescence. It wasn't the sound of a weak, helpless female.

Ian tensed, and then he swung away from her, his feet hitting the floor with a thud. He tore his underwear off while Braden's clothing flew in the other direction. And then two hulking, naked men faced her down with the promise of everything she'd ever desired flashing in their eyes.

She swallowed and lay still, waiting and wanting.

"On your knees," Braden said in a low, silky voice.

Slowly she rolled, and then she pushed herself to her knees until they were planted in the soft mattress.

"Turn to me," he said.

She turned, her fingers dug into the edge of the bed. The bed dipped behind her, and she glanced back to see Ian positioning himself at her ass. His hands gripped her hips, and there was nothing gentle about his grasp.

Braden's hand slid into her hair, and then he fisted the strands and pulled her head slightly to the side. He grasped his cock with his other hand and pumped a few times as he guided it toward her mouth.

"Open," he said.

Adrenaline-laced desire centered in her belly and fanned outward, tightening every nerve ending in its path. Her pussy fisted and tingled, and then she felt Ian nudging impatiently at her opening. There was no finesse, no gentle coaxing. He lined up and thrust deep.

She gasped, and Braden took advantage by sliding to the back of her throat. She was simultaneously filled by both men, and she'd never felt anything like it in her life.

"That's it," Braden said approvingly. "You're ours, Katie. Take it deep. Just like that."

Her body shook and rocked with the force of their motion. Neither man gave her any reprieve, and God, she loved it. She wanted to mount them both, take them hard and hungry. Her need was feral and demanding.

Braden's musky scent filled her nostrils. His taste invaded her mouth and exploded over her tongue. She sucked hungrily, matching his thrusts with the bob of her head.

Ian rocked against her ass with enough force that each stab into her pussy was an exotic mix of intense pleasure and sweet pain. His swollen cock dragged over her entrance, stretching her mercilessly. He felt bigger than before, as if only now had she plumbed the depths of his desire.

And then she realized that she wasn't feeling the sleek latex of a condom-covered cock. Every ridge, every swollen vein slid over the walls of her pussy. Flesh to flesh.

She ripped her head from Braden's cock only to have his hand tighten in her hair, his displeasure over her action evident as he shoved his cock back to her lips.

"Condom," she said hoarsely. "Ian. Condom."

Ian stilled against her and then cursed vividly. Then he pressed a gentle kiss to her spine. "Sorry, baby."

He left her, and cool air brushed over her behind, chilling her as she lost his comforting warmth. Braden's hand softened in her hair and he stroked, caressing the strands between his fingers.

She looked up, an invitation. He touched her cheek with his other hand and then shifted his hips so that his cock brushed across her lips. She tongued the head, lapping in a circle as she tested the contour of the flared tip.

He plunged, taking her breath in one forceful thrust. He lodged in the back of her throat, and she swallowed to accept him. His hand tightened again in her hair, all softness gone.

He fucked her mouth with rapid, hard strokes. For several long seconds, she didn't breathe. She just felt. Absorbed. And then he tore himself away, and both their ragged breaths filled the room.

"Come here," he rasped.

She got off the bed, her legs shaking. He yanked her to his chest and kissed her fiercely. Then he walked her back until she met the bed.

"Lay down."

She sat first, her palms going down to brace her fall. Slowly she reclined until her head was pillowed in the tangle of sheets. He hooked her legs over his arms and pulled until her ass was aligned with the edge of the mattress. And then he let her down and stepped back.

Ian loomed over her, picking her legs up as Braden had done. He spread her wide and moved in, his cock brushing her clit. He let one leg go long enough to grasp his erection and position it at her entrance. Then he reclaimed her leg and surged forward.

She cried out. Standing as he was, leaning over her, he had more power in his thrusts. He was deep. So deep. For a long moment, he stood there, wedged tight, staring down at her with eyes that burned.

His fingers fluttered over her stitched cut, his gentleness in direct contradiction to every other action.

"Don't let me hurt you," he said in a low voice. "Take what we give you, but don't let me go too far."

She nodded.

"Promise me. I want you. I want to fuck you long and hard, but I won't hurt you."

"I promise," she whispered.

At that he closed his eyes, reared back and then slammed into her so fiercely that her entire body jerked. Her hands came up, grasping at air, needing, wanting something to hold on to, to anchor her as she spun out of control.

Braden caught her wrists and pulled until her arms were over her head. His face appeared over hers, and he kissed her, his lips upside down against hers.

"Do you have any idea how sexy you look all laid out beneath us, your body ours to do with as we please?"

He moved to the side, gathering her wrists together with one hand as he shifted his big body. With his free hand, he cupped and kneaded her breast.

"You like pain, but how much, Katie? You love it when I nip and bite, when I pinch and twist your nipples."

She moaned softly, her entire body awash in soft euphoria. She shook again as Ian retreated and powered forward, his thighs slapping against the backs of her legs.

"Tell me," Braden ordered. "Tell me what you want. I won't give it to you until you do."

"God," she whispered. "Please, Braden. I need..."

"Tell me what you need."

"Bite me," she begged. "Hard. My nipples, my neck. Make it hurt." She looked down at Ian. "Harder."

"Oh hell yeah," Ian said in a strained voice.

He rammed, hard and fast just as Braden's teeth descended, a flash of white against her skin. They sank into her nipple, and pleasure, white hot and piercing, exploded through her body. Her vision blurred, and her mouth opened in a soundless scream.

He alternated, roughly biting and sucking the taut peaks. The friction caused by Ian's huge cock abrading the walls of her pussy sent spears of heat and indescribable ecstasy shattering through her groin.

Hard, rough, hot. Ian slammed ruthlessly. Braden's mouth slid like silk to her neck, and then sweet agony seared over her skin when he sank his teeth into the column just below her ear.

Her entire body bowed, her back arching off the mattress. She sailed in an endless freefall into a bottomless canyon. Her orgasm shattered, rained slivers of pleasure like the skies opening after a drought.

She had no knowledge, no thoughts except the softness of

the mattress as she floated gently downward. Her pussy throbbed around Ian's cock as he continued to rock against her.

Braden knelt up and then leaned over her as he turned her head to the side. His cock bumped against her lips and he pressed inward until she opened and let him in. He thrust, arching up over her so that he had a dominant angle.

His hand left her head as he braced himself with his palms flat on the mattress. He was over her mouth, pumping, mimicking Ian's movements between her legs.

The two men fucked her ruthlessly, and she surrendered to the mindless euphoria that swept over her. Ian shuddered against her, thrust hard and then stilled, his legs shaking as he gripped her hips with bruising strength.

Braden slipped deep, bumping the back of her throat. She swallowed, holding him there with her tongue. He pulsed and then hot liquid filled her mouth. She swallowed rapidly and sucked as he thrust frantically, his balls slapping against her jaw.

He powered deep once more and held himself rigid as he finished emptying himself into her mouth. Then he carefully pulled away and rolled his body over her head to collapse onto the bed.

He touched her hair, caressing softly as he cradled her head against his chest.

She glanced down to see Ian's eyes closed in agony as he leaned into her. When he opened them, his expression was one of complete satisfaction. He leaned to brush his lips across her belly and then stepped back, slipping from her still trembling pussy.

His hands slid over her hips and underneath to pat her ass affectionately before he walked over to dispose of the condom. Braden reached down and urged her to cuddle into him, and she turned readily, aligning her back to his chest.

Ian returned to the bed and slid his knee onto the mattress as he climbed toward Katie. His eyes were intent as he settled on his side to face her. Braden's hand glided lazily back and forth over her hip, and he kissed the curve of her shoulder.

Ian put a palm to her cheek and hesitated a moment before leaning in to capture her lips in a kiss so tender that she couldn't reconcile his actions with the animalistic way he'd possessed her.

"No, you didn't hurt me," she said before he could voice the concern she could see shining brightly in his eyes.

"Good," he said huskily. "Because I sure as hell want to do that again."

Braden's teeth sank into her shoulder, sending a shiver cascading down her spine. She closed her eyes and moaned.

"Hell," Ian muttered. "Give me a minute to recover before you make those kinds of sounds."

She snuggled a little closer to Braden even as her hands went out, seeking Ian's body. "Give me an hour and we'll do it again," she said as a huge, contented yawn split her lips.

Chapter Twenty-Nine

Katie came awake as her legs were spread and one long finger rimmed her anus. Her eyes widened as she processed that she was flat on her belly, her ass splayed open to seeking fingers.

Cool gel contrasted with the spark of heat and edge of pain when another finger pushed bluntly at the tight ring.

"Don't tense," Braden murmured next to her ear.

She turned her head to see him lying beside her, which meant Ian's fingers were the ones inside her.

"Relax, let him in."

"How is your stomach?" Ian asked from behind her.

"What stomach?" she asked as she tried to squeeze breath into her lungs.

Braden chuckled. And then his hand smoothed over her back, warm and sensual.

"We're going to fuck your ass, Katie. Did Paulo ever do that?"

Slowly she nodded.

"And did you enjoy it?"

She nodded again.

"We won't be gentle," he said silkily. "It'll probably hurt."

Her shoulders shook as a spasm overtook her. She had to close her eyes and breathe deep through her nose.

Ian pressed a third finger, stretching her until her ass twitched in pain.

"And you'll lay here helpless while we fuck your ass,"

190

Braden continued. "First Ian. Then me."

She whimpered as Ian worked his fingers back and forth.

"How much hurt can you take, Katie? How rough do you want it?" Ian growled.

"Hard," she whispered. "I want it hard."

Both men sucked in their breath.

Braden yanked her arms above her head and quickly tied them to the headboard. She jerked her head up in surprise, blinking when she saw her wrists bound. She couldn't be in a more helpless position. On her belly, unable to move.

Braden left her side and disappeared from her vision. Hands gripped her ankles and spread her wider. Oh God.

The heat of a body, male flesh, covered her back. A huge cock, blunt and pressing, striving to gain entry into her body. There was no easing, no gentle wooing. He thrust forward, opening her wide.

She screamed hoarsely, her head rearing back as her entire ass caught fire. Pain. Wonderful, excruciating pleasure. Oh God, it hurt. She'd never felt anything more exquisite.

She panted and curled her fingers into her palms, tugging at the bindings around her wrist.

Ian didn't give her any time to recover. He planted his hands on either side of her waist and pulled back before slamming his hips against her ass again.

Her vision blurred. The headboard swam in front of her and she squeezed her eyes shut to try and prolong the sensation, the burn. She grabbed it and held on, not wanting to let go, fearing the sharp edge would subside as her body stretched to accommodate Ian's size.

He withdrew, easing out as her body clutched greedily at him. She released him with a small sigh. He paused just a moment before ruthlessly opening her again.

"Yes, oh God, yes," she panted.

He hunched down over her and began riding her, his hips undulating and slapping against her ass over and over. Braden's hand tangled in her hair, pulling her sharply back until her gaze found his.

His eyes glittered with lust as he watched her, as he forced her to watch him. He lowered his head to hers and kissed her, his teeth sinking into her lip. She bit him back, taking him every bit as hard as he took her. Their kiss was no loving meeting of mouths. It was a battle, fierce and ungiving.

"I'm next, Katie," he breathed against her mouth. "I won't be as gentle."

She closed her eyes and moaned. Anticipation flickered like flame to dry wood. "Don't make promises you can't keep," she taunted in a hoarse voice.

He yanked her head back and stared at her with glittering eyes. "You'll beg for mercy."

"I don't beg."

And the challenge was laid.

He let go of her head, and she slumped forward as Ian slammed into her again. Her orgasm lurked, building, each burst of pain and raw pleasure sending her ever closer. But she wouldn't go. Not without the right stimulation. And it was killing her. She couldn't last like this, and they both damn well knew it.

Ian leaned down, his body covering hers, his weight blanketing her. His teeth sank into her shoulder as his body trembled with his release. She writhed, needing her own release, but Braden merely laughed softly as he left her side.

Just as she squirmed in protest of Ian's weight pressing her wound into the bed, he propped himself up with his hands and eased out of her body.

She moaned and lay there limply, trying to collect herself, to steel herself for Braden's assault. She was a fool to think she could. He was on her, fast and furious, his hands spreading her as his cock found its target.

No, he wasn't as gentle as Ian, and Ian hadn't been a bit easy. Braden ripped into her and never gave her a moment to react. He knew what she needed, maybe even better than she did. He knew she wanted even more than she thought she could take.

His thumbs spread her cheeks impossibly wide and with each thrust, he pulled completely out only to ram inside again. It was torture. She dangled so precariously close to her orgasm, but something held her back. If they would only touch her. Her breasts, her clit, anything.

Back and forth, he opened her, then pulled away. Opened her again. Retreated and held her open before tucking his cock back and sliding inward.

She jerked at her bonds, needing to be free. If only she could touch herself.

And then suddenly her hands fell. Ian had untied her. Braden yanked out of her body and flipped her over. She spread her legs wide, arching upward, seeking what, she wasn't sure.

"Please," she whispered, and then she remembered saying she never begged and that she'd done just that minutes ago. Her lips clamped shut, refusing to let another word pass. But they'd heard her.

Ian leaned down and sucked a nipple into his mouth just as Braden parted her folds and thumbed her clit. She went crazy. Her release billowed up, and she screamed then screamed again.

Braden lifted her, bent her legs back and thrust into her ass again. The final edge of pain sent her spiraling into a black void. Shadows overwhelmed her vision. Freedom from the unbearable pressure that had built as the two men fucked her mercilessly.

As Braden jerked and trembled against her in his release, she floated free. Her eyes fluttered closed, and she reached for sweet oblivion. She felt so good. Wrapped in tendrils of pleasure.

She barely registered Braden pulling free of her body or the two men carefully tending to her. Fingers brushed over her wound, light and seeking. Then lips kissed a line across her stitches.

Ian gathered her in his arms, laying her head against his shoulder. His hands stroked and caressed her body as she snuggled deeper into his embrace.

"That was incredible," she murmured.

"I take it we didn't go too far," Ian said into her hair.

She shook her head. "Perfect. You were perfect."

His hand smoothed over her tingling ass, and she moaned all over again.

"Where's Braden?" she said, her voice muffled by Ian's chest.

Ian kissed the top of her head. "He's coming. Getting cleaned up."

"Going to sleep for a while," she said groggily.

The heat from Ian's body enveloped her. She wrapped her arms and legs around him and dove into the comforting veil of sleep.

Chapter Thirty

Damiano stared out at the rugged outline of the snow-capped mountains. There was no glass to block the chill. Just a simple cut-out with a crude flap that could be drawn down to prevent a draft. This place that Marcus had brought him to was stark and beautiful, but the accommodations were lean.

The floors were made up of packed dirt, made smooth by repeated footsteps. Just a makeshift hut erected on the ground. Sturdier than a tent but nothing that would withstand a strong storm.

Surely they had them at this elevation. The snows would come in but a few weeks.

Fatigued from the journey, from the weight of his worry, he pulled clumsily at the flap and turned away to the pallet on the floor. Remnants of the sedative still traveled sluggishly through his veins and tugged at him, calling him to rest.

He might need more. What if he woke on the fringe of a shift? Marcus hadn't seemed worried. He said they waited for Nali. Whoever that was.

Damiano lay down on his back and stared at the poorly constructed roof. How had this place lasted as long as it had? It wouldn't surprise him if the ceiling fell in on him during the night. Or was it day? It was a testament to his state of mind that he had no idea if it was morning or evening. He only knew he wanted to close his eyes for a while and forget all that he'd become.

He drifted tiredly toward sleep. But in the shadows he saw the tiger. He saw Ty and himself as children on the streets of Prague as they looked in sympathy at the caged predator.

"We should free him," Damiano said fiercely.

Ty looked at him with big, worried eyes. She twisted thin fingers nervously in front of her. "It's dangerous."

He hugged her to his side in an effort to reassure her. "He is like us, Ty. He wants to be free. The orphanage was our cage."

The rich gold and amber eyes stared at them from behind the bars of the too-small cage. They called to Damiano in a way he didn't quite understand. He only knew that somehow he and the tiger were connected.

He walked forward, and the tiger's keeper immediately issued a sharp reprimand to stay away.

"He eats children like you!" the man jeered.

Damiano scowled. "I wish he would eat you," he muttered.

"Let's go, D," Tyana whispered urgently. "We don't want to be caught. I don't want to go back to the orphanage."

Reluctantly, Damiano turned away and took Ty's hand in his. But to the tiger, he silently promised that he would return.

He turned restlessly on the pallet, the fingers of sleep pulling him deeper into the twisted myriad of his dreams. He saw himself standing on the street in the black of night, only he was alone. Where was Tyana? The streets were completely deserted, and when he looked again at the cage, the tiger was gone.

This wasn't how it happened. He'd freed the tiger. With Tyana's help. He turned, his bare feet scraping against the jagged cobblestone, and there it was.

Standing a few feet away, the tiger stared thoughtfully at him. Damiano froze, afraid to move, afraid to breathe. And then they were no longer standing on the streets of Prague. Damiano was on the island, in the game room, watching helplessly as Tyana fought for her life against the tiger. Why had he attacked her?

He tried to lunge forward as the tiger ripped the crutch from Tyana's hands, but he was frozen, paralyzed. Never before had he felt so utterly helpless.

And then it was just him and the tiger, face to face in the rugged Nepalese mountains. Damiano stood naked before him, his hands at his sides, his palms facing forward. An eagle swooped down behind the tiger and landed on a tree branch a short distance away. From behind rock outcroppings, more animals appeared. He knew them. They were all the animals he fought so desperately when the shift came over him.

"You are one of us," the tiger said, startling Damiano. "Why do you fight us so?"

"Our brother," the eagle cried.

"No," Damiano whispered. "I'm just a man."

The tiger tossed his head. "You are flesh, but your spirit cannot be confined to your human form. Free yourself as you have freed me."

Damiano shook his head. Sweat beaded his forehead as he struggled with invisible bonds.

"Damiano. Damiano! Wake up."

He heard Marcus's voice from a distance. He stared back at the assembled animals. One by one, they disappeared until only the eagle and the tiger remained. Then the eagle took flight, circled once overheard and disappeared into the clouds.

Embrace us.

Damiano's eyes flew open as his body jerked to awareness. Marcus knelt over him, his brow creased with concern.

"Are you all right? Do you need another injection?"

"No," he croaked.

Slowly he sat up with Marcus's assistance.

"What happened, D?"

Damiano shook his head. The images so vivid before now blurred into a mass of confusion.

"I don't know," he admitted. "God, I don't know."

Marcus put his hand on Damiano's shoulder and squeezed. "You're going to be okay. We're going to beat this. You have to believe that."

He looked up into Marcus's eyes, and for the first time let all the doubts and fears flood him. Before he'd kept a positive attitude, more for Ty than for himself. But she wasn't here. He was alone, and there was no reason to keep living a lie.

"I'm not okay, Marcus. I'll never be okay. What are we

197

trying to do here? How is any of this going to change what I've become? Am I looking at spending the rest of my life anticipating the next time someone sticks a needle in my arm? Will I have to forever separate myself from the people I love for fear that I might kill them?"

Marcus blew out his breath and let his hand fall from Damiano's shoulder. "You can beat this, D. I believe that, and you have to believe it or you're going to lose. That's all I can offer you. Tyana believes in you and so do your brothers. Don't let them down by giving up. Don't let yourself down."

Damiano reached for Marcus's hand and grasped it tightly. "I don't know that I've ever thanked you for everything you've done for me and Ty."

"Falcon saved me," he said simply. "There's nothing I wouldn't do to repay that debt."

Damiano shook his head. "You're family now. There are no debts among family."

A sound outside the small room had Marcus turning his head. He got awkwardly to his feet and extended a hand down to Damiano. "That'll be Nali. Come, and I'll introduce you."

Chapter Thirty-One

Her stomach growled, and she remembered breakfast had been forgotten. And now it was well past lunch as well. Katie got out of bed and hurriedly dressed. When she stuck her head into the living room, she found it empty.

Distant noise from the kitchen told her where they were, and she headed in that direction. She rounded the corner and found both men in the process of making lunch.

"Hey, there she is," Braden said when he looked up. "We wondered if you'd slipped into a coma."

She grinned and leaned against the cabinets close to the stove.

Ian walked over to her and pressed inward, crowding her with his big body. He bent to kiss her. "You okay?" he asked, his eyes bright with concern.

She reached up to touch his face, her fingers trailing down the slight stubble at his jaw. "It's been a long time since I've been better."

"I'm glad," he said simply.

"Have a seat," Braden called. "I'm about to dish it up."

Ian kissed her quickly again before backing away so she could go to the table. Braden's gaze followed her as she slid into her seat, and she smiled up at him, allowing the full force of her contentment to shine through. A dimpled grin was her reward as he ambled over, skillet in hand to scoop out her omelet onto her plate.

Not to be outdone by his older brother, evidently, he cupped her chin with his free hand and gave her a lingering kiss. She savored it, his taste and the heated feel of his lips over hers. It was a possessive kiss, one meant to remind her of his ownership of her body.

As much as she should have balked at such a notion, she couldn't help but enjoy a delicious shiver.

"You're ours, Katie," he murmured as he released her mouth. "Whatever you're thinking or feeling, you remember that fact."

A flutter started deep in her stomach. She loved that they were so possessive, and she loved it even more that they didn't treat her like a piece of glass. Sex with them had been volatile. Edgy and rough. They'd treated her like an equal.

Braden returned to the stove while Katie dug into her food. Moments later, both men joined her with their own plates.

"How is your wound?" Ian asked between bites.

Both were looking at her like they'd prefer to have her for lunch. Her cheeks went warm, and a flush worked over her body at the blatant sensuality in their stares.

"It's fine," she said. It was a lie. It ached like a bitch, but there was no way in hell she was telling them that. Not when the promise of more really scorching sex reflected in their emerald stares.

"I'll have a look at it after you finish eating," Ian said in a tone that suggested he'd be looking at a whole lot more.

She slid the last bite over her tongue, letting the tines linger at the tip. The bitch of it was, she could really get used to being taken care of by these two men. As much as Gabe had taught her never to rely on anyone but herself, surrendering her wellbeing to Ian and Braden was so potently tempting that she'd begun to fantasize about it in her waking hours.

And that sort of fanciful mess was what had gotten her into trouble with Paulo and Ricardo. Because at the heart of her abrasive, bitch-on-wheels attitude was a woman who wanted to be loved and cared for. Apparently she was like every other woman out there, and quite frankly, it pissed her off that she couldn't be smarter than that.

"Don't you know that sex should never be analyzed, only enjoyed?" Braden drawled.

She jerked her gaze to him to find him watching her,

analyzing *her*. Then she smiled ruefully. "Busted."

"I love an honest woman," he said with a grin.

"I don't like an overly analytical one," Ian said in amusement. "Kind of takes the fun out of really good sex."

"Make you a deal. You don't analyze me and I won't analyze sex," she said evenly.

"Deal," Braden said. "I think we should shake on it in the bedroom."

She stood and pushed back her plate. Resting her palms on the table, she leaned forward, letting her gaze slide suggestively over the two men. "Last one there is a rotten egg."

She turned away, even as the scrape of chair legs over the wood floor echoed across the room. With a laugh, she bolted into a run only to be overtaken in two steps.

Oh, she loved it that they weren't all careful and cautious with her. Ian yanked her up and tossed her over his shoulder. She looked up to see Braden following, his hands unfastening his jeans with every step.

She landed on the bed with a thump, her back meeting the still-tangled covers from earlier. Both men loomed over her in various degrees of undress.

"How rough do you want it?" Ian rasped as he pulled at his shirt.

"As rough as you can make it."

Braden crawled onto the bed, his erection heavy and swaying between his legs as he made his way up her body. "We like it rough, Katie. Not some fake, half-ass crap. Be damn sure you know what you're in for."

"Haven't we had this conversation already?" she asked in exasperation.

In response, he yanked her pants down, mounted her and stroked deep. Her breath caught in her throat. She tried to move her legs, but her pants were bunched around her ankles. God, she was full, stretched so tight around him that every nerve ending in her pussy pulsed and vibrated around his thick cock.

Ian pulled at her pants and underwear, tossing them aside as her legs came free. Braden tugged at her shirt, impatient as her breasts bobbed into view. Still embedded deep, he lowered his head and nipped sharply at the puckered tips of her breasts.

Then he reared back, nearly sliding free before ramming forward again. She groaned, part in pain, part in delicious ecstasy.

"Hurt?" he asked with a grin.

"Yes," she whimpered.

"Good," he said as he captured her mouth.

Then he wrenched free and climbed upward, positioning his knees on either side of her breasts. His cock touched her chin, and he reached behind her head to grasp her hair.

His fingers tightened painfully as he yanked her forward to meet his thrust. "Suck me," he said. "Open that pretty mouth and take me deep."

Just as he thrust, hitting the soft tissues at the back of her throat, her legs were spread wide again and Ian mounted her. Both men rode her body, rocking back and forth, their cocks penetrating with ease.

They weren't easy. They weren't gentle. They took. She didn't offer her surrender, they demanded it.

Braden's fingers relaxed and gentled in her hair as he leaned forward and held himself there for a long moment. She opened, accepting, trusting that he wouldn't stay too long, cutting off her air supply.

"Open wide," he said in a strained voice. "Just open and let me fuck your mouth, baby. I want all of it."

She tilted her head back as much as his grip would allow and relaxed, letting him take control. He arched over her, positioning himself above so that he had leverage and power.

And then he started fucking her without mercy. Relentless. Ian paused, deep in her pussy, and she knew he watched as Braden brutally fucked her mouth.

Her body hummed in response to the erotic position, her underneath him, so submissive, so powerless. Her breasts swelled and her pussy tightened around Ian's cock. She wanted him to move so badly. She'd come with the slightest touch. But he held still as Braden owned her mouth.

Then his hand came down and he slipped free of her lips. "Keep it open," he rasped. He jerked frantically at his cock, the tip bouncing off her tongue.

Hot liquid surged, splattering across her lips. Then he sank deep as more come, hot and salty, flooded her mouth. He arched his hips, fucking her with ease as he forced his creamy release past her tongue and into her throat.

"Oh, fuck yeah," he breathed. "Taste it. Take it all."

As he slowed, he continued long, slow strokes, dragging his cock over her tongue. "Lick it," he whispered. "Clean it off me, baby."

She sucked at his length, tasting the tangy drops as she licked them from his skin. She took him all, his balls resting softly against her chin as he held himself there for a long moment. Then he withdrew and rolled away, leaving her panting for breath—and want. She was so close and she needed release.

She found herself staring back at Ian who was still lodged in her pussy. His eyes glittered with savage intensity, enough that she realized whatever Braden had just done to her was going to pale in comparison.

"Be sure this is what you want," he said in a voice that sent shivers cascading over her entire body. Before, Braden had always been the one she feared while Ian was the one she drew comfort from, the one more likely to take care of her and worry over hurting her.

She swallowed nervously, but she was excited. God, she was so excited. She was going to orgasm just from the thought of what he'd do.

He pulled out of her and got off the bed to stand at the foot. He studied her with hard eyes. Goose bumps puckered and spilled over her. She swallowed again.

"Come here," he ordered.

Without thought, she obeyed, coming to her knees and crawling to the end of the bed.

"Clean me," he said. "Taste yourself and lick me clean."

She allowed him to cup her head and guide himself into her mouth. Her taste exploded on her tongue, creamy and slightly sweet. Not as tangy as Braden had tasted.

For a moment she sucked and licked as he thrust forcefully into her throat. Then he pulled away and gripped her shoulders.

"Turn around," he ordered.

She complied, her knees shaking as they dug into the mattress. He gathered her hands in his and tugged until they were behind her back, resting just above her ass. Then he pulled upward, linking his fingers with hers just as he rammed into her pussy, forcing her forward.

Braden was there to catch her. He placed his body in front of hers, blocking her so that she didn't fall to the mattress. He was semi-hard, and he wasted no time fitting himself to her mouth again.

Fucked from both ends. Two huge cocks dove deep into her body, stretching her mouth and her pussy. Ian held her arms tightly behind her as his hips slapped against her ass. He yanked out of her, his body quivering as he sucked in deep breaths. "I want her ass," he demanded over her head to Braden.

Braden slipped from her mouth and got off the bed. In the distance, she heard the crackle of wrappers. Braden crawled back onto the bed, lying flat on his back.

"Ride me, Katie."

He didn't have to tell her twice. She climbed over Braden's legs and eagerly sheathed herself on his latex-covered cock. They both groaned as she sank down. It was too much. He was too big. God, he felt good.

Firm hands gripped her hips then slid over her ass, impatiently spreading the globes. Ian's huge dick prodded her back entrance, and she gasped as he tucked himself against her. There was no lubrication this time. Her body tightened in anticipation even as she braced herself for the pain. Oh God, the imminent pleasure.

She started shuddering as the first waves of her orgasm rolled over her, and he hadn't even gotten inside yet.

"Slow down, baby," Ian murmured in her ear. "Make it last."

She took several steadying breaths as she fought the breaking wave. Her body heaved, and Braden stilled for a moment as he let her come down slightly.

Then Ian's hand twisted tightly in her hair, and without warning, he thrust past the tight ring of her anus, seating himself deep in her bowels.

She screamed as her body bowed forward, and the orgasm she'd so desperately fought exploded with the force of an atomic bomb. Braden surged. Both men were buried so deep in the most sensitive parts of her body.

She sobbed desperately, begging them to stop, not to stop, to move, to fuck her, to hurt her. She writhed uncontrollably, her body on fire as they slammed in unison.

Braden reached up and twisted her nipples, plucking the stiff tips with enough pressure to cause a wave of pain and exquisite, numbing pleasure to throb through her veins.

Instead of subsiding, instead of the orgasm breaking sharp and gradually lessening, the men drove her higher. The sensation of both their cocks, rubbing against the thin separation between her pussy and anus, stroking and fucking with no mercy, merely sent her higher, the pleasure sharper, the pain wonderfully excruciating.

Her only regret was that they both wore condoms, and she wanted to feel their release, wanted their come deep and hot in her body.

As if reading her mind, Ian pulled out, and suddenly come splattered her back and ass. He'd torn off the condom and come on her body.

With a moan, she looked down at Braden. "You too," she whispered. "All over me. Please."

Braden surged up, holding her against him. They slid from the bed until her feet hit the floor.

"On your knees," he ordered.

She fell to her knees as he yanked at the condom and tossed it across the room. No sooner was it off than he grabbed clumsily at her jaw, squeezing it in his hand and then plunging deep into her mouth with his dick.

For several long seconds, he thrust fiercely and then he pulled out. The first rope of come landed across her cheek. She closed her eyes as more coated her breasts and then her lips.

The tip brushed over her mouth, pushing incessantly until she opened and he slid back in. He thrust forward, rocking up on his heels, burying himself and then stilling as the last of his release quivered over her tongue.

She knelt there, sucking in air through flared nostrils. Come coated her front and back. She felt exotic, beautiful and desirable. She felt powerful in a way she'd never experienced. Not even with Paulo in the early days. Utterly feminine. Wanted.

As Braden eased from her mouth, she turned her gaze upward. Ian moved into view, his heavy cock dangling. She reached out to touch him and then Braden, cupping them both in her palms. Ian moved forward, giving her easier access, and she had both men in front of her.

Gently she stroked, loving the softness over the turgid steel of their shafts. Her fingers traveled up to fondle their balls. She loved the supple give, the silky, pliable pouch that responded to her every touch.

"We want to taste you now," Braden said in a husky voice. "Every inch."

She took her hands from their cocks and slowly cupped her palms over the wetness that streaked her body.

Their eyes followed her every movement. Their dicks came to life at the erotic sight of her rubbing their thick cream into her skin.

She cupped her breasts and circled her nipples then coated the tips until they shone.

Ian groaned and lifted her up.

"Shower?" she asked innocently. "As much as I want you to lick every part of me, I doubt you're interested in tasting your come."

Braden laughed. "You got that right, sister. It's fun to play with, but I draw the line at consumption."

"Who gets to bathe me? I feel rather weak. I'm not sure I can stand in the shower."

"Manipulative heifer," Ian muttered, but he grinned the entire time. "Come on, we'll all rinse off, and then I plan to give you a bath of a completely different kind."

Chapter Thirty-Two

Katie got out of the shower shivering, but not for long. She was enveloped by two male bodies, warm and comforting. They sandwiched her between them as they dried her hair and rubbed the dampness from her skin.

"I'll go build up the fire," Braden said as he slipped out of the bathroom.

Ian tucked his hands over her bare shoulders and pulled her into a leisurely kiss. It lacked the urgency of their earlier lovemaking. It was unhurried, sensual, sweet where before there had been so much roughness.

Gentle fingers tucked damp strands of her hair behind her ears then stroked over her cheekbone. This man was a study in contrast. That he could be so bone-meltingly gentle after being so hard, so relentless—it was enough to make her go weak in the knees. She didn't know how to handle this softer side of him.

"I know you hurt," he murmured as his hand brushed ever so lightly across her stitches. "We're going to go in the living room, you're going to take something for it, and Braden and I are going to give you so much pleasure that you'll forget all about the pain."

"Oh..." she said on a soft intake of breath. There was nothing else to say.

"Come here." He bent down and tucked an arm underneath her knees then hoisted her up against his chest.

He walked into the living room where Braden was still tending the fire. He'd added logs until it burned briskly, the flames leaping upward.

Ian laid her on the couch, and Braden came over to stand next to her head. Neither made an effort to disguise their arousal, nor did they seem abashed to be standing in the nude. They could have been completely clothed for all the attention they gave it. No, their attention was focused solely on her.

"I'll be back," Ian said.

First he returned with a glass of water and some of the pain medication Marcus had left for her. After he made sure she'd downed it, he turned and left the room again.

She watched in confusion as he left only to come back a moment later with several blankets and pillows. He positioned them on the floor in front of the fire, making a comfortable pallet. Then Braden bent and lifted her from the couch.

He carried her over and settled her among the blankets. The warmth from the fire skittered over her skin and seeped into her bones. It felt wonderful.

She settled against a pillow with a sigh of contentment. When she looked up, two naked, hugely aroused men stood over her.

Ian moved first, kneeling at her feet. Braden positioned himself beside her and cupped a hand to her breast.

Without a word, Ian carefully spread her legs, bending her knees just slightly so that she was comfortable. He lowered his head, pressing his lips to her ankle just as Braden's mouth closed around one nipple.

She moaned soft and low as warm pleasure shot through her body. Ian took his time, kissing a line up her leg, paying careful attention to all her sensitive spots. The inside of her knee, the back of her knee. Then he spread her thighs and lapped softly at the inside of her leg, just inches from her pussy.

She arched involuntarily as he licked and nibbled, keeping just far enough from her clit to drive her crazy. He pressed his tongue to her skin, starting at her knee and sliding it upward, leaving a damp trail all the way to the soft folds of her mound.

Braden circled each nipple, showering her with kisses and soft licks. Never once did he bite down or even suck too hard. He regarded her so tenderly that it brought tears to her eyes, and then she blinked furiously, dismayed at the welling emotion.

And then he moved to her mouth, kissing her with reverence. Sweetly, so sweetly, like the kiss of a first lover. He licked the moisture from her cheek that she'd willed not to leak down, and then he kissed both her eyes, fluttering the softest of lips over her lids.

What were they doing? And why?

Ian parted the plump folds of her pussy and pressed his tongue to her quivering entrance. He licked upward with one long swipe, ending over the sensitive bundle of nerves tucked under the hooded flesh.

Her hips came off the floor. Her fingers curled into tight fists at her sides. And still he continued, lapping, licking, sucking and probing with his tongue. He hadn't lied when he said he was going to taste every inch of her. There wasn't a part of her lower body he hadn't covered with his tongue, and Braden was doing his damndest to cover the top.

As Braden swirled around each nipple again, Ian mimicked his brother's actions around her clit.

"Oh!" she cried.

"That's it, sweetheart, let it go," Braden softly encouraged. "Don't fight it."

She closed her eyes tight and arched into both men, wanting more of their intoxicating sweetness. Light. So light. Like a feather stirring in the wind. Each lick sent her higher until finally her entire body tightened and clenched. Then, deafening still. She shattered, her body going slack.

The ceiling blurred above her. Tears swam in her eyes, and for the life of her, she couldn't figure out why she was crying. But weep she did. At first it was light. Silver tears trickled down her cheeks. But then those quiet tears gave way to noisy, messy sobs. Her shoulders shook with abandon.

Strong arms gathered her close. Two men, holding her between them as they petted and caressed her. Murmured words against her hair, soft and understanding. But she didn't understand. How could they?

So much had been released, let go. For so long she'd held it all in, and now it flooded out, a broken dam that had no hope of being repaired.

Braden held her to his chest, rocking back and forth as he kissed her hair. Ian's hands were at her back, rolling over her shoulders, his lips pressing to her spine and upward to her nape.

Then Braden relinquished her into Ian's arms, and Ian held her as Braden had, touching her, reassuring her. And still she cried, for who or what she didn't even know. All she knew was that the relief was so strong, so sweet. It felt like the first rain in summer after a long July.

Ian made no effort to hush her. He just let her go, holding her, lending her his strength.

When finally she quieted, she went limp against him, her strength gone. She tensed, waiting for the questions, the judgment or even the analysis, but they said nothing. Ian continued to stroke her hair as the fire died down to brightly glowing embers.

He arranged the covers around them, content to just hold her. Nothing had ever felt better. She'd never felt as whole as she did in this moment, as if she'd spent her entire life searching. For this.

She reached for him, reached up and curled her arms around his neck, wanting to hold him as he'd held her. She tucked her head against his shoulder and looked over at Braden who still sat to the side. Their eyes met, and she found warm acceptance in the liquid green of Braden's gaze.

She didn't smile but neither did he. And then she reached out her hand. He lifted his to meet her halfway. Their fingers twined and their palms met, flush against each other.

Still holding his hand, she let her eyelids flutter softly downward. They drooped even as she fought to keep them open. Braden rubbed his thumb across the top of her hand then pulled it up to his lips.

She snuggled deeper into Ian's arms as his warmth bled into her heart...and soul.

Her last conscious image was of Braden's lips pressed to her hand.

"She's asleep," Braden murmured a long moment later.

Ian shifted carefully and looked down at Katie's closed eyes. His heart turned over and did funny things in his chest. Then he looked back up at Braden.

"What just happened here?" he asked quietly.

Braden lowered her hand, careful not to awaken her. "I think I just decided that I can't let her go."

Ian tensed and held onto her a little tighter. She was draped over him, her body warm and limp. Her soft breathing filled his ears, and he realized that there was no way he would let her go either.

"What the fuck are we going to do?" he murmured.

"Fuck if I know," Braden said grimly. "I'm not going to risk her, Ian. She means..." He broke off and looked away. When he glanced back, Ian could see the emotion swirling in his eyes. "She means too much, more than Esteban. More than a cure."

Ian leveled a stare at his brother. "I agree."

Braden lifted one eyebrow in question. Ian merely nodded. They both wanted her.

"Is that going to be a problem?" Ian asked evenly.

Braden stared for a long moment then finally shook his head. "No," he said slowly. "It's not a problem."

Chapter Thirty-Three

Katie opened her eyes and blinked to clear away the cobwebs. She'd slept and slept hard, thanks in part to the drugs Ian and Braden had given her, but also their sweet lovemaking.

She glanced around the living room to see it empty. The fire had been built up again, but the men were nowhere to be found. No sound came from the kitchen, and she frowned as she swung her legs over the side of the couch. Wrapping a blanket around herself, she got up and headed across the living room to the kitchen and did a quick check, but didn't see them by the stove. She saw movement out of the corner of her eye and zeroed in on the front window.

She carefully pushed aside the worn curtain and peeked out to see Ian and Braden in conversation with Eli and Tits. They were standing beside sleek snowmobiles, and they all wore grim expressions. Had Esteban found them?

Adrenaline surged. She moved to the door and eased it open the barest of cracks. Given their propensity to protect her, chances were they'd shut up the minute she made her presence known.

Cold wind blew in, and she levered the door so that it was barely open a slit. Their voices carried to her, faint at first but then louder at intervals.

"Esteban is on the move. We recorded a sudden burst of activity from men known to be loyal to him. They're coming here," Eli said.

"The bait worked then," Braden said with a satisfied nod.

Tits looked up at Ian and Braden. "Does Katie know she's

being used to draw Esteban out?"

Ian shook his head. "There's no reason for her to know."

"I'd think she'd need to know so she doesn't inadvertently do anything to endanger herself," Tits said.

Braden scowled. "We're perfectly capable of taking care of Katie. She's done what she needed to do which is stay with us in one place long enough for Esteban to pick up her trail."

The wind kicked up, blowing a smattering of snow. She strained to hear but only caught words.

Trap.

Bait.

Expendable.

Sacrifice.

She stared woodenly at the men as they continued to converse, and then Ian and Braden turned to stare at the door. She eased it closed, making sure there was no noise, and then she hurried to the bedroom.

She sat on the edge of the bed so it would appear she'd just gotten up from the living room and come in here to get dressed. All the while her mind raced to make sense of what she'd been able to pick up from their conversation.

One part of her was pissed. She wanted to feel angry and betrayed, but that emotion was reserved for relationships. She had nothing invested in them and vice versa.

She closed her eyes and swallowed the deep disappointment, the betrayal she shouldn't feel but did. They'd made her no promises, not verbal. They'd made plenty with their bodies, though, promises she'd taken to heart. She didn't want to feel hurt, but the truth was, she was devastated.

Still, she didn't appreciate being a sitting duck. They hadn't told her anything, and once again, in her naïve stupidity, she hadn't demanded more. She'd been too caught up in the idea that finally, after years of running, she was enjoying a moment's respite. A brief escape from fear. When in fact, danger had never left her.

She was to blame for being too trusting when Gabe had taught her never to trust anyone.

She blew out her breath and willed herself not to become

too emotional. Ian and Braden were doing what it was they did best. Act the mercenaries and use whatever means necessary to take down their target. Even if they'd become everything to her, she wasn't anything to them, and she couldn't fool herself into thinking she was. That would get her into a lot of trouble, not to mention turn her into a spineless moron. Who was she kidding? She was already there.

So what was she going to do? It was obvious they didn't mind sacrificing her if it achieved their objective. She didn't particularly want to die nor did she want to end up in the middle of a fight that wasn't hers. Which meant the best idea was to get the hell out of here.

A few problems. She was in fucking Austria. In the mountains. Lots of snow. No money, no ID. She could stay and wait it out, but if she did, there was no question that she'd place herself in danger. Esteban was coming. For her.

Her gaze went to the bag on top of the dresser. She did have some cash. Dollars, but still, it was better than nothing. She had her bankcard.

Excitement stirred in her belly. Braden or Ian, she couldn't remember which, had mentioned a fake passport when she said she didn't have one. It hadn't registered at the time because she honestly hadn't believed she was leaving the country. But they would have needed something for her.

She hurried over and rummaged through her bag. Just her stuff, money, cards, her clothes. Not that she thought they would have put her passport with her junk.

With a quick glance in the direction of the door, which still remained closed, she tore through their bags. There, in the bottom, three passports. She opened one and discarded it, going on to the next.

Brenda Mullins. A picture that could have been Katie or not stared back at her. It was fuzzy but passable. The woman had the same hair color and features. Someone only giving it a passing glance would be fooled. Bingo.

She grabbed the passport and stashed it in her bag underneath her clothing. She needed time to formulate a plan of action which meant she was stuck here pretending that nothing was wrong and that she was the same clueless moron she'd been since she arrived.

At least the sex would be good.

Braden stood in the biting cold as he, Ian, Eli and Tits formed their plan of action. The Falcon secondary had positioned itself in a wide radius around the cabin. If Esteban or his men got close, they'd know about it.

"We need someplace to stash Katie after he's made his move," Ian said grimly. "I don't want her around when the shooting starts. I don't want her anywhere that she's in danger. Nothing is worth risking her."

Eli nodded. "I understand, but we may not have a choice in the matter. You and Braden can cover her. Tits and I will take care of Esteban. We want him alive. The rest of his men are expendable."

"Just understand I won't sacrifice her for him," Braden cut in. "We don't know that he has a cure, and I'm not throwing her to the wolves in order to find out."

Ian nodded his agreement.

Eli studied Braden for a moment and then included Ian in his scrutiny. "You guys seem...calmer. More stable. I don't know. Something's different. Are you still taking the sedative?"

Ian frowned and looked at Braden. Realization was slow in coming. Braden wasn't sure he understood the implications.

"We haven't taken it in days," Ian said in a low voice.

"You haven't shifted?" Eli asked sharply.

Braden shook his head. "No. I haven't even felt one coming on. I haven't felt threatened."

Ian continued to stare at Braden, a brooding look on his face. There was hope but also a sense of confusion.

Braden looked down at his hands and up his arms as if he expected his skin to come alive, the crawling incessant itch that signaled a shift. And yet he felt nothing. He felt...normal.

"I don't understand," he said numbly. "Just days ago we were both so unstable that we had to take turns knocking each other out. Ian killed a man."

Tits shrugged. "Don't knock good fortune. Just keep the drugs handy, unless of course you're staring at Esteban, and then feel free to let the kitty rip."

"Alive," Eli reminded Tits. "We need him alive. Too much is riding on what he knows."

"You know how to ruin happy thoughts," Tits grumbled. "I was getting all warm and fuzzy over the image of Esteban being kitty food."

"I was rather fond of the idea myself," Braden said.

Eli offered a half smile. "You can kill him after we've extracted the information we need."

"I think I just came in my pants," Tits said.

"You sure you just didn't piss yourself in fear?" Braden smirked.

"Fuck you." Tits shoved Braden's shoulder. "Or better yet, let me fuck your girlfriend."

Ian's lip curled into a snarl. His eyes glittered with a feral light as he advanced on Tits.

"Well, shit," Tits muttered. "How long did you say it had been since he shifted?"

Eli grabbed hold of Ian's arm. "Calm down, man. He was joking." He glanced at Braden for help, and Braden stepped forward, his hand going over Ian's shoulder.

"Why don't you go back inside," Braden said quietly. "Check on Katie. Make sure she's okay."

The blaze died in Ian's eyes and then he swore as he ran a hand through his hair. "Christ," he muttered. "It's her. She has us all sorts of fucked up."

Tits chuckled. "That's what a woman does, my man. Puts more knots in your dick than a climbing rope."

"Keep us posted, Eli," Ian said as he started toward the cabin. "I don't want to be caught with our pants around our ankles."

"We'll let you know if something goes down," Eli said. "You and Braden stay safe."

Braden watched as his brother mounted the steps to the cabin, and then he turned back to Tits and Eli. "He's right. There's something about Katie that either soothes us or sets us off. Doesn't make a lot of sense, but there it is. Ian is particularly affected. If he thinks Katie's in danger, he's completely unpredictable. I'm saying all this because I'm not sure that when this all goes down that either of us will be any help. Which means Katie will be vulnerable. She's going to need your help if Ian and I are out of commission."

Eli put his hand on Braden's shoulder. "We'll keep her safe, Braden."

Tits nodded his acknowledgement. Then he held up his fist to Braden's. "We're going to get on out of here and wait for Esteban to do his thing. Check you later."

Braden bumped his fist. Eli and Tits climbed onto the snowmobiles and roared off over the snow, leaving Braden standing there in the cold. He turned and slowly climbed the steps to the cabin.

In theory, the idea of using Katie to draw out Esteban was sound. In reality, it sucked. When she was a faceless entity, he had no compunction about using the sister of the man who'd betrayed them to flush out a rat. But she wasn't a faceless, unimportant factor anymore. He didn't want her at risk. He didn't want her here at all. He wanted her someplace safe. He wanted her to have the security she'd never experienced.

Katie had posed the question. What happened after Esteban was no longer a threat? It was something he'd asked often enough himself. Only now he had the answer. He wasn't letting her go. Her future was inexorably tied to his and Ian's.

Chapter Thirty-Four

Tension she couldn't ascribe to her own feelings had permeated the cabin. Katie glanced warily in the direction of Ian and Braden. Both men sat at the small table next to the window, eating in silence.

She'd done an admirable job of pretending complete ignorance. She'd been flirty, casual and relaxed while Ian and Braden had both been quiet, withdrawn and moody. And more protective than ever. She couldn't piss without one of them hovering. If she hadn't heard directly from the horse's mouth what their plans were, she'd still be floundering in ignorance, accepting whatever they doled out and begging for more.

She shook her head in disgust. Time was running out, and now she was going to be forced to make *her* move.

Without a glance in their direction, she slipped into the bedroom. She pressed her hands to her pants to stop the trembling and to dry the sweat from her palms.

She touched the two syringes full of the sedative and placed them on the dresser. Then she made sure her bag was packed, her cards, money and passport on top of her clothing. An earlier check outside had yielded two snowmobiles, both with keys in the ignition.

She could see lights of a distant village further down the mountain from the cabin deck. She'd head there and then get what transportation she could. By the time Ian and Braden regained consciousness, she'd be three countries away.

New life, fresh start. A chance at redemption.

Without Gabe. Without Ian and Braden. Pain sucked the air from her lungs. She closed her eyes and held back the dismay clogging her throat. *Without Ian and Braden.* Nothing had ever hurt so much.

Ian closed the satellite receiver and glanced up at Braden. "Esteban is moving in. Personally."

Braden's gaze sharpened and a light of anticipation flared in his eyes. "Arrogant son of a bitch."

"He's moving with a small band of men. If the Falcon secondary can get a bead on him, they'll eliminate his team and take Esteban alive. Eli and Tits are on their way here. If Esteban makes it all the way to Katie, we want to be sure she doesn't get caught in the crossfire."

"We need to tell her what's up," Braden said.

Ian nodded as he pushed away from the table. His own brand of anticipation singed along his skin. "How are you feeling?" he asked Braden as he paused outside the bedroom door. "We need to be at our best, and our best is not drugged."

"I'm good," Braden said. "Other than the fact that I'm looking forward to kicking some serious ass, I feel pretty calm."

Ian blew out his breath in relief. So far so good. Now to stash Katie somewhere she would gain the least amount of exposure.

The two brothers walked into the bedroom to see Katie sitting on the bed, her hands tucked underneath her legs. She looked up with wary eyes, and Ian couldn't blame her. He and Braden hadn't exactly been warm toward her for the last two days.

He approached her with Braden and cupped a hand to her cheek. "Katie, we need to talk."

She launched herself forward, her hands flying out in a blur. Ian felt a stab of pain in his arm even as he stared dumbly at her.

"What the hell?" Braden roared just as realization of what she had done hit Ian full force.

Ian staggered back and yanked at the needle still stuck in

his arm. She'd pushed the stopper to its limit and injected him with a full dose of the sedative.

She shot up but Braden grabbed her arm and tossed her back onto the bed. She scooted backward on the mattress, her eyes wild.

"Katie, what the fuck?" Ian demanded, and then he shook his head. He didn't have time to ask questions. He had to make her understand what was about to take place. That danger was coming, and now he and Braden would be out of commission.

Braden staggered and braced himself against the bed. "What have you done?" he whispered. "Why?"

"I'm not expendable," Katie said quietly. "My life may not be important to you, but I'm not giving it up that easily. I've run too hard for too long to give up now. I won't be used as bait for Esteban. I'll no longer be used by any man."

Ian's muscles twitched and seized as the predator locked within the man fought for freedom, fought against the sedative coursing through his veins. Beside him, Braden lunged for Katie. He landed on top of her but she lay there calmly, waiting for him to succumb.

Ian held his hands to his ears to dim the roaring. He shook his head, trying to shake off the sluggish lethargy stealing over his body.

"Katie," he whispered. "You don't understand. Esteban...coming."

"Yeah, I know," she said bitterly as she stared at him with hard, glittering eyes. "He's coming for me. I just don't plan to be here when he arrives."

Panic surged, and for a moment he thought the adrenaline would overpower the sedative. "No," he slurred. "You can't go. Dangerous. He's out there. Stay where safe."

He felt himself falling, and then Katie was over him, shoving him until he faced the ceiling. Her face loomed close to his. And then she kissed him. Lingeringly. With regret. Soft. A goodbye. He tried to reach for her, to hold her against him but she pushed aside his hands as if they were nothing.

Darkness clouded his periphery and still he fought. She didn't stand a chance on her own. She thought he and Braden had betrayed her.

"*No,*" he croaked out.

Katie hurried to the dresser to collect her bag. She pulled on Ian's heavy sweatshirt and snagged a jacket from the floor. After she'd donned the heavier clothes, she chanced one last look back at the two unconscious men.

The knot grew tighter in her throat. For just a little while, she'd allowed herself to become ensconced in the fantasy of having these two men care about her. Worse, though, she'd allowed herself to care about them. Men and sex were her biggest weaknesses, apparently. The fact that she clearly hadn't learned her lesson with Paulo told her she was as careless as ever when it came to jumping into a situation.

But she'd survived, and this time she was getting out on her own terms. She squared her shoulders, collected her bag and grasped one of the assault rifles. Slinging the strap over her shoulder, she walked briskly toward the cabin door.

She stepped into the cold night. The chill was a slap in the face in a good way. An awakening from her morose thoughts and regrets. Her survival was all that mattered right now. Ian and Braden would be just fine.

Unless...

She stared back, indecision wracking her cluttered mind. Had she left them completely vulnerable to Esteban? If he came here looking for her, he'd find two unconscious men.

For a woman who'd had only herself to consider for so long and no compunction about doing so, it was extremely unsettling to realize that Ian and Braden could die because of her. No matter that they'd callously used her for their own purposes.

She didn't want them to die.

Her fingers tightened around the rifle, and then in the distance, roaring closer, the sound of snowmobiles shattered the still of the night.

Chapter Thirty-Five

Lights nearly blinded her as two snowmobiles roared up to the cabin. As soon as the riders stepped clear, she could make out their outline in the pale moonlight. Eli and Tits. And then Eli simply disappeared.

Tits started for her, his expression fierce. Indecision tormented her for all of two seconds. An eerie sensation wrapped around her body, her neck and her wrists, momentarily paralyzing her.

And then she remembered that Eli could shift to smoke or mist.

Her hands shook as she warred with the need to hold onto the rifle while Eli exerted steady pressure on her wrists.

"Drop it, Katie," Tits ordered as he trained his gun on her. "Where are Ian and Braden?"

A shot cracked the night, and Tits staggered then fell to his knees. He squeezed off a series of shots into the trees before he fell face-forward into the snow.

Esteban was here.

Fear, cold like the snow, trickled down her spine. She thought of Ian and Braden inside the cabin and knew she couldn't allow them to be killed.

"I know you can hear me," she whispered to Eli. "Don't shift back. Ian and Braden are unconscious in the bedroom. You have to protect them. I'll lead Esteban away."

"*No.*"

She felt more than heard the faint whisper as it trailed over her ear.

"You know I'm right," she hissed. "Let me go. You have to cover Ian and Braden. They're defenseless right now. At least give me a chance to live, Eli. Give us all a chance."

The pressure lessened at her wrists, and she didn't waste any time. She leaped off the porch and threw herself on the still-running snowmobile. She gunned the engine and spun the machine around, sending a spray of snow arcing into the air.

As she headed around a clump of trees, she saw a group of four snowmobiles headed straight for her. She had always loved a good game of chicken. And it wasn't like she had anything to lose.

She yanked her rifle up with her right hand and gripped the wheel with her left. She gave it everything she had.

The snowmobile lurched forward and flew toward the oncoming lights. When she was impossibly close, she laid down a line of fire and aimed straight for the middle.

At the last second, the one on the far right spun out and turned end over end into the trees. The second and third split right and left to avoid her, and she skimmed past, kicking up snow in her wake.

She lowered her head, blinking against the stinging wind and the water forming in the corners of her eyes as ice pelted her face.

She hit a soft patch of snow and the snowmobile bogged for a moment. She gunned it, fishtailed and finally broke free. A glimpse behind her told her that she had at least three men on her tail.

She turned in the direction of the village and prayed she'd be able to find her way in the darkness. The headlight bounced off the snow but didn't give her much lead time to avoid pitfalls.

Lights reflected off the snow in front of her. They were getting closer, flanking her as they closed in. Out of the corner of her eye, she saw the one on her right creep up. She veered sharply in front of him. His machine clipped her back end as she cut him off.

It yanked her right but she recovered while he careened wildly into the path of one of the other snowmobiles. A loud crash splintered and then an explosion rocked the night. A ball of flame shot upward, bathing the area in an orange glow.

She jumped a rise, becoming airborne. She hit the ground with a resounding jolt and skidded sideways, bogging down in the snow. She yanked the wheel, gave it some gas and righted herself. As she chanced a look over her shoulder, her spirits sank. How many more were there?

Four sets of headlights bore down on her. Did they reproduce like bunnies? Every time she took one out, two took its place.

And then a loud rumble reverberated over her ears. The ground shook, causing the snowmobile to vibrate wildly. She looked behind her again only to see a wall of white envelope the headlights like a suffocating cloud.

Panic welled, fierce and nauseating.

Avalanche.

One of the snowmobiles raced before the steamrolling wave of snow. She was no longer the man's aim. Survival was. He raced in front of her as they both stayed barely ahead of the rumbling crush.

She leaned forward and let loose. She surged past the other snowmobile, her lights dancing over the snow like a drunken ballerina. Trees, rocks, bushes bounced up and down, puppets on stiff strings. She rocked over inclines, nearly thrown free of her seat.

She looked again just in time to see the other snowmobile go under the rolling white death. The machine flipped and then rolled end over end, the man's body bouncing with it before finally being thrown clear and quickly buried under several feet of snow.

Her heart sank. She couldn't outrun it.

Not wanting to become entangled in the snowmobile, she made a quick decision. Closing her eyes, she dove right, hitting the ground with a bone-jarring crunch. She rolled as both she and the snowmobile were swallowed whole. White descended and all went silent inside her icy tomb.

Eli simmered through the air, a thin plume of smoke, and

streaked toward where Tits had fallen in the snow. Blood, brilliant red, stained the pristine white on the ground as the snowmobiles bounced by in pursuit of Katie.

"I know you're there, you crazy bastard," Tits grunted out. "Leave me and go after her."

When he was certain the snowmobiles had passed, their engines echoing in the distance, he came to form beside Tits, his hands already going out to staunch the flow of blood from Tits' shoulder.

"Why'd you let her go?" Tits asked in halting stutters.

"Because she was right," Eli said grimly. "Ian and Braden are our priorities, and they're lying in the cabin out cold."

"Why'd she go crazy?"

"Hell if I know. She could have shot us both. She could have left Ian and Braden to die."

"But she didn't."

"She didn't," Eli agreed.

Holding his palm to Tits' bleeding wound, he pushed at the larger man, helping him to his knees. "Come on man, let's get you into the cabin before you bleed to death."

"It's not bad," Tits said as he hoisted himself to his feet. "I've had worse."

Still, he stumbled as they started for the cabin, and Eli dug his shoulder under Tits' arm to support the larger man.

They slowly climbed up the steps, and Tits paused for a long moment, catching his breath before they headed for the door.

Eli maneuvered it open with his free hand and started to haul Tits forward when a loud rumble had them both turning around. The entire porch shook. The sounds of breaking glass came from within as plates fell from the counter and splintered on the floor.

"What the fuck?" Tits demanded.

"Oh hell," Eli muttered.

He and Tits exchanged looks of horror as the realization hit them both.

"Avalanche!" Tits yelled.

"Get in, now!" Eli shoved Tits forward just as the spray of snow hit him in the back. He fell to the floor but kicked at the door with his foot and prayed like hell it would hold.

Chapter Thirty-Six

"Getting out of here should be a snap for a man of your means," Tits said darkly.

"I never said it wouldn't be," Eli returned.

The two men sat in the dark with only a penlight to illuminate the interior of the cabin. The door had miraculously held. The windows had not. Broken glass littered the living room along with piles of snow and ice.

It was cold but not unbearably so.

"I need to check on Ian and Braden. Are you going to be okay?"

Tits waved the penlight in a dismissive gesture.

"I'll make sure they're all right, and then I'll see if I can use the satellite uplink to reach Jonah. I'd prefer they got here before any local rescue effort. If I can't raise him that way, I'll shift and go out the chimney. I'll go to the village and get word to them that way."

Again Tits waved the light, and Eli got to his feet and made his way to the bedroom.

There was only one window, and it too was busted out. Snow was steadily dribbling and shifting onto the floor from the strain. Ian and Braden were sprawled on the bed, out like a light. Damn, but he needed them awake and aware.

"Hey Tits, can you come back here, man, or are you too weak?"

Eli almost laughed at the snarl that followed. A few seconds later, Tits thumped into the bedroom holding his shoulder with one hand.

"Thought that would get your ass in here," Eli said.

"Hey, fuck you. What the hell do you want, anyway? I was comfortable."

"I need you to see if you can wake up the sleeping beauties while I raise Jonah."

"I could always stick their faces in the wall of snow at the window," Tits said with a shrug.

"Do what you have to do. I'll get Jonah on the way."

"They ain't going to be happy about what happened to Katie," Tits said quietly.

Eli grimaced, knowing full well that surviving the avalanche on a snowmobile was next to impossible. "I'll let you tell them," he muttered.

"Gee thanks. You're all heart, man."

Eli turned away and then dug into his pack for the satellite transmitter and tiny keyboard. No, he didn't want to be the one to tell Ian and Braden about Katie. She was a lot more to them than just an assignment. He didn't want to break the news that she was dead.

Ian pulled his way sluggishly from the heavy blanket of sleep. Someone was yelling his name and shaking him. His limbs were lead-filled, and none of them were cooperating with his command to move.

"That's it, man, open your eyes. Look at me, damn it."

"What the hell?" he slurred out then licked his dry, cracked lips.

A palm slapped sharply at his face, and Ian snarled in irritation.

"Get mad all you want. I'm not going away."

"Tits?"

Ian opened his eyes to see Tits staring down at him, pain etched in his face and blood smeared over his shoulder and chest.

Remembrance slammed into him. He bolted upright, Katie's name on his lips. He stared over to see Braden still unconscious on the bed.

"Where is she?" he growled.

Tits glanced warily at him. "Don't try any of that shifting shit on me, man. I'll knock your ass out again, and I'll make sure you sleep for three days straight."

"Where. Is. She."

"She's gone," Tits said softly. "Now help me get your brother awake. We're up shit creek without a paddle here. I'll explain the best I can as soon as we figure out how the hell to get out of here."

Ian looked around the darkened cabin in confusion. There was light from a flashlight standing upright on the nightstand, and another smaller light sat on the dresser. It was just enough that he could make out Tits and the area immediately surrounding him, but beyond that, there was nothing.

He saw the glass lying in a puddle of water on the floor, and then he saw the bulge of snow against the shattered window.

"What the ever-loving fuck?"

"Avalanche," Tits said grimly. "We're snowed in until Falcon gets here to pull our asses out. Eli's on the horn with them now."

Tits turned his attention to Braden, shaking him like a rag doll as he shouted at him to wake up. Ian shook the cobwebs from his own head and put the pieces back together in his mind. Katie had drugged them. She thought... She'd obviously overheard some of their conversation with Tits and Eli. It was the only explanation for why she thought they were using her to get to Esteban, or at least why she'd assumed the worst.

Hell.

"Does Esteban have Katie?" Ian asked hoarsely.

Tits shot him a grim look. Braden stirred and muttered as Tits continued to harass him.

Frustrated, Ian reached over and hauled Braden up by his shirt collar. He shook him then slapped him repeatedly on the cheek with his open palm. Braden's eyes shot open belligerently, and he shoved at Ian.

"What the fuck is your problem, man?"

"Wake up. We've got problems," Ian said brusquely.

Braden rubbed his eyes wearily and shook his head a few times. Then he bolted to awareness, grabbing Ian by the collar.

"Katie. Where is she?"

"Tits is just about to tell us." He glanced over at Tits, not liking the uneasy look on the other man's face.

"What the hell happened to you, Tits?" Braden demanded as he took in the blood all over his shirt.

"Took a bullet from Esteban's men," Tits said shortly.

"Katie?" Braden asked hesitantly.

Tits looked up in relief when Eli strode into the room. "You get Jonah?"

"Yeah, they're on the move. ETA six hours. An extrication team will reach us first. No idea on the Falcon secondary who were with us on the mountain. Jonah's afraid they were all buried by the avalanche."

"Katie?" Ian asked again. He was beginning to sound like a damn parrot.

Eli shot Tits a scowl. "You haven't told them yet?"

"I was getting to it," Tits mumbled.

"Why don't you tell us since Tits is having a hard time with the English language all of a sudden," Braden said, his voice hard.

Eli ran a hand through his shoulder-length hair and shot the brothers a look of sympathy. "We don't think she made it."

A fist slammed into Ian's gut, knocking the breath right out of him. Braden didn't look any better. He paled, and his fingers curled into tight balls.

"What do you mean she didn't make it?" Braden asked in a deadly quiet voice.

"When we rode up, she was on the porch with an assault rifle and her bag. She was about to bolt," Eli began. "I shifted so I could gain position on her. Then Tits took a bullet. They obviously had staked out the cabin. Katie told me to let her go so she could lead Esteban away from you and Braden. She said you were unconscious and helpless. She asked for a chance to live. For all of you to live."

"*And you let her go?*" Ian shouted.

"I had three men down," Eli said calmly. "She was right."

"What happened?" Braden snarled.

"She took off on the snowmobile, and Esteban's men took off after her. Several minutes later as I was getting Tits into the cabin, we got hit by the avalanche. She couldn't have been far enough away to have avoided it," he finished quietly.

"Mother of God," Ian said hoarsely.

No. She couldn't be dead.

"What are you so worked up about, man? She screwed you over. Drugged your asses and was all set to ditch you."

"Because she thought we'd fucked her over first," Ian bit out. "She had to have overheard our conversation outside the other day and misunderstood."

"What was to misunderstand?" Eli asked. "You *were* using her. Or did I miss something here?"

"We were protecting her." Grief was thick in Braden's voice. "We would have never let Esteban get to her. That wasn't the plan. That was never the plan."

"How long?" Ian demanded. "How long since the avalanche? How long has she been out there in the cold?"

Eli flashed him a look of sympathy. "Three hours. She couldn't survive that long."

Braden shot up from the bed. "Where's the locator?"

Ian looked up, his brow creased.

"The tracking device," Braden said impatiently. "I had Marcus put one back in when he stitched her up. It should show up on the locator."

"Braden, man, it's been three hours," Tits said.

"I don't care," he roared. "Even if she's dead, I'm not leaving her out there to rot. She deserves better than that. She's always been left behind. This time she won't be."

Ian stood, his mind numb. He moved jerkily, like an automaton with no clear direction. His gaze scoured the room in search of the locator. He staggered to the two bags by the window and ripped into them. Everything was soggy from the melted snow. God, let the locator still work.

He yanked it out and hit the power button. Nothing happened.

"Goddamn it!" He hit the button again.

"Let me have it," Braden demanded as he strode over. "I can take it apart and dry it out. It might work again."

"Jonah will have another," Eli said.

"We don't have six hours to wait for them to come rescue us," Ian seethed. "If we can get a bead on her location, you can shift and get out of here."

Eli and Tits exchanged uneasy glances which only enraged Ian further. They'd already given her up for dead.

He tossed the unit up to Braden. Braden snatched one of the lights from the dresser and went back over to the bed.

While he worked feverishly, Ian paced, his gaze going to the blocked window.

"Have you tried digging out? Have you shifted and gone above to see what we're facing here? Have you tried digging down from the outside?"

Eli put a hand on Ian's shoulder. "The cabin is covered, Ian. We need more than one man with a shovel. Jonah's on his way with back-up. We'll get out, I swear."

"Yeah, but will we be in time?"

Eli shook his head. "You have to know, Ian. The chances of her surviving...they aren't good."

Ian closed his eyes. "Why did you give her up for me?"

"You know the answer to that," Eli said patiently. "If you think about it, you'll know I didn't have any other choice. I had a wounded man and two more out of commission. There was no way I could stave off all of Esteban's men alone. Katie led them away. Don't take away from her sacrifice."

"I just don't understand why she did it." Ian dropped his head as grief and anger surged over him. "She told me...one of the last things she said was that she wasn't expendable. That her life mattered. So why then did she suddenly decide she gave a damn about the fact that Braden and I were sitting ducks here?"

"I can't answer that," Eli said quietly. "But I bet you can if you look deep enough. It was probably for the same reason you're considering digging out of here with your bare hands. She's more to you than a job, Ian. And I'd say you were more to her than just someone her brother sent to save her ass."

Anguish, harsh, so heavy that his knees buckled, hit him. He turned, his hands flying to his face in an attempt to make the reality go away.

He sagged, and Eli caught him. They both fell and their knees hit the floor with a jolt. Eli caught the back of Ian's neck as Ian's forehead hit Eli's shoulder.

"I'm sorry, man," Eli said. "I know how I'd feel if someone told me Tyana was out there. I wouldn't accept it either. But it wouldn't change a damn thing."

Ian's breaths roared from his lungs like fire. Each inhalation hurt, hit him with such savagery. He hadn't kept her safe. He'd failed her just like everyone else in her life. And too late, he realized he wanted to be different. He wanted to be the one she could trust. Love. Rely on.

"Don't you fucking give up," Braden snarled.

Ian's head came up, and he saw Braden staring at him, answering grief simmering in his eyes. They glittered with moisture, and his entire mouth twitched. His jaw jumped and spasmed, and Ian realized how hard he was hanging on to his control.

Slowly, he stood, using Eli for leverage. He walked over to the bed where his brother was piecing together the locator.

"I won't give up," he vowed as he locked gazes with Braden. "I won't give up until we find her. Even if it's just to recover her body and bring her home. She deserves that much."

Braden nodded and held out his hand. Ian grasped it. A current of power passed between the two men. In that moment, Ian knew that Braden had fallen as hard and fast for Katie as he had. And now neither of them would have a chance to take care of her—to love her—the way they both wanted.

Chapter Thirty-Seven

Braden stared at the array of waterlogged parts to the receiver with a tenuous grip on his fury. He wanted to hurl them against the wall and then he wanted to hit someone. Several times the beast inside had risen, snarling to be set free. The edgy, sharp sensation prickled along his skin, raising his hairs. The signal of an impending shift. He'd never fought so hard in his life to remain calm, to ward off the panther. Never before had he been successful.

Too much was riding on his ability to remain human. Katie was depending on him.

For the umpteenth time, he carefully wiped down each individual wire, each piece and then put it all back together in an effort to make it come to life.

When he finished, he hit the power button and held his breath.

Nothing.

With a snarl of fury, he hurled it across the room, and it shattered on impact. He thrust himself up from the bed, crossed to the wall and punched it for all he was worth.

The wall caved and dust from the sheetrock slid down and skittered onto the floor.

"Hey, lighten up," Eli said as he put his hand on Braden's shoulder.

Braden held up his hand, a clear warning for Eli to back off. He did.

"Don't tell me to lighten up. Would you lighten up if it was Tyana out there? Cold. Alone."

"No, man, I wouldn't," Eli said quietly.

"How's Tits?" Braden asked as he turned around. He sucked in his breaths, trying to soothe the fury that singed his veins and thundered in his ears.

"A little weak, but we stopped the blood. Looks like a flesh wound. He'll bitch and moan, but he'll be fine."

"I can't stand it, Eli. I can't stand to stay here any longer. I've got to get out of here."

"It won't be much longer," Eli soothed. "Jonah and Mad Dog and the rest of the Falcon secondary are getting here as fast as they can. The extrication team he already had on the ground should be here anytime."

Braden stared across the room to where Ian sat slumped in a chair, his head down, palm covering his forehead. What a fucking mess.

"I'll go out and have a look around again," Eli said. "It should be getting light soon."

Braden nodded, and Eli faded from view. Only a slight shadow streaking across the room signaled his departure. Ian looked up at Braden.

"We lost her, man."

Braden swallowed and willed himself to remain calm, not to let the anger—and the grief—tear out of his chest. He was pissed. If only they'd been upfront with Katie from the beginning or even later on, after they'd arrived in Austria. Hell, even after they'd started sleeping with her.

They'd had countless chances, but they'd been arrogant, too confident in their ability to control the situation. And neither had realized what they stood to lose until it was too damn late.

Braden turned away from his brother, no longer able to stand the pain in Ian's eyes. They mirrored his own agony too much.

A few minutes later, Eli strode back into the bedroom, his expression tight. "There are rescue crews further down the mountain. Nothing up here yet, but then we're pretty far out of the way. Chances are no one knew anyone was in this cabin."

"Have they recovered any survivors?" Ian asked, hope

edging into his voice.

"Just bodies," Eli said grimly. "Esteban's men and a few of the Falcon secondary. No sign of Katie. There's a team of men heading in our direction. Most likely Falcon, but we can't be too careful. Stay on your toes and have your guns at the ready."

The men walked back into the living room where Tits was propped up against the wall, his gun leaned against his uninjured shoulder. He stared at them with slitted eyes, monitoring their progress across the floor.

"How you holding up?" Eli asked.

"I'm good. Ready to go. No wimpy ass bullet's gonna take me down."

Eli squatted beside Tits. "We've got a team moving in."

Tits nodded and grasped the stock of his rifle, sliding the barrel down his body and then tilting it forward. "Well, let's do it, then."

Eli grasped his good arm, and Ian leaned in to help pull Tits to a standing position. Tits stared at Ian eye to eye, his expression serious.

"I'm sorry about Katie."

Ian swallowed and nodded shortly.

Thirty minutes later, they heard the sounds of equipment hitting the roof. Then light shone in the broken window on the left. A hand appeared as it scooped out snow, widening the beam of light.

"Guess it's time to greet our guests," Eli muttered as he strode to the window.

Ian moved in behind Eli and pointed his rifle toward the opening. Eli disappeared in a thin vapor trail and filtered up through the window. Braden joined Ian with Tits close behind.

"That shit makes me nervous," Tits muttered. "What if I inhaled the man?"

Braden shook with laughter despite the raw grief carved on his face.

A few seconds later, the hole got bigger, and a hand thrust a small receiver through the opening. Ian lunged for it, his hands shaking as he powered it up.

"We'll get you out shortly," one of the men hollered down.

Ian ignored him, turning away as he punched in the code for Katie's tracking device.

"Come on, come on," he murmured impatiently as he waited for the map to load.

The graphic flashed on the screen and the lines spread out, signaling the layout of the area. A hundred-mile radius. He frowned and keyed the code in again.

"What the fuck?" Braden demanded as he looked over Ian's shoulder.

"That's impossible." Ian keyed it in for the third time. "Something's wrong."

"What is it?" Tits asked as he too came over to look.

"She's not showing up," Braden said.

"Maybe all the snow interfered," Tits offered cautiously.

Ian shook his head. "That thing would work on the bottom of the ocean."

"Could it have fallen off?" Braden asked.

"It would still show up on the receiver," Ian said. "Marcus sewed it into her damn stitches. It didn't just fall out. The only explanation..."

He turned to Braden, afraid to hope, afraid to let Braden see his hope.

"What?" Braden demanded.

"The only explanation is that she's beyond the search radius," he said slowly.

Light sparked in Braden's eyes. "Widen it."

Ian rapidly keyed in the coordinates for the world map and held his breath. And then a small dot on the display screen started to blink.

Excitement exploded in his chest. Relief so profound he felt lightheaded. He yanked his gaze to Braden to see the same excitement burgeoning in his eyes.

"Where is she?" Braden asked hoarsely.

Ian frowned as he crosschecked the latitude and longitude. Then he looked back up at Braden and Tits.

"If my coordinates are correct, she's somewhere over the Atlantic."

Chapter Thirty-Eight

It really pissed Katie off that she had to be grateful to this creepy jerk for saving her life. She stared over at the worm who'd introduced himself as the notorious Esteban and curled her lips in disgust.

At least she'd stopped shaking. Finally. And the interior of the plane was nice and toasty. Which was good because she was convinced her skin had turned permanently blue.

Still, she hitched the blanket higher around her chin, more of a protective measure than one of true discomfort over the temperature.

Esteban's stare raked over her, and he locked gazes with her. She stared boldly back, refusing to let him cow her. She'd faced down enough bastards to recognize that he wasn't anything special in the sleaze department. Just a typical man full of himself and assured of his own importance.

He smiled, flashing crooked teeth. "You don't look very happy that I pulled you from the snow, Katie. I could have left you there, you know."

"I'm glad you pulled me out. I just wish you'd left me alone once you did," she snapped. "Where the hell are you taking me, and why do you want me so badly? I can't possibly have anything you want."

"Oh, but you do," he said softly. "You have something I want very much. You are, in fact, key to my success. Perhaps *the* key."

She furrowed her brow in genuine confusion. He was utterly serious, and for a moment, he even seemed sane. Which was scary in its own way. She didn't want to relate to this creep or even see him as half a human being.

"You'll have to forgive me if I'm not feeling too charitably toward you. You gassed my brother and his team. You made them what they are, and you're responsible for my brother's death. That makes you a son of a bitch, and I'd just as soon see you rot in hell than ever be the key to your anything."

"I regretted Gabe's death very much," Esteban said tightly. "It was senseless. He was vitally important to my program. He chose his path, and he chose to sacrifice himself for two failed prototypes."

"Prototypes? What the hell? They were men. Men you fucked over and made into unpredictable wild animals."

Esteban rubbed his face tiredly. "I don't expect you to understand. You're not a scientist."

"And you are?" she scoffed. "From what I heard, you own a pharmaceutical company, and you like to play God in your spare time. How the hell does that make you a scientist?"

She leaned forward. "Why do you want me? What part could I possibly play in all of this, and how could I be of any importance to your program?"

"You're Gabe's sister," he said evenly. "That makes you extremely important. You share the same genetic material. He was one of my successes while the Thomas brothers were dismal failures. How do you explain the stability of one man and the instability of another when they were introduced to the same set of conditions?"

She stared at him in shock. She opened her mouth to speak, but she honestly couldn't formulate a single word.

"You're getting the picture," he said with a small smile. "If Gabe was a success then chances are you will be too. And any children you have."

Nausea welled in her stomach. "You're not changing me into some wild animal," she whispered. "And I won't be a breeding machine."

He shrugged. "There's nothing to say you'll turn out to be a wild animal. Gabe could become invisible. Part of what makes this so interesting is learning what your gift will be. If you'll share the same traits as Gabe did or if all we'll be guaranteed is your stability, your ability to control your shifts and retain human cognizance in shifted form. It will be a fascinating experiment. Your eggs will be harvested for breeding purposes, so you don't have to worry about losing your figure to a pregnancy."

She was too horrified to protest, too dumbstruck to do anything but stare at him in absolute disbelief. Was he joking? He said it so flippantly, like he was doing her a grand favor by sparing her a pregnancy. And who the hell did he plan on fathering those babies?

A shudder rolled over her shoulders, and bile rose in her throat. She'd never been more disgusted in her life, and Ricardo de la Cruz was plenty heave-worthy.

"I'm not planning to hurt you, Katie," he said in a cajoling voice. "You're far too important to me. I plan to take very good care of you."

"Why?" she whispered. "Why on earth do you want people who can shift? Why would you force that on anyone?"

"It's merely a starting point," he said idly. "If I can alter human DNA and make a man a hybrid between human and beast, what else can I create?"

"You want to be God?"

"No, I wouldn't want his job," he said seriously. "It's not my place to judge, to make life or death decisions. Who gets to live, who gets to die. I'd rather offer humans choices."

"Oh, dear heaven," she groaned. "I take it you don't believe in the whole theory of free will? You believe in predestination? And if that's the case, don't you think God would have to be pretty stupid to preordain someone who could change all his rules?"

She hugged her knees to her chest, ignoring the pain in her ribs and the raw wound that had partially reopened in her fall from the snowmobile.

Esteban smiled ruefully. "You intrigue me, Katie. I hadn't expected you to be so difficult. I think you'll make a fascinating addition to my experiment."

"And what will you do once you've turned me into a trick pony?" she asked softly. "Are you just going to let me go? Let me go back to my life?"

His lips pressed together in an expression of regret, and

then he shook his head. "I'm sorry to say that your life as you know it is over. The sooner you accept it, the better off you'll be."

She eyed him coldly, allowing the full force of her hatred and disdain to bleed into her expression. "You've made some ambitious plans," she said in a mock congratulatory tone. "But you forgot to factor in one little variable. Make that two."

Esteban's eyebrow went up. "Oh? And what's that?"

"Ian and Braden Thomas," she said evenly.

"You think they give a damn about you?"

She smiled tightly. "I don't have any illusions where they're concerned, but I know how much they hate you. They're not going to give up hunting you."

For a moment annoyance flickered across his face, and then he shrugged nonchalantly. "If they do, they'll die."

"But I thought you didn't make life or death decisions?" she taunted.

"If they go after me, they choose death, I don't choose it for them," he said in a chilling voice. "Their deaths will be a consequence of their choices."

She stared at him calmly, confidence radiating. "And maybe your death will be the consequence of *your* choices."

Chapter Thirty-Nine

"The last time we went into a compound like this, I lost a man," Eli said grimly as he looked at the gathered men. "I don't want that to happen this time."

Jonah stood to the side, his arms crossed over his AK-47. He looked almost bored. Except for his eyes. They flickered alertly over the assembled group as if he were measuring each one.

Mad Dog and Tits flanked Ian and Braden, and Tits slapped at another bug, real or imagined, Ian wasn't sure.

"Goddamn it," Tits muttered. "The entire jungle is determined to have me for dinner."

"It's the fresh blood," Mad Dog drawled. "If you're not careful, they'll suck you dry. They grow 'em big here in South America."

"Hey, fuck you," Tits said. But he pressed a hand to his wound as if to prevent any bugs from invading the bandage.

"You boys done?" Jonah asked dryly. "We've got a job to do here. I'd just as soon quit fucking around and get it done."

Braden nodded his agreement. He was tense and edgy. Ian worried that he might be close to shifting, but neither of them wanted to risk taking a sedative and not being a hundred percent when they went in for Katie.

Her signal had led them deep into the Venezuelan jungle to a compound undetected by satellite. Mostly underground, what was above the terrain was hidden by heavy growth and lush foliage. Thank God for the tracking device or they would've never found her.

If Esteban had hurt her there would be no mercy. Obtaining a cure was no longer a priority, at least not for Ian and Braden. Ian knew that Falcon was still keenly interested in Esteban because of Damiano. All Ian cared about at this point was extracting Katie. Alive. Esteban could live or die.

Jonah looked toward Eli, a concession to the fact that he led this mission. Ian wasn't in the mood for a pissing match or a contest to see whose dick was bigger. The merger wasn't his idea. He didn't give a shit who called the shots as long as Katie got out alive.

"Let's go," Braden growled.

"I'll shift and find a ventilation system to get in. Give me a ten-minute head start so I can take down the security system," Eli said.

Tits stepped forward with a glance sideways at Mad Dog. "Our recon points at four possible entrance and exit points. Could be more."

"Katie's signal was pinpointed in the heart of the compound," Ian said. "We're going to need those exits secured and the paths clear. I don't want to rely on only one way out. I want a plan, and then I want plans B, C and fucking D. We can't afford to fuck this up."

Eli nodded. "If I fail to override the security, then those entrances will need to be blown. We lose some of the element of surprise which means you have to get in and move fast. Shoot first, sort bodies later. Esteban has proven what a complete and utter coward he is. He won't stick around to get caught in the crossfire."

"Okay, enough with the chitchat," Braden said. "Let's do this."

Eli took quick stock of his gear and then dissolved into the thick, humid air. Jonah checked his watch and began the countdown.

"I want the secondary manning those exits as soon as we gain access," Jonah said. "Two will remain outside to provide cover and to make sure no one crawls up our backsides." He looked at Mad Dog and Tits. "You two set the place to blow. I want this to be an in-and-out job. Our objectives are Katie, information and Esteban. In that order."

He pinned Ian and Braden with his hard stare. "Don't make this personal. Get in, get your girl, get the hell out. You'll take the central entrance and hone in on Katie's location. The other half of the secondary will be moving ahead of you to clear a path. You'll have back-up in front and behind you."

He glanced down at his watch. "Let's move. We have three minutes to go time. Take your positions and get ready to kick some ass."

Katie hunched down in the corner of the cold, sterile, glassed-in observation room, knees drawn up to her chest as she rocked back and forth in an effort to get warm.

The thin hospital gown she wore offered little protection from the bone-aching chill. It was as though Esteban had stored her in the freezer.

She laid her forehead on her arm and closed her eyes as she rocked harder. Her belly still cramped from the procedure performed just hours earlier. She'd been restrained on an exam table, her legs forced apart, and she'd lain there helpless as the first egg extraction had been performed.

Esteban had been delighted to discover that she was at the perfect time in her cycle. The discovery of two mature eggs ready to be released during ovulation had been enough for him to go ahead with the procedure instead of putting her through a regimen of fertility drugs as he'd threatened. Why he hadn't taken both at the same time, she didn't know. An important piece of the puzzle was missing, but she couldn't wrap her brain around what.

She couldn't feel more violated than if she'd been raped. This was worse. Much worse.

She ignored the tapping on the glass wall. It would be Esteban. Asking once again how she was doing. As if it mattered.

His voice filtered over the intercom system. "Prepare yourself, Katie. This next part...is not pleasant."

Her head came up, and she stared dully through the glass

to see Esteban standing by the speaker, his hand on the button.

"It will be over soon, though, and then you can rest," he said in a soothing voice.

What the hell could be worse than what she'd already been subjected to?

A hissing sound, like an airlock being broken, sizzled over her ears. She yanked her gaze up in alarm to see a cloudy vapor seeping into the room from every vent. She scrambled up, panic beating at her mercilessly.

The bastard was gassing her.

She turned and began to pound at the glass. "No! You son of a bitch. You can't do this!" she screamed. "This isn't my choice. I don't want this."

Esteban pressed his hand against the glass, mirroring hers. An expression of regret framed his face. He looked almost...sorry.

Fire raced over her skin. She inhaled as she cried out in pain and then coughed and choked as the chemical entered her lungs. Oh God, she was on fire from the inside out. Burning.

Her hands slapped and wiped frantically at her skin. She was melting. Her skin was going to slide right off her bones.

Her eyes singed, and tears poured copiously down her cheeks. She fell, writhing, to the ground. Agony. She couldn't take it.

Razor blades scoured her flesh, marking her, but she didn't bleed. She had no blood to give. It boiled in her veins. Burned like acid.

She clawed frantically, trying to relieve the pressure, to give the poison somewhere to go, to escape. Her throat closed in. Her tongue swelled, and she tried in vain to draw a breath.

She was going to die. She *wanted* to die.

Numbly, she lay there, her entire body twitching as her nerve endings fired. The floor felt cool against her cheek and she rubbed, trying to infuse more of the blessed chill into her tormented body.

Saliva pooled in her mouth, odd against her dry, cracked tongue. It leaked onto the floor as her eyes became fixed and unblinking, focused blindly on the opposite wall.

Her hand. It wouldn't quit moving. It jumped, her fingers extending and hopping. She curled them into a ball in an attempt to make it stop.

Ants. She was covered in fire ants. They were eating her alive. A sob escaped her lips.

"Let me die," she whispered.

Rain, sweet and refreshing, poured down on her. Water hit her with bruising force as it fell from the ceiling. She curled into a ball and held her hands over her face. After a moment it stopped and then quiet descended.

She tried to move, but her body wouldn't obey her commands. She was locked in the worst kind of hell. On the inside the pain still raced, surging through her veins like a brushfire. The bitter chill, made worse by the soaking she'd received, encased the outside of her body.

But worse than the pain was the fear of what he'd turned her into.

Chapter Forty

Ian and Braden made fast tracks through the low-slung corridors that snaked toward the middle. Convoluted was apparently a favorite design of Esteban's. This one mirrored the building in Switzerland almost exactly.

Using the signal from Katie's tracking device, they navigated the twists and turns. Halfway in, everything went dark. Braden slapped on night vision goggles with infrared sensors and continued forward, his gun up.

A few seconds later, track lighting along the ceiling flickered and bathed the hallways with a dull glow.

Ian stopped outside a closed doorway and held up a finger and pointed. Braden gripped his gun tighter and nodded for Ian to go in. According to the locator, Katie was in the next room.

Ian slapped on the explosive, set the timer and then motioned for Braden to get down. Three seconds later, the door blew, and he and Ian rushed through the entry.

Braden staggered back when brilliant white light accosted his vision. He put a hand up to ward it off before making a sweep of the room with his rifle. It was empty. Save for a cylindrical platform in the middle of the room. A red beam illuminated a tiny container resting on the surface.

He and Ian exchanged glances. Where the fuck was Katie?

Dread tightened his gut as he walked slowly toward the platform. He knew what he'd find before he ever got there.

Almost invisible, sitting in what looked to be a Petri dish, was the thin, needle-like tracking device that Katie had worn.

"Mother fuck!" Ian swore as he spun around.

And then from the tiny holes that ringed the platform, smoke seeped upward, drifting higher and spreading out, faster and faster.

"Get out of here!" Braden shouted as he bolted for the door.

He was nearly there when rails slammed from the ceiling, barring his exit. He yanked around only to be enclosed by another set as they dropped like bricks, imprisoning him in a large square box.

Ian fared no better.

The two brothers stared at one another even as Braden felt every muscle go limp and unresisting. The room swam in his vision, and he felt himself fall. His head rolled to the side. His last conscious thought was of Katie and whether she'd died on the mountain after all.

Braden opened his eyes and saw only a blurred blob of vague color and slight movement. He blinked and blinked again, each time clearing some of the film from his vision.

He saw Katie, lying on the floor inside a glass enclosure, her eyes glassy and unfocused, fixed on some distant object. She was soaked, the thin gown she wore plastered to her body. She shivered uncontrollably, her body jerking as she clutched her arms to her chest.

Relief surged, sweet and soothing. She was alive.

Then rage followed, replacing the calm. It curdled in his veins, whispering and calling to the killer inside him. To the predator.

"What did you do to her?" he demanded as he saw Esteban step to the glass to stare at Katie.

Esteban turned, a smile on his face. He looked oddly calm, not at all the demented, frantic man they'd confronted in Switzerland.

"Ah, you're awake."

"What did you do to her?" he bit out again.

Esteban glanced back at Katie, his expression almost

regretful and as strange as it seemed, tender.

"I regret the pain I caused her, but that's over with now. She won't feel the second egg extraction."

"*What?*" Braden shouted. He tried to strain forward and only then did he realize that he was restrained standing up, his ankles secured to an iron plate with metal cuffs and his arms banded on either side of his head.

"Getting worked up won't help you," Esteban said calmly. "You can't shift. I've injected enough paralytic that I rather doubt you'll do much more than drool occasionally once it takes effect. It should be hitting you any time now."

Movement beside him alerted him, and he glanced over to see Ian similarly restrained. His eyes came open slowly, and he blinked as Braden had as he tried to bring his surroundings into focus.

"Leave her alone," Braden demanded. "You don't need her."

"Oh, but I do," Esteban said. "It's you I don't need. Your men have done a good job of gaining access to the compound and my security system, but the inner shell operates independently. It's steel reinforced and completely closed off from the rest. As soon as the outer perimeter is compromised, the inner hull goes into lockdown. I delayed it long enough for you to arrive."

"I thought you didn't need us," Braden said. "Why the elaborate hoax? Why bother leading us here at all?"

Esteban glanced back at Katie one more time and then he pressed a button and spoke rapidly in Spanish. Two men immediately walked into the containment room where Katie lay, both wearing biohazard suits.

Oh God, Katie. What have they done to you, baby?

He stared in agony as the two men carried her out of the glass enclosure. A few moments later they walked into the room where Esteban stood and laid her on the exam table. She lay there listlessly, her body shaking, her eyes unseeing.

Esteban tended to her, his motions gentle. He touched her cheek at one point and carefully pried her wet hair from her face.

And then he turned back to Braden. "It was actually something that Katie said on the plane. That I hadn't factored you and Ian into the equation. She was right. I gave you no thought other than thinking you a nuisance. Your instability made you unacceptable for my needs—or so I thought. My scientists are intrigued by you, though. They'll use you for research, and when you've served your purpose, you'll be disposed of. My concentration, however, will be on Katie."

"You'll never leave this place alive," Ian broke in, his face tight with anger.

Already, Braden could feel his limbs grow heavy. Lead traveled sluggishly through his veins. It was all he could do to lift his head.

"You're crazy," Braden slurred. "Certifiable."

"I assure you, I'm completely sane."

He turned to one of the men in a lab coat. He rattled off an order in Spanish, and Braden was too disoriented to follow the different dialect. But the intent was clear. One of the men gripped Katie's ankles and spread her legs.

She whimpered and put a hand out to ward him off. Esteban cupped his hand to her face and whispered soothingly to her. She only became more agitated.

When the other man took a metal speculum and started to move between her legs, Ian went crazy. Braden closed his eyes and did what he'd never done before. He called to the panther. A soft plea. Unfettered acceptance. He embraced his beast and surrendered to the shift.

Chapter Forty-One

Katie fought against the bile rising in her throat. Pain, so much pain. Every touch to her skin was like a branding iron, a hot coal pressed against her flesh.

Her legs were spread, and she felt the cool metal brush against the inside of her knee. She arched off the table, unheeding of the soothing words whispered in her ear. His touch was wrong. It was evil.

And then as they overpowered her, her head lolled to the side. A single tear slipped over her temple, wetting the surface of the table she lay on. Her gaze flickered, and she saw Ian and Braden, their faces contorted in rage.

She continued to stare, sure she'd imagined them. Why weren't they helping her?

And then Braden disappeared. A huge black cat flew over the table, taking down the man who held her ankles. A scream split the air. Esteban tried to push himself away, but the cat rose with a low snarl. His scream of fear died in his throat when the panther lunged, his jaws closing around his neck.

Blood, bright red and warm, splattered onto her chest. She rolled, trying to push herself upright. She collapsed on her side, too weak to do much more than lie there, staring down at the horror reflected in Esteban's eyes.

The cat let out a hiss and moved away from Esteban as he stalked the remaining man.

She tugged at her slack and unresisting body, trying to force herself into motion. She rolled and went down on the floor in a puddle of Esteban's blood. She raised her hands, staring in horror at the sticky, red stain on her palms.

"Katie!" Ian cried.

She looked up to see him straining sluggishly at his bonds, his face a wreath of torment. A gentle nudge at her side, soft and warm. She glanced down to see the panther rub his head over her arm. Then he raised his head and licked her cheek.

She stared into his green eyes and found calm. Slowly she reached out to touch his head. He ducked and butted against her palm and then leaned further in to nudge against her cheek again.

"Katie, get away from him," Ian shouted hoarsely. "He'll hurt you."

She leaned against the panther's neck and buried her face in his soft fur. She closed her eyes and weakly held on. After a moment, she glanced back up at Ian. "Shift," she said softly.

His eyes flashed in helpless rage. "I can't. I won't hurt you, Katie. Get up. Get out of here."

Her hand trailed over the panther. Braden. "You won't hurt me. He won't let you. Don't you see? He's protecting me. I can't free you, Ian. I'm not even sure I can get up. Trust in yourself. In what you are. Let the jaguar free."

Ian closed his eyes, his jaw ticking with strain. His fingers curled and clenched, his arms bulged and contorted. He let out an anguished cry, and then he seemingly stopped fighting.

She watched in wonder as his body reshaped. His arms slipped from the cuffs as they became slim paws. He fell forward, hitting the floor as he tore his hind legs free of restraint. His big head reared and flexed, his jaw opening and then closing in a snap of teeth.

He prowled to the fallen man, the last that Braden had taken down, and sniffed cautiously. Then he padded to where she sat. He tried to insert his heavy body between her and Esteban, steadily pushing her back with his strong shoulders. He leaned over Esteban and growled menacingly.

A low hiss escaped from the panther when miraculously, Esteban stirred, his eyes fluttering open. They were glassy and nearly fixed in death. Blood seeped from his torn neck, and Katie couldn't countenance how he was still breathing.

He raised a shaking hand and let it flutter down over her arm. The panther hissed again, and the jaguar let out a menacing growl.

A gun lay at his side, one he'd tried to raise to shoot Braden. Katie dove for it, mustering all her strength in a final bid to make sure the cats were safe. Her fingers closed around it, and she dragged it weakly into her grasp.

But Esteban never made a move for it. He stared at her, blood trickling from the corner of his mouth.

"I wanted to be free," he whispered. "God..."

"You should have never tried to play God," she said bitterly.

"Your God made me what I am," he rasped as more blood frothed and foamed over his lips.

She leaned down, her body trembling with pain and rage. And fear for what this man's actions had wrought. "God is no respecter of persons. He doesn't make one man evil and another man good. He gives us choices. Control over our own destiny. And you chose wrong."

"*You're* wrong," Esteban whispered. "He made me imperfect. A mistake."

"No one's perfect," she snarled.

Another stab of pain rolled over her body, and she closed her eyes against the urge to vomit.

"But some are mistakes," he said. "Freaks of nature. Like me..."

He raised his hand again, his fingers twitching and pointing to the table across the room. "Take it," he choked out. "The journal. Explains...everything..."

The last whispered past his lips, a long hiss, the sound of finality. Blood burbled and spit over the edge of his mouth, and his eyes lost the spark of life.

Then his body began to shake and tremble. She backed hastily away. The two cats placed themselves between her and Esteban, briefly obscuring her vision. They both hissed, and an eerie yowl sounded.

She shoved at them so that she could see. She wanted to be certain he was dead.

What she saw shocked the breath from her lungs. Lying on the floor where Esteban had lain just seconds before was a beautiful silver wolf. Blood smeared his fur and matted his jowls. The blue eyes were fixed in death.

She wrapped her arms protectively around her chest and stared as tears filled her eyes. The entire world had gone mad. Nothing was as it should be.

The gun lay useless in her lap, and she looked down, wondering how she could get herself and the cats out of the compound.

Taking a deep, steadying breath, she squared her shoulders. Ian and Braden had risked everything to save her. They hadn't betrayed her, hadn't left her to Esteban. She wouldn't leave them now.

She'd survived. She could feel sorry for herself later. Right now she had to overcome the mind-numbing pain ricocheting through her body like a short-circuited electric system and get the hell out of here.

She thumped the butt of the rifle down on the floor for leverage and shoved herself to her knees. She promptly bent over, vomiting as her stomach curled and squeezed relentlessly.

The two cats bumped incessantly at her legs, urging her forward. They flanked her protectively, forming a tight circle around her with their bodies. And to think she'd once worried about them killing her. As had they.

Sucking air through her nose, she gritted her teeth and pushed herself to her feet. She nearly went down in a heap and had to lean heavily on the rifle to keep her footing.

The cats followed her to the door, pressed tightly against her legs in an effort to keep her upright. Didn't retain human cognizance, her ass. They knew precisely what they were doing. Maybe they didn't remember afterward, but it didn't mean they were mindless killers.

Her gaze fell on the leather-bound journal lying on the table by the door. Part of her had no desire to know anything about Esteban, but the contents might help Ian and Braden and their teammate Damiano. She might need help every bit as much as they did now that Esteban had probably turned her into a shape-shifting being.

She curled her hand around the spine and tucked it to her breast. Slowly and painfully she headed across the room to the small corridor that she knew led to the lower level. There was a tunnel leading to the outside. She'd heard Esteban talking. Maybe it was to her. She couldn't remember. He'd spoken to her often, as though he was trying to win her over, to make her understand.

She closed her eyes as more tears simmered in her vision. What had he done to her? And why? What was he? Had he experimented on himself only for things to go horribly wrong as they had with Ian and Braden? Was his mad search for her an attempt to correct his mistakes, to find a cure?

They descended into the cooler, darker tunnel. A sound in the distance sent a wave of adrenaline through her body. Somehow she found the strength to raise the gun as she and the cats moved steadily forward. At the end, two men appeared. As they raised their rifles, she fired off a volley of shots. They went down and she shot again, not taking chances as they drew closer.

The cats sniffed at the bodies and growled but urged her over them.

Deeper and deeper, further down until she was certain they were entering the bowels of the earth. The tunnel wound and narrowed, and at several points she had to stop and lean heavily against the wall.

Tears of rage, of pain and frustration, of fear and of sorrow flooded her eyes, and she angrily brushed them away, furious that now of all times she was breaking.

And then the tunnel sloped upward. The going went slower as she struggled to put one foot in front of the other. Agony seared her muscles. They contracted and protested, shook like a newborn colt's legs.

Sunlight. Just a beam shining and bouncing off the tunnel wall. She extended her hand, touching the slight trail of warmth along the cooler surface.

It grew brighter, and then she saw the small entrance ahead, a simple trap door in the ceiling, old enough that intermittent splashes of sun leaked through.

A few feet away, her legs gave out, and she fell headlong onto the floor. She lay there gasping, her eyes closed as pain raced and rebounded through her body like a current with no outlet.

The jaguar leaned down, his warm tongue lapping gently at her cheek. He nuzzled her jaw, pushing upward. The panther butted her in the middle of her back, nudging her forward, impatient.

She raised her arm, and the jaguar looped his head underneath, giving her purchase. The panther slid his head underneath her other shoulder and lifted.

With renewed strength, she rose unsteadily, her weight borne by the two large predators. She reached up to shove at the old wood. When it didn't budge, she picked up the rifle and extended the butt, ramming against the doorway.

When that didn't work, she stepped back several feet, took aim and fired a series of shots. The wood splintered and rained downward. She busted out the remaining pieces with the rifle and squinted as the sun shone in.

Now for the most difficult part. Getting out. When she started to reach, the jaguar issued a warning growl. She stepped back nervously, but he simply leaped into the opening first. The panther then nudged her forward, obviously wanting her to go next.

It took her a long time to hoist herself through the opening. Her entire body was bathed in sweat, and she was in so much pain, she nearly passed out. When she finally pulled herself out, she rolled to clear the entrance for Braden, and she simply lay there, her energy spent.

It wasn't long before the cats started to nuzzle her again. Gently, probing and inquisitive. Then more firmly when she didn't respond. They wanted her up and away from danger.

Her hand going automatically to the gun, she dragged herself to her knees but when she tried to stand, she found she simply lacked the strength. So she crawled. Between the two cats. They guarded her carefully, their gazes always seeking. They matched their pace to hers.

She headed into the lush foliage of the jungle. Shelter. A place to hide and to rest. And finally, she was at her end.

She crawled underneath a tree into a bed of damp leaves. Water dripped from the canopy overhead, soft and soothing.

The panther inserted himself between her and the tree so that she leaned into his warm body. She went without hesitation, pressing her back into his fur.

The jaguar settled himself a few feet away, his head up and staring, his ears perked and alert.

She just wanted to stop hurting. Just for a little while.

Chapter Forty-Two

Ian came awake, the sounds of the jungle humming incessantly in his ears. Awareness of everything else was slow in coming. He moved with marked lethargy, and he moaned softly as blackness swirled.

He turned his head, his cheek scraping against the damp ground. Oh God. "*No*," he whispered when he saw Katie lying several feet away.

Blood covered her body, bathing her in scarlet red.

He scrambled for her, grief and confusion clouding his mind. Memories splintered and came back rapid fire. Braden had shifted and killed the men in the laboratory. Katie had looked up at him with pain-filled eyes. He'd allowed the shift to happen.

He'd done this to her.

He crawled to her body, ignoring Braden who lay just beyond her, his back against a gnarly tree trunk. With shaking hands, Ian reached for her, his fingers feathering over her pale face.

Tears clouded his vision as he gathered her in his arms. Ignoring her blood-soaked clothes, he crushed her to his chest and buried his face in her hair.

She stirred softly, her body trembling against his. His hopes soared. Then he began to shake uncontrollably as he gently put her back down so he could judge the extent of her injuries.

God, there was so much blood. Had he ravaged her? Had he turned on her and attacked her?

He pushed at her clothing with impatient hands. He found the wound Marcus had stitched, countless bruises, but no gaping wounds, certainly nothing capable of producing the amount of blood on her clothes.

"Ian?" Braden asked groggily. "What the hell are you doing?"

"I must have attacked her," Ian said in a broken voice. "There's blood everywhere."

Braden pushed himself upward, his brow creased in absolute confusion. "But you didn't." He stared down at Katie in horror and then back up at Ian. "Ian...I remember."

Ian stared back. "Remember what?"

Braden opened his mouth but seemed to have great difficulty in forming what he wanted to say. He palmed his forehead and closed his eyes for a moment.

"I shifted on purpose, Ian. And I remember what happened while I was the panther. I remember *everything.*"

Ian shook his head, sure he wasn't hearing right.

"I remember killing Esteban. And the others. And then you shifted. The blood isn't hers. It's Esteban's. She was in so much pain, and we tried to get her out."

"How can you remember that?" Ian asked in disbelief.

"I don't know," Braden whispered.

Braden pushed himself forward and leaned over Katie. He touched her cheek and then bent down to kiss her temple. "Katie," he choked out. He stroked her face, his fingers skittering lightly over her skin.

He glanced back up at Ian. "She's so clammy. She's trembling all over. She's not doing well, Ian. We have to get her out of here. I don't know what the hell they did to her, but it wasn't good."

Four men burst out of the dense jungle foliage, their guns pointed at Ian, Braden and Katie. Braden dove over Katie, his body shielding her while Ian grabbed for the rifle at her side.

"Whoa, man, stand down," Eli barked. "It's us, Ian."

Ian stared up through the red haze crowding his vision to see Eli, Jonah, Mad Dog and Tits standing in a tight semicircle. They lowered their guns.

"Christ," Mad Dog grumbled as he dug into his backpack. "It's getting to be a chore keeping you two in clothes."

Ian glanced down, only now noticing that he was nude. Mad Dog tossed a pair of fatigues and a T-shirt at Ian and then to Braden. But Braden focused solely on Katie, anguish etched into his features as he stared down at her.

"What happened, Ian?" Eli asked softly.

Jonah and Eli both squatted down beside Katie. Braden ignored them in his distress.

Ian shook the cobwebs from his head. "I don't know everything," he said honestly. He stared up at his brother. "Braden said he shifted on purpose and that he remembers everything that happened while he was the panther."

Eli and Jonah jerked their gazes to Braden.

"Is that true?" Eli asked.

"Think, Braden," Jonah said urgently. "This could be important."

"They were hurting Katie," Braden said simply, his voice breaking with emotion. "Ian and I were helpless to save her. Esteban had us shackled and drugged. I knew I had to shift and so I did. Then I killed the man who was trying to hurt Katie. Then Esteban and finally the third man in the room."

Eli exchanged glances with Ian, his brow creased in concentration.

"Did you mean to kill them? What I mean is did you know what you were doing? Did you plan it?"

"Yes," Braden said simply. "I went after them. I wanted them dead. Katie fell from the table. There was blood everywhere, on her, on Esteban."

He stared up at Ian. "You told her to get out, that I would hurt her. She touched me and then she buried her face in my fur. Then she told you to shift. You refused and said you didn't want to hurt her. She told you that I wouldn't let you, that I was protecting her. It was true. When you shifted, I put myself between you and her. I didn't know what you would do. But you immediately went to help her. We both were just trying to get her out of there. She barely made it down the tunnel."

He returned his gaze to her. "She was in so much pain. I

don't know what they did to her, Ian, and it's killing me."

Katie moaned again. She shook, seemingly wracked with a chill, but sweat bathed her body, beading on her forehead. Her face was pale, and her muscles twitched like a junkie in withdrawal.

Her face contorted, and her lips drew together in a fine line, going white as she battled what seemed to be unbearable pain.

And then her eyes flew open, and she stared up at Jonah and Eli. Her pupils went wide with fear, and then she turned away, her eyes staring unseeingly into the jungle. Her leg jumped, and the nerves in her arms spasmed uncontrollably.

Eli's expression hardened while Jonah's face softened when he stared down at her shaking body. Jonah reached out and gently touched her face.

Slowly her eyes moved until she locked gazes with him.

"What did they do to you, *habibti?*"

His voice was strained. Uncharacteristic emotion simmered in his eyes.

She stared dully back at him. "They took my eggs," she whispered.

Jonah's head came up in shock, and the other men all stared at each other. Had they understood right? Ian's face tightened in horror as he remembered the scene right before Braden shifted. The spreading of her legs and the metal device the man had put between her legs. Dear God.

She closed her eyes as tears seeped from the corners, leaving damp trails down her pale face.

Eli turned to stare up at Mad Dog. There was steel in his eyes. "Give me some time before you blow this place to hell." Then he turned to the others. "Get Katie to the helicopter. I'll meet you there."

Jonah carried Katie through the jungle, with Mad Dog taking point and Tits bringing up the rear. Ian and Braden were still weak and shaky from the drugs and the prolonged shift.

Jonah glanced down as Katie jerked and spasmed in his arms and wondered for the hundredth time what the bastards had done to her. And why? She clutched a worn leather journal to her chest, and murmured a weak protest when he tried to take it from her. So he left it, not wanting to cause her any more distress.

Her eyes had the vacant, distant look of the women brutalized under his father's reign of tyranny. She looked...like his mother had the day he'd found her huddled in the bedroom of their palace home.

He stared stonily ahead even as his grip tightened around Katie's slight form. He hadn't been able to save his mother or the many others his father had crushed. In the end, he'd fled, shedding all association with Adharji and his dictator father.

Funny how things had a way of coming full circle. All things began in Adharji.

"Slow up, Jonah," Tits called. "We're nearing the landing site. Let Ian and Braden go ahead and make sure the area is clear. I'll hang back and provide cover for you."

Jonah slowed his pace and loosened his grip around Katie's body. "Poor *habibti*," he murmured as he stared down at the perspiration glistening on her face. "You've had it way too hard for one so young."

"She needs a doctor," Tits said.

Jonah jerked his head around to see Tits standing at his right shoulder. Then he glanced back at the strain on Katie's face. "Yes, she does."

"She's really messed with you, dude," Tits said casually.

Jonah lifted his head to stare at Tits. After a moment Tits shifted uncomfortably and looked away.

"I would hope that any woman treated so abominably would mess with any man," he said tightly.

Tits nodded. "True enough. I'm just not used to seeing you so..."

"So what?"

Tits shook his head. "Nothing, man. Forget I said anything."

Mad Dog shouted an all clear, and Jonah strode forward

into the clearing where the helicopter would land shortly. On cue, the *whop whop* of an approaching chopper sounded from low over the horizon.

"Give me your shirt," Jonah said to Mad Dog.

Mad Dog dropped his pack and shrugged out of his mesh button-up. He thrust it toward Jonah, and Jonah nodded his head down at Katie. Mad Dog carefully arranged it over her shivering body while Ian and Braden hovered close by.

Ian and Braden both wore expressions of men who'd been tortured a dozen times over. Jonah studied them, in awe over the fact that two men could both so obviously love the same woman. They made it seem so natural. Even Mad Dog and Tits hadn't blinked an eye over it. Everyone just accepted it and went on.

Love was an interesting, multifaceted thing.

Jonah turned and shielded Katie's body as the helicopter dipped and lowered several yards away. Mad Dog threw open the door and motioned for Tits, Ian and Braden to get in. Jonah walked slower, taking care not to jostle Katie. When he got close, Ian leaned over, his arms outstretched. Jonah relinquished her to the other man and turned to wait for Eli.

He simmered impatiently, checking his watch at five-minute intervals. He didn't like having his team exposed, sitting ducks. He was getting antsy and impatient with each passing minute. After ten minutes, Eli strode from the jungle, a silver cylinder in his hand.

He hurried past Jonah and climbed into the waiting chopper. Jonah climbed in after him, and they lifted off.

Eli knelt on the floor in front of Ian. He picked up Katie's hand and placed the canister against her palm. Then he gently pressed her fingers until she gripped it.

"You've left nothing of yours here, Katie," Eli said in a low voice. "Do you understand?"

Tears filled her eyes once more. "Thank you," she whispered.

Mad Dog pulled out a transmitter and yanked the antenna up.

"Take us low over the compound," Mad Dog yelled toward the pilot. Then he glanced back at the others. "Let's blow this joint, shall we?"

As they zoomed over, explosions rocked the air. The compound disappeared from sight as orange balls of flame shot skyward. Smoke billowed and clogged the air. For a long time, Jonah stared out the window as they got further away.

Esteban was dead and with him any secrets he harbored. D's condition was a very uncertain thing. There was no miracle cure for him. No quick fix.

There was only Braden's sudden ability to shift at will and retain the panther's memories to give them any hope for the future. But was it a one-time aberration spawned by desperation? Or was it possible that the man might gain control over the beast?

Chapter Forty-Three

Katie slowly closed the journal and lowered it to her lap, her fingers trembling as she fiddled with the worn edges. She raised her head to stare out the window at the ocean spreading out as far as the eye could see.

The window was cracked so she could hear the waves rolling in. The sound soothed her and eased some of the hypersensitivity she still experienced from the chemical Esteban had exposed her to.

She stared back down at the journal and then closed her eyes against the fear that tightened her chest. With a sigh, she uncurled her legs and pulled herself out of the plush armchair that Ian and Braden had positioned by the window. The others would want to know what the journal contained. They would need to know.

Fatigue weighed heavily on her. She'd worn herself out gauging her every mood, analyzing each twinge, each shift in temperament. She lived in fear that at any moment, with no provocation, she could turn into a wild creature. Not knowing what she might change into was killing her.

Marcus knew what had happened to her. The others still did not. It was time to tell them everything.

She headed down the stairs of the south wing. The island estate was huge, with stairs from all the wings converging into a central foyer. Most of the time, however, the members of Falcon and CHR gathered in the game room. They weren't opposed to a little imbibing and some pot smoking, and pool was always a hot commodity.

She paused inside the doorway, suddenly unsure of herself,

of her place in this crew of mercenaries. They were tougher than her, more ruthless. She admired that, wished she embodied more of their traits.

She wished she wasn't so terrified.

Tyana and Eli stood at one corner of the pool table watching as Jonah leaned over to take his shot. Tyana leaned on one crutch while Eli supported her by wrapping his arm around her waist. Mad Dog stood back, cue in hand, and made a jeering noise when Jonah's shot went wide. Ian and Braden leaned against the bar. Braden's hands were shoved into his pockets, and he nodded at something Ian said.

Then he looked up and saw her. He straightened immediately, concern flashing on his face. Did she look as fragile as she felt?

He shoved off of the bar and crossed the room. He came to a stop just in front of her and reached for her hands.

"Hey," he said softly. "You okay?"

She offered a faint smile and nodded.

"Come here."

He tugged her against his chest, tucked her head under his chin and wrapped his arms around her. For a moment she relaxed into his hold, absorbing his strength and the comfort he offered. Then she carefully pulled away. She trembled as he smoothed his fingers down her arms and then captured her hands again.

"I finished the journal," she said. "There are things that everyone should know. And other things..."

Braden studied her intently then tugged her forward. "Come over here where you'll be comfortable."

He wrapped an arm around her shoulders and led her toward the couch in front of the bar where Ian still stood.

The others stopped to look at her. Jonah's gaze followed her, and when she met his eyes, his expression softened.

"I'd rather stand," she said when Braden started to sit her down on the couch.

She slipped her fingers from his and took a few steps back. Ian's hands clasped her shoulders, and his mouth brushed close to her ear.

"Are you okay?" he asked quietly. "Are you feeling well?"

She nodded and turned to face the others. She'd start with Esteban. Maybe by the time she'd explained all she'd read, the part where she divulged that she might turn into an unpredictable shifter might actually seem normal.

Tyana, Eli, Mad Dog and Jonah all stared at her expectantly. She wiped her palms down her jeans and took a deep breath.

"Esteban was a shifter. A wolf, to be more exact. Not a werewolf like the movies or legends. A real wolf."

Shocked silence ensued.

Jonah stepped forward. "You want to run that by us again?"

"I saw him," she said. "When he died. When he took his last breath, he shifted." She glanced at Braden. "Do you remember?"

"I thought that part was a delusion," Braden muttered. "So much of that time was so scattered. It all happened so fast, and when I look back it's with such a sense of detachment, like I'm seeing something that happened through someone else's eyes. Honestly I thought I was a little nuts."

"According to his journal, he's a natural shifter."

Eli surged to attention, and Tyana put her hand on his arm.

"A what?" Mad Dog demanded. "What the hell is a natural shifter?"

"He was born that way," Katie said softly. "Unfortunately, he had no control over when and how he shifted. He spent most of his life in seclusion. He began experimenting with a chemical that altered human DNA in early adulthood. I say he, but he only funded the research. He had no scientific background."

She glanced at Eli and then Ian and Braden. "You were his first successful experiment. But only Eli and Gabe achieved the results he was interested in. Stability. He couldn't accept that his genetic make-up couldn't be changed, that there was no cure for his instability."

"Christ," Tyana muttered. "We've all been searching for the same thing. The bastard created his own problem in D and the others."

Katie nodded. "Except, for whatever reason, Gabe and Eli gained full control of their abilities. Esteban became obsessed with reproducing that result. Which is why he came after me. I shared Gabe's DNA. Eli had no family. He wanted my..."

She swallowed, and Ian's hands tightened around her shoulders.

"What did he want?" Jonah asked.

She looked down as tears threatened. This part terrified her—admitting it—out loud. It made it real, and now she'd face a very uncertain future. What if...

"Baby, what's wrong?" Braden asked, concern evident in his voice.

"He exposed me to the same chemical agent that you were exposed to," she said in a low voice.

"*What?*"

The demand exploded across the room from at least three different places. Ian spun her around, his eyes wide with horror.

A tear rolled down her cheek as she shook in his arms. "I'm scared," she whispered.

"Dear God, that's why..." He broke off and dug a hand into his hair. "Jesus, that's why you were in such pain, why you're still so weak."

"Son of a bitch," Braden swore.

She found herself between the two men, their hands shaking as they stroked her arms and her back. They touched her face, her hair, held her close.

"I'm terrified of what will happen," she choked out. "What am I going to do?"

She leaned her forehead against Ian's chest, and he pressed his lips to the top of her head. His entire body shook against hers.

"Come sit down," he said. "We'll figure this out, okay? I don't want you to worry."

She smiled wanly at his attempt to infuse her with hope. But she allowed him to lead her to the couch. The others all gathered in the small sitting area. Tyana and Eli sat on the opposite couch while Mad Dog parked it on the arm of the chair that Jonah sat in. Ian and Braden flanked her on the couch, Ian holding her hand while Braden clasped her leg above her knee.

Jonah leaned forward, his expression serious. "You won't be alone, Katie. Falcon will help you in any way we can."

"She'll have *us*," Braden said softly.

Jonah nodded, his expression easing.

"I think everyone is missing a very important question here," Mad Dog said. "Was Esteban really a natural shifter or was he bat-shit crazy? Is it even possible? Does that change anything for Eli, D, Ian and Braden or is all hope for a cure gone?"

Eli propped his elbows on his knees and scrubbed at his face.

"Eli, don't," Tyana pleaded. "You don't have to do this."

He grimaced and then reached over to squeeze her hand. "Yeah, sugar, I do."

He focused his weary gaze on Ian and Braden, regret brimming in his dark eyes.

"I've been lying to you guys for a long time."

Katie glanced anxiously at Ian and Braden as confusion darkened their faces.

"What?" Braden asked.

"The chemical that turned you into cats…it didn't affect me."

"Of course it did," Ian said. "Hell, I've seen you shift."

"I was born a shifter," Eli said quietly. "It's a secret I've carried since I was ten years old. It just became easier to disguise after what happened in Adharji. I no longer had to hide my ability from you because suddenly I was provided an explanation. Gabe was stable so it didn't stretch probability that I was too."

"Holy fuck," Mad Dog breathed. "Has the entire world gone crazy? That shit just doesn't happen."

"So Gabe was the only one who truly turned out the way Esteban envisioned?" Katie asked painfully.

"Apparently so," Ian muttered.

Braden held up his hand. "Whether or not Esteban was a natural shifter is irrelevant. The fucker is dead. What we need to be worried about is the fact that the son of a bitch gassed Katie."

Ian nodded and then he turned to her again. "Does Marcus know?"

She nodded slowly.

"What did he suggest?"

She closed her eyes. "He said all I could do was wait and see. There's nothing he can do." Her voice cracked. "No tests he can run. No cure if I'm affected."

Braden cursed and turned away, his fists rolled into tight balls against the couch.

Tyana stared across at her with a stricken expression. "I'm sorry, Katie."

"We're getting ahead of ourselves here," Jonah said. "We don't know that Katie will be affected. I say we don't borrow trouble. Take it one day at a time."

He glanced sorrowfully at Tyana. "We already knew that finding a cure was a long shot."

Tyana looked away, tears brimming in her eyes.

"We can't just give up," Ian said fiercely. He gripped Katie's hand and brought it to his lips. "We can beat this, Katie. What happened at the compound with Braden. Explain that. It was a breakthrough. Maybe a step forward."

"You're not alone," Braden added as he took her other hand.

"Aren't I?" she asked. "Sometimes I feel like I've always been alone. Gabe was all I had left, and now he's gone. I have nothing to go back to."

Ian and Braden went completely still next to her. She felt the stares of the entire group, and she shifted uncomfortably on the couch under their scrutiny.

"Maybe we should leave you three alone for a while," Jonah said as he stood.

Eli helped Tyana to her feet. Mad Dog slid off the arm of the chair and ambled to the door. And then she was alone with Ian and Braden.

She leaned forward and buried her face in her hands. She was so tired. Her body still fought the effects of the chemical. Moving hurt, more than she let on. All she wanted to do was curl up in a ball and sleep.

"You're hurting," Ian said quietly.

She nodded without opening her eyes.

"Katie, look at me," Ian prompted.

She opened her eyes and turned her head to stare at him.

"I love you."

Such powerful words. No one had ever said them to her before. They were staggering. She'd heard them, been flip about them, but hearing them now, directed at her...it shattered her.

"I love you," Braden whispered next to her ear.

She turned, her breath held in her chest. She stared in wonder at him and then turned back to look at Ian.

"I—"

"Shhh." Ian placed a finger gently over her lips. "Hear us out."

Braden scooted up so that he was in her line of vision. Ian reached over and curled his fingers around her palm and stroked lightly with his thumb.

"We want you to go back to Argentina with us. CHR has a house there. A compound, really. Eli doesn't have a need for it. His life is here with Tyana and Falcon."

She swung her gaze back to Braden to gauge his reaction. There was calm in his expression. Sincerity.

"We want you with us, Katie."

"But what if...what if I become—"

"What if you become what?" Ian prompted. "Like us?"

She nodded.

"Whatever happens, we're going to be with you," Braden said.

His voice slid over her, a promise she reached for and held tight.

"You won't be left behind, Katie. Not ever again. Do you understand that? We want you with us. Always."

She wrapped her arms around Ian and held on tight. "I love you too," she whispered against his neck.

He gathered her close and buried his lips in her hair. He stroked the back of her head with his hand as he murmured in her ear. She pulled slowly away and then turned to Braden.

"I love you."

He touched her cheek and smiled, his teeth flashing his boyish grin. Then he leaned in and kissed her, long and sweet. So exquisitely gentle, as though she'd crumble with the slightest touch.

"I want you to get better," he said. "I want to make love to you again."

Her face fell and she looked away.

"Hey," he said softly. "What was that for?"

"I'm just afraid of what will happen if the chemical affected me badly. What if it ruins everything?"

Braden and Ian both reached for her hands until she held both of theirs in her lap.

"No matter what, we'll always be together," Ian said. "Believe that if you believe nothing else."

"We'll make it," Braden added. "Together."

Some of her fear lifted, and she smiled a shaky smile. She squeezed their hands and then brought them up to kiss them both. "Together," she agreed.

Chapter Forty-Four

"She's getting worse," Ian said wearily as he and Marcus stood watching Katie and Braden from inside the glass doors leading to the deck.

Marcus frowned. "How so?"

Marcus had flown in to perform his regular check-up and physical on Katie. These days he spent his time between Damiano in Nepal and Katie in Argentina.

"We're having to use the inhibitor far more frequently, and we've had to sedate her three times in the past two weeks. I'd hoped..."

Ian broke off and rubbed a tired hand through his hair. "I hate this, man. I love her and I hate to see her suffer."

"And what about you and Braden?" Marcus asked.

Ian gave him a startled look.

"Any unexpected shifts? Further instability?"

Ian shook his head. "Braden shifts regularly. He's pretty good at doing it at will now. He hasn't made a single move toward me and Katie. We've tested his recall, and it's odd. At times he can clearly remember events that occur while he's in panther form. Other times, however, it's all a blank. When that happens, he backs off shifting for a while, and he gets edgy. It scares him when he can't remember. He's too afraid he'll hurt Katie or me."

Marcus nodded, a thoughtful look in his eyes. He started to speak, but was interrupted when Braden knocked over his chair getting up. Katie sat stock-still in hers, her face pale, her hands shaking violently. Tremors rocked her slight body, and she looked at Braden in panic.

Ian made a grab for the syringe that lay on the table inside, and he threw open the door. He made it over to Katie, prepared to inject her when Marcus caught his arm.

"What the fuck? Let me go, man."

"Don't give it to her," Marcus said calmly.

"What?" Braden demanded.

Katie clutched her arms, rubbing almost violently. Fear shone vividly in her eyes. She was terrified.

"I promised her, I *swore* to her that I'd never let this happen," Ian bit out.

"Listen to me," Marcus said. "You don't know if she's stable or not. You've never let her explore the depths of her abilities. She's understandably frightened. We don't even know what her ability is. What if she's like Gabe and can control her shifts? We have to let her try. She can't go on like this, living in terror, being sedated every time the urge comes on."

"Christ," Ian muttered.

He looked up at Braden, seeking his input. Braden looked tortured with indecision. Finally he closed his eyes and nodded.

A strangled cry burst from Katie's throat. Ian reached for her, grasping her shoulders. "We'll be right here, Katie. We'll help you through this."

"I don't know what to do," she said desperately.

Braden shoved in and framed her face in his hands. "Just let go, baby. Surrender to it."

She closed her eyes then bolted upward. She stepped forward and then back as if she had no idea where to go. Then she crumpled. Ian lunged for her, but Braden held him back.

"Let her go," he said in a strained voice.

They watched in agony as her body spasmed, and she cried out in pain. It was like watching a battle between human and animal. And finally the beast won.

Tawny fur rippled across her skin. Hands became paws. Black spots appeared. Her clothing ripped and fell away. Her head twisted, and her jaws opened wide as a sound that wasn't quite human or animal escaped in an eerie howl.

And then where a human woman had fallen, a cheetah arose, graceful and sleek. Yellow eyes stared calmly back at the men.

"Amazing," Marcus breathed.

"A cheetah," Ian whispered.

So much made sense now. His and Braden's reaction to her from the very beginning, how she called to the cat inside of them.

"She's beautiful," Braden said, his voice barely above Ian's.

Slowly she closed the distance between her and Ian. She sniffed delicately, her head bobbing as she stared up at him. He fell to his knees, and she moved in close, butting her head against his chest. She rubbed and nudged at his chin and then along his cheek.

Braden knelt beside him and extended his hand. The cheetah closed her eyes and began to purr as he stroked her head. Then she sidled close and rubbed her jowls over his shoulder and chest.

She finished with a lick to his cheek before she moved around him and took off in a lope.

Both men stood and turned around to see her streaking across the back of the compound. She was magnificent, wild and running free.

"I'll be damned," Braden murmured.

"It is through you and Ian and Katie that I have hope for Damiano," Marcus said. "The fact that you can shift at will and that you retain memories of being the cat. And now maybe Katie will enjoy control over her shifts as well. My theory with Damiano is that if he can train his mind, he can control the beast. I'd say you learned that yourself in your own way."

"Or maybe I just knew Katie needed me," Braden said with a smile.

He turned to watch her again, and then with a mischievous grin, he closed his eyes and fell to his knees. In a matter of seconds, the panther rose and loped after the cheetah.

The two raced across the ground, nipping and swatting at each other.

Marcus turned to Ian and smiled. "Damn fine family you

have, Ian."

Ian grinned, his heart soaring with such profound relief. He wanted to laugh and cry all at the same time. "That I do, Marcus. That I do."

About the Author

To learn more about Maya please visit www.mayabanks.com. Send an email to Maya at maya@mayabanks.com or join her Yahoo! group to join in the fun with other readers:

http://groups.yahoo.com/group/writeminded_readers.

*One woman's mission to bring down a sexy elemental
shifter turns into a battle of wills...and hearts.*

Into the Mist

© 2008 Maya Banks

Falcon Mercenary Group, Book 1.

Hostage recovery specialist Eli Chance has a secret. He was
born a shifter. A freak of nature.

While on a mission, Eli's men and their mercenary guide
are exposed to a powerful chemical agent, and suddenly his
secret has become easier to hide. Now he's not the only one
with the gift. But for his men, this "gift" is becoming more and
more of a curse.

Tyana Berezovsky's brother Damiano was the guide for Eli's
team and was the worst affected by the chemical. As he grows
increasingly unstable, Tyana fears she's going to lose him to the
beast he is becoming.

Tyana will do whatever it takes to help him, even if it
means using her body to go after the one man she thinks holds
all the blame—and possibly the cure. Eli Chance.

*Warning: Violence, blood, guns, knives, ass kicking, people
who do mean things, bad people dying, explicit sex and smart
mouths.*

Available now in ebook and print from Samhain Publishing.

Their final mission will be to win her love.

Amber Eyes
© 2009 Maya Banks

A beautiful, vulnerable woman appears at the high country cabin where Hunter and Jericho live between assignments. They are captivated by their stunning, reticent visitor and vow to protect her—and uncover what she's hiding. Neither is prepared for the unbelievable. Their beautiful innocent is a cougar shifter who's spent a lifetime alone.

In the shelter of their love, Kaya blooms, finally willing to trust—and embrace her humanity again. Then Hunter and Jericho are called away on a mission that goes terribly wrong. Now, pregnant, and alone once more, she must find her way in a world she doesn't belong to—and hope that the two men she loves will find their way home.

Warning: This title contains explicit sex, adult language, sweet lovin', multiple partners and ménage a trois.

Available now in ebook from Samhain Publishing.

Amber Eyes is the sequel to Golden Eyes, which is available through another publisher. For further details, visit Maya's website. www.mayabanks.com

GREAT
CHEAP
FUN

Discover eBooks!

THE FASTEST WAY TO GET THE HOTTEST NAMES

Get your favorite authors on your favorite reader, long before they're
out in print! Ebooks from Samhain go wherever you go, and work with
whatever you carry—Palm, PDF, Mobi, and more.

samhain
publishing
ltd